THE AMBER SECRET

THE AMBER SECRET

SECRET

THE RELIC **3** HUNTERS

DAVID LEADBEATER

THOMAS & MERCER

Text copyright © 2019 by David Leadbeater
All rights reserved.

Published by Thomas & Mercer, Seattle
www.apub.com

Amazon, the Amazon logo, and Thomas & Mercer are trademarks of Amazon.com, Inc., or its affiliates.

ISBN-13: 9781542017251
ISBN-10: 1542017254

Cover design by Dominic Forbes

Printed in the United States of America

THE AMBER
SECRET

PROLOGUE

Early 1945

Strident thunder sought to challenge the very heavens. It was not the thunder of a glorious storm or a magnificent railroad carriage. It was the dreadful sound of Russian guns, battering and pounding the city of Königsberg. The shocking sound of war.

Ivan trudged through the wet and dirty streets, a heavy rain streaming from the skies, bouncing off his thick coat and pouring from the rim of his six-millimeter-thick field-gray steel helmet. He was a German sniper, a man who should have been in the vanguard, but today he had been called back to the city for a special mission.

Ivan didn't like it. His friends were facing the enemy even now, while he trudged these dirty pavements. They needed him. They needed the help and confidence his weapon and his skill lent to the offensive.

Except that it's fast becoming a defensive, he thought. The Russians were growing in number and onslaughts every day. They had already cut off the landward side, splitting the road down the Samland Peninsula to the Pillau port. They had trapped around two hundred thousand civilians inside the city in addition to the Third Panzer Army. As a consequence the civilians were dying, starving or riddled with disease. But it wasn't Ivan's place to question decisions made higher up the chain. It was Ivan's job to be the good soldier that he knew he was.

Hence tonight, stalking these streets with a wary eye. Civilians or not, anyone who saw him wouldn't balk at jumping him to see what possessions he might carry. With rations set at mere grams of bread, even his clothing was a prize to them.

It wasn't all bad news, he thought as he approached his destination. The Third Panzer and the Fourth Army had opened a route to Pillau. It was after this news had filtered down that Ivan had received his new orders. And here he was, removed from the front, turned from a man who knew his job to a man milling on a sidewalk, wet and hungry, wondering if he might yet get pounced upon by desperate locals.

Königsberg was a grim place, made darker and gloomier by the incessant rain. High brick walls stood on both sides. The black streets ran deep with water that pooled in the drains. A shadow moved, and Ivan almost raised his rifle.

But then Ivan saw the man was wearing the same uniform as he was. Ivan relaxed, and the man beckoned him to come forward.

Ivan moved swiftly and bent his head as he approached. *"Leutnant,"* he said, recognizing a superior officer.

"Come with me."

Together, they marched through the pouring dark. From memory Ivan knew he was bypassing Königsberg Castle. The walls were to his right, with the great spire up ahead. To his left the great river wound, and he wondered briefly what, tonight, might be the parameters of his special mission.

There were trucks parked at the side of the road and dozens of other men dressed like he was. Dark and nondescript. They didn't speak, nor did they move much as more men struggled down a set of steps to the right. The steps led right up to the castle. The men carried many boxes, all sealed shut, and shoved them into the back of one of the trucks. As he watched, Ivan saw many more boxes, rolled-up paintings, and other treasures removed from the castle.

"You will never speak of this," the man at his side whispered. "If you do, both you and whatever family you have will be killed."

Ivan frowned. He was a loyal soldier, always following orders. What right did this man have to threaten him?

He opened his mouth to find out, but then one of the men carrying the treasures stumbled under the weight of a large crate and went flying down the steps. Crying out, he landed askew. The crate toppled and fell, splitting apart. For a moment, Ivan stared, wondering if he should help.

One of the officers came forward, grabbed the man's forehead, and raised it up, baring his neck to the sky. Without warning, he cut the man's throat and pushed him to the ground, letting him gurgle and cry into the gutter, blood mixing with pouring rain.

"Now," the lieutenant beside him said, "do you have something to say?"

"No."

The lieutenant stopped all work and gathered everyone together, and there in the pouring rain, in the darkest of dark nights, surrounded by running water and muck and disease and death, he gave them a speech that finally made Ivan think he was about to be part of something tremendous, something noteworthy.

Perhaps, if Ivan did everything they asked and shone like a star, he would receive great recognition for it.

"This operation is sanctioned by the *Generalfeldmarschall*. We cannot fail. Failure will bring death not only to all of us but to our families. Do you understand?"

"Yes, *Leutnant*."

"Then go help. And men?"

Everyone looked expectant.

"Do not drop the crates. Do not look inside the crates. Be good soldiers and do as you are told."

Ivan nodded, taking the place of the murdered soldier, hefting the crate that had split. Some of its contents shifted inside, and from the corner of his eye, Ivan saw panels several inches thick and oblong, deeply colored, reflecting even the most meager light. Maybe gold. But Ivan had seen gold before and knew that these were different. Perhaps even more precious.

So much wealth in that single crate. Enough to feed a family for years, an army for months. He found it hard to conceive of the man greedy enough to want it all to himself.

And he went on to help carry eighteen crates.

CHAPTER ONE

Demons danced in the hearth.

Dante Caruso gazed into the fireplace, wondering if it might be the reflected image of what roiled inside his head. The people he knew called him half-crazy. "Look, the mad Italian's here," they would say, laughing and joking, when he approached. To them, his rhetoric was a confused stream of words, barely intelligible. Still, they often bought the items he brought back from his travels—ancient artifacts, old statues, and pottery.

The income from these sales barely kept his family clothed. Caruso knew, at some level, that he could do better for them. But his obsession was too strong. He was certain that the great prize waited for him over the horizon.

Caruso nursed a pint of beer, drawing the glass close into his chest. Its amber glow, enhanced by the firelight, brought into sharp focus everything that had taken place during the last few days.

It had finally happened. Years of failure and drudgery had paid off. He'd followed some obscure Second World War trail to look for an infamous treasure. And—he could scarcely believe it even now—he had found it.

I found it. Yes, me!

The words felt alien to his brain. Caruso wasn't used to major success. Only once before could he remember a winning day—a day when he'd felt he'd beaten everything that life could throw at him—and that had been over eight years ago now. It was the day his son, Marco, had been born. Caruso had experienced clarity for a brief span of time as he'd realized a true treasure had come into existence, but obsession was insatiable, always chipping away at the corners of his mind.

I am an explorer. A treasure hunter. I must . . . go on.

Caruso lifted the glass and swallowed a mouthful of beer. The passion inside remained strong, but it was riddled with frustration. Angrily, he replayed the first conversation he'd had with his wife, Anna, on returning from his quest.

"I have succeeded. Finally. It is everything I ever knew that I could find."

"You stink." Anna had refused to come across their small kitchen to stand near him. "Always, it is the same. You vanish for entire weeks and then come back with some insane story. And you find a goblet. A knife. A broken shield. When will it end, Dante? When?"

"I am not a good father?" he had asked. "A good husband?"

Anna bowed her head and did not answer.

Caruso took a moment to sit down at the kitchen table. "I am trying to provide in the only way I know how."

"Yes." Anna came over to him then and took his head in her arms. "I know. But since the onset of . . . of your . . . memory loss . . ."

"Do you want me to tell you what I found?" His question was muffled by her sleeve.

Anna flicked her eyes around the room. "Why not show me? You usually do that."

Caruso frowned as the jumbled thoughts inside his head focused for a brief few minutes. This tended to happen whenever he thought about his beloved treasure-hunting adventures. "I found a cave full of treasures," he said. "Each one beyond anything I have found before. Rows upon rows. But one—*the* one—could not be transported. It is too heavy."

He felt Anna become tense. "So . . . you have come home . . . with nothing?"

"I . . . I . . ." Caruso couldn't form the words. Reality hit him, and the brief moment of clarity faded.

Anna pulled away, moving to the old, stained sink and leaning over it with her head in her hands. "We have nothing left," she whispered.

Caruso immediately wanted to reassure her that this latest find would set them up for life. But again, confusion riddled his brain, and he found that his tongue was tied.

Finally, he rose.

"I will begin now," he said.

Her head lifted slightly. "Begin?"

"To put the word out. To describe my find to friends and colleagues. To customers. I will gather together a trusted group who will return with me to unearth the greatest find in history."

Anna's shoulders began to shake as she cried. "They won't believe you," he heard her whisper. "They know about the dementia, and they just won't believe you."

He walked out, determined to restore her faith in him.

The barkeep brought him another glass of beer, requesting the money first. Caruso dug it out of a small, dirt-encrusted wallet, loath to spend the cash but knowing it would only take one influential, wealthy man realizing the magnitude of his discovery to change everything. The fire demons still berated him, muddying his thought process. He recalled that the great treasure couldn't be moved by one man—but why hadn't he picked up something smaller? Something to pay the bills or even an item that might prove his claims?

Because that was who he was, and to be anything different would look wrong to the people of Siena, who he called friends and customers.

Chaos was all he remembered—the chaos of the journey, the chaos of the discovery. The disease he had came with memory loss and lapses in both focus and concentration. The doctors told him he was in stage three, which, while not totally debilitating, remained incredibly challenging.

It had taken a long time to return home from his last hunt along a necessary yet ingenious route. But he did recall a poignant moment—in his elation, all else had dwindled to nothing. The discovery of his life had stood right before him, endorsing him, saving him. Nothing else mattered now but bringing back a team—*his team*—to start the excavation.

After walking out on Anna earlier, he had remained true to his word. The people he always bartered with were his first stop. He classed them as friends. Some truth hidden far back in the recesses of his mind told him they were swindlers and charlatans. That they ridiculed him behind his back, poked fun even to his face. He imagined that he came across as a desperate man.

Not anymore.

He'd found redemption.

He spotted two of his best customers at the bar. When they had asked where he wanted them to go, Caruso had only nodded vaguely north. "That way."

"And you're talking about the *real* Amber Room, the treasure crafted in the eighteenth century and looted by the Nazis in World War Two?"

"It is considered the eighth wonder of the world," Caruso added eagerly.

He saw only stony disbelief in the eyes of the men he thought of as friends. One of them spoke. "We're having trouble believing, that's all, Dante. The Amber Room is one of the most notable lost treasures in history. Thousands have searched for it or attempted to document its travels, and thousands have failed. Experts from every race . . ." He took a breath. "How did you . . . ?"

Caruso met their harsh stares. "I said I'd found it, didn't I? My brain might be mushy, but I'm sure I said that. Didn't I?"

They drank their beer and laughed, as if thinking it a fine joke. "Yes, you did, but why won't you reveal any more about your incredible discovery?" one asked. "Why?"

It was incredibly clear to him, but perhaps they had already drunk too much. "Because," he said. "Because . . . others will try to steal it."

"Ahh." The second one grinned. "And tell me, Dante, are you requiring money up front for this venture?"

Again, a ridiculous question. "Of course," he said. "How else could we bring it home?"

"And why should we believe you?"

Caruso wasn't sure how to reply. He was sure that they were mocking him, but his ability to focus was deteriorating as they continued to challenge him. To keep his thoughts clear, he tried to concentrate on the treasure. "It is damaged," he said. "But it is still priceless."

"Damaged?" One turned his nose up. "Come on, Dante. We are your friends. Tell us more. Where is this treasure?"

"Poland," Caruso replied instantly. "No, in the mountains between . . ." And then he stopped himself, seeing clearly their smirking faces and hearing their mocking tones.

Quickly, he walked away from his friends and tried not to listen as they sniggered. Who else could he try? He reached out again, to less reliable customers this time, but nobody would part with their money. By late morning, almost everyone he knew in this part of Siena had heard the tale. Some retold it slightly differently, deprecatingly. If he'd revealed any more details, then they must have been passed on too. He worried that the local unsavory characters may have heard, but what could they really do? Most treated him as a laughingstock. Caruso paused in the afternoon and wondered where the next few steps would lead him on life's journey.

Into happiness? Or into madness? How deep was he into stage-three dementia?

His legs ached. The sun was beating down. He rested wearily on a low wall, bending his neck and staring at his feet. Life had never been good to him, but he'd expected more when he'd beaten it. When he'd won. But now every relationship he'd ever fostered here in Siena had slapped him in the face.

After a while, it seemed only one course of action remained. He remembered Anna warning him that nobody would believe this story, his latest of many. He vaguely understood why nobody would finance and embark on a long journey. *But . . . the treasure is out there.* Why couldn't they see that?

Close to the bar he'd visited earlier, Caruso found his favorite café, ordered a large black coffee, and sat down behind one of the establishment's computers. They were old, grubby machines, their keyboards thick with dust and germs, but Caruso's hands were always stained, and he did not notice. Quickly, he logged into the biggest online forum dedicated to treasure seeking and relic hunting. It was an international business. The coffee arrived, and he took a long gulp, sitting back, savoring its bitterness. Steadily, he scrolled through the index, studying the most recent threads and comments. Nothing relevant presented itself, so Caruso took some time to compose a thread of his own. The hardest part was gauging exactly how much he should reveal. How to make his discovery appear authentic and yet keep it away from the crazies, the freaks, and the bad men. Caruso racked his brains for an hour, fighting through the fog and welcoming the onset of the caffeine rush.

Finally, he felt happy with the wording and uploaded his new thread.

◆ ◆ ◆

Later, Caruso wandered home at a shuffle, a deep frown on his face, his back bent as if under the stress of a heavy burden. Darkness had fallen. A slight drizzle dampened the entire city. He walked straight into the house and let the door close behind him.

The only thing in the world that could cut instantly through his torpor greeted him.

"Dad!"

"Marco! Oh, you've grown so big. I miss you, son. I miss you so much."

The eight-year-old ran and leapt into his arms, his weight almost toppling Caruso. He held the soft, warm boy close for several perfect seconds and then let him down gently to the floor. Marco planted his hands on his hips and gave his father a child's critical stare. "Where have you been?"

Caruso knelt to meet his son's eyes. "Seeking our fortune," he said seriously.

Marco's eyes widened. He'd heard his father say that phrase before. "Did you find it?"

"I hope so." Caruso ruffled his son's dark hair. "I really, really hope so."

He caught sight of Anna over the top of Marco's head, her hard stare telling him that he was by no means safe from her ire. He also saw Anna's mother, a sixty-six-year-old white-haired lady with a considerable temper, and felt his heart sink.

Not tonight. I really need to rest now.

He pulled away from Marco, and within a minute Anna was ushering the boy to bed, ordering him to change into pajamas and brush his teeth before they came to tuck him in.

She glared at Dante as the moments slipped by. "Well? What happened? I've heard tales of your ramblings all day long."

"Me too," his mother-in-law added. "People come to me; they say, 'Greta, has Dante finally lost his last few marbles? Is this world too much for him?'" She shook her head despairingly.

"I can't make my old friends believe me," he admitted. "I wish I understood why. Despite my . . . disease, haven't I always told them that one day I will bring back the greatest treasure in history?"

"Yes," Anna sighed. "You have."

"Pah," Greta spat.

He tried to navigate through their condescension. "I remember the start point," he muttered. "And the mountains. That is all we need. What more could my friends want from me? But don't worry, Anna. We're not finished yet. I have other contacts I can use."

"Other contacts?"

"I am waiting for their reply."

"Be careful, Dante. Your ramblings one day will get you—"

"Stop!" Caruso snapped. "They are not ramblings. You make me out to be senile, a failure. I have found . . . I have found . . ."

"What have you found?"

"The Amber Room," he whispered.

Anna shook her head. "I don't even know what that is."

He nodded. "Nazi treasure," he said. "Stolen in the war. Considered to be a modern wonder. It was loaded onto a train one stormy night and never seen again. Anna, I have found that which

12

other treasure hunters have been seeking all their lives. I just need you to have faith, my Anna." He reached out to touch her cheek. "Faith that I can and will provide for my family."

She allowed him to touch her but screwed up her nose as he stepped closer. "You still stink," she said. "Go take a bath."

"And I am going to bed." Greta stalked from the room without another word.

He nodded, allowing himself to relax for just one second. Marco shouted from his bedroom that he was ready for them. His son's voice acted like a balm to Caruso's jumbled disquiet. The demons faded, and he saw his surroundings with complete clarity: the tiny, disheveled kitchen where Anna proudly made the best cannelloni that had ever crossed his lips, the dirty windows that she didn't have time to clean, the way his precious family remained aloof from him, as if expecting that tomorrow he would be gone.

It almost broke his heart. But the treasure was real, and it called to him. It was there. All he had to do was—

The kitchen door flew open behind him, crashing back on its hinges with a thud that rattled the glass. Caruso whirled to see four large men pushing through, one after another. They wore leather jackets over T-shirts and black trousers. They were all practically bald and clean shaven. They moved with purpose and with confidence. His first thoughts were for Marco and Anna, and he cried out a warning before stepping across the doorway that led deeper into the house. "What do you want?"

One of the intruders stared as if studying a photograph. "Yes, this is the right place. That is him." The man's voice was barely more than a growl. "Take him now."

"We have nothing," Caruso said. "We are only poor. Please, don't hurt my family."

"Then come quietly," the trespasser replied.

"What is going on?" Anna's voice was full of terror behind him. His heart flipped as he heard Marco asking his mother why she sounded so scared.

Caruso faced the men. "I don't see how we can help you."

"You'll find out very soon."

"And the family?" another man asked the first trespasser.

"Take them too. That should crush any urge to escape that he might develop."

"And the old hag?" One of the men laughed.

Caruso cringed and glanced around once more. Greta had walked quietly to Anna's side, behind Marco. She was holding the boy around the shoulders, trying to comfort him.

"Only the boy and the mother will be useful," the first trespasser said. "Do what you have to."

A flurry of activity made Caruso's head spin. He saw one of the large men grab Marco and pull him away. Anna followed immediately, which was what they wanted. That left Greta alone with another man, who approached from the side.

"Old lady," he said, "I take no pleasure in this."

"Wait." Caruso still couldn't comprehend the suddenness with which these invaders had ruined his life. He couldn't understand their indifference, how they were so calculating and cold in their violence.

Someone grabbed his arms from behind. He was held fast as the man beside Greta produced an eight-inch military knife and stabbed her through the ribs, twisting as the blade rammed up to the hilt. The old woman shrieked and then fell. The man dropped with her, withdrawing the knife and stabbing her again.

Then he cut her throat.

Anna struggled and tried to scream, but her captor punched her hard in the face. Marco was being led away, thankfully not a witness to the terrible murder of his grandmother.

"Do as we say," a voice whispered next to Caruso's right ear, "or we'll do exactly the same to your wife and kid."

Caruso frowned. The words didn't make sense. What was this all about? Why were these men in his house?

He didn't see the hammerblow coming from the right. It connected solidly with his temple and laid him out cold.

The last thing he knew was his head hitting the hard kitchen floor.

CHAPTER TWO

"Hey," Heidi Moneymaker said softly. "What are you thinking, Guy?"

Bodie blinked, looking over at the curly-haired, blonde CIA agent. It had been a difficult two weeks since they had found Atlantis. Bodie had found himself zoning out on more than one occasion after the loss of Eli Cross.

"It's all different without him," he said.

The room stilled. They were in the safe house's lounge: Cassidy, Jemma, and Gunn at a small circular coffee table with steaming mugs in front of them, Lucie and Yasmine on the floor in front of a leather couch, large glasses of water clasped in their hands.

Nobody said a word.

What can they say that hasn't been said? Bodie thought.

Cross had died protecting Yasmine, and now, two weeks later, they were living in a safe house. Attending the master thief's funeral had been one of the hardest things Bodie had ever done. Saying goodbye to a friend with such a good nature, watching as his coffin was lowered into the ground. Cross had been Bodie's only family, a man he'd learned to trust through years of danger and delight and world-class thievery. And Bodie had always chosen his family very carefully, ever since the tragic death of his parents, which had cruelly wrenched him away from his childhood friends. The Forever

Gang, they'd called themselves. He thought about his old friends now as he thought about the death of Cross. Somehow, the losses felt related.

I can't protect my family.

Bodie took a breath before walking over to the drinks cabinet. He poured a shot and drank it quickly. "But he'd want us to carry on," he said to the room in a gruff voice. "To finish this. How are we going to steal this bloody statue?"

The plan to steal the statue *back* from the merciless Ritter family had taken up most of their attention during the last ten days and had provided a timely distraction. Some time ago, the Ritters had hired Bodie and his team of relic hunters to steal a certain statue from an American Bratva family. It had turned out that the statue was, in itself, worthless, but it had held deep sentimental value for the aging Bratva head honcho. The old man had suffered a heart attack and died following the theft, which had put Bodie on the gang's hit list.

Through Heidi and her CIA contacts, they knew the Floridian Bratva leaders still sought them, blaming Bodie and his colleagues for the death of their father. This had led to Jack Pantera—Bodie's mentor—being compromised and Bodie being thrown into a Mexican prison. Now, the well-hidden safe house was all that kept them from the hands of the Russian brotherhood looking to settle the old score.

"We steal the statue back from the Ritters," Cassidy said. "And find a way to return it to the Bratva. Simple."

"Simple?" Jemma was busy tying her long dark hair into a bun. "I've planned easier gold heists than this."

"And there's no guarantee they will accept it in return for our lives," Gunn said a little nervously.

"The CIA will help facilitate that," Heidi said. "We can't meet the Bratva without the statue. They'd kill us outright. Returning the

17

statue will speak deeply to their code of honor. Once we have done this, we have assets who can broker a face-to-face talk with them. Whoever returns the statue to the Bratva won't be going in blind."

To Bodie's mind, that person would be him.

Cassidy was trying to catch his eye, and he knew that she would insist on being his bodyguard. Ex—cage and street fighter, she was their most capable warrior and one of his best friends.

The only warrior, Bodie admitted to himself. Though he was practiced, his combat talents were limited. On the other hand, when it came to relieving anyone in the world of a prized possession—there was nobody better than Guy Bodie. At least, not since they'd lost Eli Cross.

He nodded at Cassidy. "You okay?"

"I thought we were invincible," she said softly. "Yeah, we got cuts, bruises, sometimes worse. But we never got dead before. I don't know if I want to put myself, and others, in that position anymore."

Bodie frowned. This wasn't the old Cass. Ever since he'd first met her, she'd been a gung ho kind of girl, always up for the risk. "It'll take time," he said. "For all of us. We're poorer as a team now too. Cross was our master thief. He'll never be replaced."

"I wouldn't want him replaced," Cassidy said. "And I think something's changed for me."

"We're still working for the CIA," Bodie reminded her.

"For now," Cassidy said quietly.

"So where are we?" Bodie turned to the others, gripping the bridge of his nose between two fingers. "I have to admit it, guys— I'm finding it hard to concentrate."

Heidi nodded. "Just being cooped up in this safe house all day is hard labor," she said. "We should get out. Take a break."

"Disney World?" Gunn asked.

Bodie attempted a smile. Cassidy forced out a laugh, trying to lighten the mood. But then Lucie Boom rose to her feet and, ever candid and emotionally detached, waved a folder at them. "This is our best chance," she said. "The Bratva are going to find us sooner or later. We have three-quarters of a plan to steal back the statue from the Ritters here. Let's get it finished."

Bodie knew the newcomer to their team was right. He also knew that if you looked past the blunt manner, the blonde pony-tail, and the curious choice in sweaters, you would see a scared, fatalistic young woman. Lucie had proved invaluable to their team during the search for Atlantis. A savvy historian, she knew her history in the same way Bodie knew his safecracking.

"Miami," he said, and they all knew what he meant. The Ritter family lived just outside the sprawling city, only an hour's drive from where they were right now.

The team appeared ready to start thrashing out the final details of their plan when Yasmine, who had been quiet until now, cleared her throat. Bodie could see by the taut look on her face that the Moroccan needed to vent.

"Should the Bratva truly be our first priority? Are you all for-getting the Frenchman, Lucien, who was responsible for the death of your friend? I was Cross's lover—the one that got away—but you all claim to have loved him too, and I say that we use all our resources to make the Frenchman pay. Then we can deal with the Bratva."

Heidi stared at her. "But you can't do that right now. And what do you mean by 'pay'?"

"There is *nothing* that I—" Yasmine began, but Bodie thought it prudent to cut her off.

"We all want that," he said. "Believe me, Yasmine, nothing matters more than seeing the man ultimately responsible for Cross's death . . . brought to justice." He paused. He didn't want to talk about this right now. Didn't want to admit to everyone how emotional he really felt about the death of his friend. "But it can't happen just yet. We will deal with Lucien after we handle the Bratva; you have my word."

Yasmine looked ready to say more, her tanned face still rigid with grief, but then she chose diplomacy and took a long gulp of water. Bodie jumped in to fill the deathly silence.

"Let's get back to the Ritters and the statue that we stole *for* them, which we now have to take back. We know they are the poisonous head of a serpentine network of ruthless gunrunners. We know they are a long-standing Miami-based family, coming from old money. We know they have a daughter, whose twentieth birthday party is in two days. Preparations are vast and intricate. Even the guards are helping." His uninterrupted flow of words seemed to help calm the room, which was his intention. It even helped calm him.

Lucie waved her folder again. "Armed guards," she warned. "Eighteen of them. Plus, family members and friends who will know their way around a firearm. We have no idea where the statue is. Hence . . ."

"The first incursion," Gunn continued; Bodie was relieved, as this was the longest conversation they'd had regarding their next mission, "is to locate the statue. The second incursion is to steal it. To match our own exacting standards, the Ritters should never know who has taken it from them." He paused. "Or at least never know it was us."

"The FBI have had the Ritters under surveillance for years," Heidi said, "but haven't been able to find anything concrete to help put them away. It's always the usual barriers we're faced with— they're well connected, have influence, and will brutally retaliate against anybody who crosses them. But . . . I have been given access to a bunch of recent surveillance photos"—she waved her own folder at Lucie with a slight grin—"which will help in more ways than you can imagine."

Bodie smiled at her. Heidi's deep-blue eyes returned the sentiment. Their feelings were complicated, muddied by their principal relationship—the CIA were compelling the relic hunters to locate ancient artifacts in return for breaking Bodie out of a Mexican prison. Heidi was in effect his boss and the person who could help to support or damage all their futures. But that didn't change how he felt.

He recalled a meaningful exchange they'd had a few days ago, when Heidi had tried to contact her daughter but had twice been rejected.

"She'll open up one day," he'd said. "I'm sure she loves you."

Heidi had regarded him with sad eyes for a moment before visibly shrugging off her sorrow. "How are you doing?" she'd asked. "I know what Cross meant to you. I know he was a father figure. And I know . . . it must be incredibly hard to lose him now."

Bodie had tensed, unwilling to open up too much. "I can't speak about it. It's just too raw."

"I understand. But I'm here, Guy, right here. Anytime. I'm always here for you."

He recalled thinking it was a significant choice of words. It revealed deeper feelings. "Thank you," he'd said, kicking himself a little. He'd wanted to explore those feelings but couldn't sort through the turbulent emotions rattling around his brain fast enough. Right now, they couldn't afford to reflect on Eli Cross's death. Grief was a long-term thing, he knew. He'd lost his parents when he was eight and still mourned them every day.

"The surveillance photos are good," Jemma said, shuffling through them with Lucie. "We can track vehicle and people movements. Obstacles . . ."

"But I," Gunn said, running a hand through his gelled hair, "have the best part. I get to play with the Ritters' smart home."

"You sure you can handle that, kid?" Cassidy asked with a glint in her eye.

Gunn looked ready to defend himself but quickly realized she was teasing. "I guess we'll have to wait and see."

"If I die because you pressed the wrong button, I'm gonna haunt you for the rest of your days."

Bodie reached for a bottle of water. "Let's get some food and an early night. Tomorrow's the first incursion and puts the relic hunters back in action as they were meant to be." He glanced over at Heidi. "Which is stealing treasure from privileged criminals who'll never know the difference. It's gonna be a big day."

CHAPTER THREE

Bodie slumped in the passenger seat of the van. "Anything?"

"No," Cassidy said patiently. "In the last thirty seconds we have received no phone calls."

"Shit, I'm sorry. I'm finding it so bloody hard not to think about Cross and the bloody Bratva."

"Well, get it together, Flash. If we put one foot out of place inside that house, we're liable to lose it."

Bodie shuffled, trying to get comfortable, but only succeeded in making the leather squeak. "I know; I'll be fine. But if I relax, all I can think about is Cross and what happened on that boat."

"Nobody could have saved him. He chose to sacrifice himself for Yasmine. I guess we're the ones who have to live with that decision."

Bodie stared at the side of her head. "I don't know how I feel about Yasmine."

"Wow, aren't we feeling sharey this morning?" Cassidy said quickly, then sighed. "She needs time just like we do."

"And you?" Bodie peered at her. "You said you felt . . . different."

"I'm struggling," Cassidy admitted. "I mean, I don't mind a fight, and I'll always be there with you, but now . . . I'm feeling something else. I think it's fear."

"You've never known fear before?"

"I don't know. Most fighters or soldiers don't know fear in its rawest form until they love something. A wife or husband. Family. Children. Love makes you weak, I guess, and I loved Cross."

Bodie straightened his frame, considering her words. They were sitting in the parking area of a gas station several miles from the Ritters' home. It was 11:15 a.m., the sun was shining, and the skies were clear. Bodie was glad for the steady air-conditioning. Their uniforms were new but clingy, a bit restrictive. He wondered if he'd put weight on through comfort eating. They had decided that the first incursion would consist of just Cassidy and him, with the others lending support from outside and Gunn close enough to hop onto local Wi-Fi signals to infiltrate the Ritters' smart home.

His eyes fell upon the coffee-and-doughnuts sign. Caffeine and sugar sounded like the perfect therapy right now.

"I'll be—"

As Bodie reached for the door, Cassidy's phone rang. The redhead answered immediately. "Yeah?"

Gunn's voice came through the speaker. "I'm ready to go. How close are you guys?"

"Fifteen minutes max."

"All right, I'll cut the air-con and turn up the heat. Just wait for Heidi's call."

"Got it."

Bodie knew their plan was far from perfect. The Ritters would have a manual heating override, for instance. But as both Cassidy and Heidi insisted, you had to put yourself into the mind-set of a wealthy, self-important, murderous gangster. Would he go sort the problem himself, would he divert his men to solve a domestic problem, or would he expect expert help?

They were counting on the latter.

"Don't hit the doughnuts, Flash," Cassidy said. "I'd hate to see those pearly whites start to rot."

Bodie winced. "Gotta love that bluntness, Cass."

About an hour later, the phone rang again. Heidi's voice filled the van.

"The Ritters are getting all hot under the collar," she said. "You guys are up."

Bodie fought for focus as Cassidy exited the gas station and followed a short route to the Ritters' house. Traffic was scarce, and soon she was slowing alongside a ten-foot-high brick wall that followed the bend of the road. Along the top, Bodie saw rolls of barbed wire and occasional CCTV cameras. Presently, they came to a set of gates where, at the right side, a guard station was being operated by two large individuals.

Heidi pulled into a waiting area and wound down her window. "MBA Heating," she told one of the men and flicked a thumb toward the logo on the side of the van. "We hear you got problems?"

"Who sent you?" he asked, consulting a clipboard.

Cassidy rattled off the name of the smart home service provider.

"Wait there." The guard spoke into a shoulder-mounted radio, announcing their arrival. The squawk of irritation he received made him practically stand to attention. "You'd better get it done real quick and keep the hell out of the way," he said, addressing Cassidy. "And trust me, that's my friendly advice."

Cassidy waited for the gates to slide open and then drove through. Sculpted gardens lay to both sides of the meandering tarmac path, and soon a sprawling mansion could be seen ahead, dominating the skyline. The lawns to the front bristled with marquees and people setting up for tomorrow's birthday party. Bodie could also see a small stage being erected as technicians worked on the lighting.

"Some celebration," he said.

"Yeah, let's hope it keeps them busy." Cassidy touched her ear, opening a comms line to Gunn. "We're here," she said. "I'll let you know when you can reverse your magic with the air-con."

"Ready and waiting."

They parked, climbed out, and made a show of grabbing their gear—two small carryalls. Bodie's feet crunched over small, pristine chunks of white gravel as he walked. They were met at the front door—an eight-foot-wide, ten-foot-high all-glass arrangement that could have been the entrance to an office building—where two armed men flanked the opening.

"Are you MBA?" one of them asked, not bothering to check the side of the van. "Just wait here. Dwayne will be out in a minute."

They waited in the heat for a short while before being ushered inside by a small sweating middle-aged man wearing a suit and a harassed glare and sporting a limp. Inside, the house was sweltering.

"You know the problem? Heating's stuck on full and the air's out. It's not often in Florida that you go outside to cool down. Mr. Ritter won't be kind to idiots the day before his daughter's twentieth, so I hope you two know what you're doing. Follow me."

Bodie and Cassidy stayed quiet as they followed Dwayne through the house. They took everything in—the placement of tables, chairs, sculptures, mirrors, and paintings. The CCTV array, alarm wires, and infrared points.

Not that they would need any of that right now, but from experience they knew that those who held a wealth of information were far richer than those who held a wealth of coins. Dwayne led them to the air-conditioning unit, told them where the boiler was, and then stalked away.

"If you need me, just grab one of the guards," he said as he left.

Bodie tried not to smile. *Perfect.*

Bodie saw a single guard keeping an eye on them from one of the doorways.

"No statues so far," he informed Cassidy from the corner of his mouth.

"Me neither," Cassidy said. "Time for the distraction." She walked purposefully toward the guard, excuses at the ready.

"Well, if you need extra muscle . . ." Bodie flexed an arm. Cassidy smiled, recognizing a weak but valiant attempt at humor, his first in a while. Bodie slipped out of sight, taking his carryall with him. If he was seen, the carryall would add to his credibility. Quickly, he examined three rooms, staying away from the windows, but found nothing that resembled the statue he'd once stolen from the Bratva.

Why does this place have three bloody floors? He paused, listening, spotting an unassuming staircase ahead and guessing it led to the second floor. The owners probably used it for quick access rather than the grander, wider ones. He was aware that one of the best resting places for the statue was Ritter's master bedroom.

A mix of blueprints and surveillance photos had revealed exactly where that was.

They hadn't come in here blind. Bodie hurried to the foot of the staircase and went up two steps at a time. The second floor appeared to be empty; everyone was outside helping set up the party. Bodie saw two maids tidying guest rooms but scooted past them without making a noise. He also saw a guard staring out a far window down at the front lawns. Soon, he stood before the double doors of the master bedroom, which were, unfortunately, closed.

So far, he could probably talk his way out of this incursion. But if he opened those doors . . .

Bodie didn't hesitate. It wasn't just daring. It was knowing Cassidy was downstairs, working to keep him safe. It was knowing that Gunn had his back too and would be manipulating the CCTV feed, ensuring its fuzziness was blamed on the intensifying heat inside the house. The team had his back.

The right-side door opened easily. Bodie slipped through the gap. It took only seconds to determine the statue wasn't there. For the first time frustration struck, coupled with a chronic awareness that Cassidy could buy him only a limited amount of time. He appraised the space again, ignoring the glitz and trying to imagine where a man like Ritter would store such a prize.

A den? Something like a man cave, perhaps?

Yeah, but that could be practically anywhere. And this place was bloody enormous. It was then, as his mind fixed explicitly on the job at hand, that he saw the small alcove off to the left, away from the windows. It was darker over that side of the room, as the floor stepped down a level. Bodie entered the alcove and spotted a concealed door.

Man cave close to bed, he thought. *Makes sense.*

The door opened easily, and beyond, on the top shelf of a trophy cabinet, he saw the only thing guaranteed to make him smile.

"I've found it," he whispered in Cassidy's ear through the comms. "Tell Gunn to switch the heating off and the air back on. Oh, and tell him we're coming back tomorrow night to do our thing properly."

"Any chance you can swipe it now?"

"No way. We're out of time. They know we're inside. And tomorrow—the whole focus will be on the daughter and her party."

"Sounds good, Guy. Now get your ass back here. I can't go any further with his friggin' guard without actually removing something."

Bodie smiled and walked out of the room, already looking forward to tomorrow night.

CHAPTER FOUR

The next evening, before darkness had fully blanketed the skies, Bodie, Cassidy, and Jemma scaled the brick wall that surrounded the Ritter property, used thick blankets to negate the effect of the barbed wire as they rolled over the top, and dropped into the grounds. Gunn thwarted the CCTV feed until they found cover, and then everything—apparently—returned to normal.

Bodie lay in the undergrowth, listening. The party was in full swing, with pumping background beats and a live singer on stage entertaining what sounded like a large crowd of guests. Multicolored lights were stabbing both at the skies and at the expensive cars parked in a single line down the driveway.

Bodie looked at Cassidy. "Ready?"

"Yeah, I used to attend this kinda thing back in Hollywood. With all the stimulation they have up front, nobody will be looking back here."

Jemma nodded. Bodie scanned ahead with a handmade device that used stabilized liquid crystal technology to find infrared beams. Nothing appeared on the small screen. Cassidy told Gunn to scramble the CCTV for fifteen seconds as they made their way to the rear wall of the house.

Once there, they stood and waited, backs against the wall.

Bodie breathed easily, savoring the darkness and the cool breeze that played across his face. The faint breathing of his friends came from his left. He felt the bulk of a small pistol pressing into his back at the base of his spine. Nobody had wanted to carry weapons tonight, but Heidi had insisted on it, talking them around in her persuasive way. They ended up packing knives too, as well as a few smoke grenades and spare ammo. "Bloody CIA," Bodie had grumbled.

"Just trying to keep you safe," Heidi had said, smiling.

"The Ritters are no more than gunrunning, murderous thugs, despite all their airs and graces," had been Gunn's response. "Never forget that."

Now, Bodie followed as Cassidy led the way to what was usually the simplest access point to a house—the patio doors. Many weren't even alarmed, but the team expected that these would be. Jemma gave it the once-over first and then turned, sending Bodie silent confirmation that they would need to employ a bypass device. A career thief, Bodie usually kept all these items close to hand, but even if he didn't have direct access to a piece of equipment, he could usually build something in a matter of hours. Of course, Eli Cross had excelled at that . . .

Bodie shrugged away the memories of his friend and used a circular glass cutter to punch a hole in one of the door panels, then redirected the infrared alarm beams using a specially designed prism. Once the alarm was neutralized, they quickly hefted the PVC door off its hinges and leaned it up against the house. Brash, but it was the quickest and most effective way, utilized by thieves and moving companies all over the world. Jemma slunk in first, looking every inch the cat burglar Bodie remembered. They all wore black outfits with ski masks to hide their identities. Bodie followed Cassidy through the new gap. The interior of the house was quiet, the celebrations now muffled.

Jemma led the way. She traversed a narrow corridor, then saw the rear staircase and paused for a moment, crouched in darkness, looking back. "This is actually fun. Just like the old days."

Bodie straightened his mask. "Reminds me of a few good nights on the King's Road," he said. "The art of the steal, I mean, not the surroundings."

"Less talk," Cassidy murmured, "and more progress. I don't feel like a fight tonight."

Jemma sneaked onward. "That makes a change."

"Guess I could manage a nightclub, though."

Jemma remained silent, still resisting the redhead's efforts to find her a date. Cassidy sighed quietly. "Ah, that shut her up."

They reached the foot of the stairs and stole a brief glance through a tiny oval window that overlooked the front lawn. To their left they saw revelers talking and dancing in groups and the multicolored play of strobe lights. No guards were in evidence, but Bodie guessed they would be mingled with the crowd, positioned around the daughter, and watching the guests' perimeter.

In darkness they slipped up the back stairs, reached the second floor, and paused to check for signs of life. Gunn whispered in their ears that he'd seen the routine night patrol begin through the CCTV feed—but that left them a whole twelve minutes before it would reach the back of the house. They were in the clear.

"We're almost there," Cassidy whispered back.

"All right," Gunn said. "Scrambling their camera feed in three . . . two . . . one . . ."

Jemma clicked open the door of the master bedroom. Bodie watched as she reassured herself that it was empty before moving in. They crept over to the alcove and pushed at the door, so close now to the statue that the expectancy of stealing it had raised all their heartbeats.

Jemma stopped. Bodie peered over Cassidy's shoulder. "What?"

"It's locked."

"Bollocks." Of course, Bodie had already factored in that Ritter would secure a personal man cave during a party of this nature. It made sense. The problem was that their time was short.

"Keypad?" he asked.

"Yeah, it's nothing we haven't prepared for, though."

Bodie passed her the little machine that would mate the keypad to its processor and feed them the code. Three minutes went by before he saw a four-digit readout.

"Hurry," Cassidy said. "I don't want us to have to fight our way out of here."

Bodie blinked at that. Normally, she looked forward to the combat. It was clearer than ever that Cross's death had badly affected her.

"You have six minutes or so before the patrol gets here," Gunn said.

Bodie checked the time. Jemma punched in the code and opened the door. "Got it." She crossed to where the statue was displayed among several other objects and lifted it clear before transferring it to a rucksack.

"I'd love to be able to check the provenance of those other items," Cassidy said.

"No time," Bodie urged them. "Five minutes."

Leaving everything as they found it, the relic hunters returned to the ground floor. With no change to the muffled revels outside or to the interior lighting and ambience of the house, they headed for the rear patio door. Bodie led cautiously but saw that nothing had changed.

"All good," he whispered back.

"CCTV back to normal," Gunn informed them.

Bodie imagined somebody inside the CCTV control room might be harboring suspicions by now, but with all the party preparations, the heating breakdown of the day before, and tonight's added burden to security, they might well be doubting themselves too. And, of course, tonight was the perfect time to steal the statue, as there were hundreds of suspects. He entered the final room, inching toward the open door, enjoying the slight breeze that wafted through. Cassidy and Jemma were right behind.

"You must be crazy, trying to rob this house." A disembodied voice floated from a corner of the room. "Old man Ritter will rip your spine out."

Bodie's heart leapt as four armed men stepped out of the shadows, two from the left and two from the right side of the room, with weapons pointed. He hadn't seen them, but the recesses back there were deep, the darkness thick.

"Whoa, steady." He put both hands in the air.

One spoke: "We have many guests here tonight. Who are you?"

"We came down here for a dare," Jemma said quickly. "We are sorry. We took nothing."

Her words brought the guards three steps closer. Their guns didn't waver. Bodie faced their leader, a hard-eyed blond man whose face was carved into a harsh expression.

The man said, "I hope you are telling the truth. But even that might not save you."

"Save us?" Jemma allowed her voice to waver.

"Take off the masks," the blond man said.

Gunn whispered in their ears: "Get ready for Heidi. Five . . . four . . ."

Bodie shrugged, relaxing the muscles. Cassidy closed the gap between herself and two of the men.

"Right," she said reluctantly.

"Left," he said.

Heidi initiated her distraction by throwing a flashbang over the far wall. The sound and the flash were loud and bright enough to make all four guards whip their heads around, giving Bodie and Cassidy a chance to attack.

Bodie went left as she went right. Jemma hung at the back, reaching for her pistol. Bodie grabbed the barrel of the blond man's rifle and jerked it straight up. The metal smashed into the man's face, drawing blood. Bodie used him as a barrier between himself and the second man, who had managed to level his gun. With a yell Bodie ran forward, pushing the first guard into the second and propelling them across the room. They all fought and struggled and collapsed into a heap. Bodie fell between them, reaching desperately for one of the fallen guns.

No luck. The blond man, face bloody, leveled his barrel right between Bodie's eyes.

"Wait. I—"

The blond man squeezed the trigger.

CHAPTER FIVE

Deafening noise filled Bodie's senses. He saw the guard's finger tighten on the trigger, heard the sound of a gunshot, then saw the blond head jerk back, blood spraying, as the gun flew upward and discharged its own deadly cargo at the ceiling.

He saw the second guard trapped under the blond's bulk, the weapon wedged underneath.

Bodie breathed deeply as Jemma's voice cut through the chaos. "I got him. Move!"

He focused on her voice and made his limbs work. In that terrifying instant when the gunshot had rung out, he'd thought he was dead. Energy flooded through his limbs, and the movement of the second guard, struggling underneath the blond man, galvanized him some more. Bodie crawled over and punched him right between the eyes, feeling relief as the man slumped.

Rising, he surveyed the room.

Cassidy had already knocked one man to his knees and was fighting another hand to hand. Jemma was breathing heavily, wide eyed, distressed by what she had done. Bodie staggered to her side quickly. Jemma had never killed anyone before.

"You saved me." He hugged her, trying to get her moving rather than offering sentiment.

He pulled; she acquiesced. They passed behind Cassidy, who dealt a heavy blow to her opponent's right temple. Bodie saw the guy's legs buckle.

"Cass, come on!"

She was already running, face harsh with stress. They ran to the open patio door and squeezed through. Behind them, at least one guard was groaning and reaching for his radio. Time was short. Bodie helped Jemma along until she pushed him away, still holding her gun.

Cassidy scanned the lawns. "We're not going to make the wall."

To their right, in the direction of the night's festivities, the music abruptly paused. It was a sudden, striking absence of sound, a warning that Bodie took to be a death knell. Cassidy was right—they weren't going to reach the wall.

They kept running, putting some distance between the house and themselves. Cassidy spoke a word of warning just as Bodie saw guards appear around the front corner of the house.

As they raced across the lawn, spotlights flashed on, flooding the area with light and illuminating their escape. Bodie saw three guards exiting the patio doors to their right.

"Any ideas?" Cassidy asked.

"Just one, but it's a little rash," Bodie said.

"Rash is good," Cassidy said. "I prefer rash to sane any day."

"Stay with me, then."

Bodie ran for the front of the house, to the left of the oncoming guards. The gap closed quickly. Cassidy and Jemma were a step behind, feet pounding the well-trimmed lawn.

"You headed for the driveway?" Cassidy asked.

"There's no other way out of this place."

The partygoers came into view, along with the huge marquees and stage. The team had brought party clothes with them, giving them an option to mingle with the guests, but that option was now dead.

And so will we be if they catch us, Bodie thought.

The odds were stacked against them. Guards were converging from two directions, guns in hand, probably refraining from shooting only because the guests were watching. Despite their fast sprint, Bodie saw they would be cut off before they reached the long row of cars.

He slowed. "Bollocks."

"No choice," Cassidy said. "We'll plow through them."

It was a great attitude, but it wasn't going to happen. With six guards ahead and three behind and the open expanse of the lawn around them, they were out of options.

"We can't just stop," Jemma agonized. "They'll just take us to some basement and kill us."

Bodie agreed, but sometimes a change of scenery offered new options. The guards were so close now that individual faces could be distinguished. Bodie saw callousness in every expression. Was it worth a firefight out here on the lawn?

Cassidy would think so. She'd never been a woman who would give in or let herself be taken, but that had been before Cross had died. What would she do now? She halted in front, handgun held loosely by her leg, pointing down. Bodie put a hand on her shoulder.

"You planning to fight?"

The guards approached, raising their weapons, shouting in guttural tones, indicating that the team should lie down on the ground.

"I don't do well in restraints," Cassidy answered.

Bodie saw another option. They couldn't hope to beat nine armed men. Their only chance lay with the crowd that was gathering around the edge of the lawn, some with phones trained on the scene.

"Be confident," Bodie said and started walking toward the people.

"How the hell is this gonna help?" Jemma asked, at his side.

"No matter what the guards do, just keep walking."

Cassidy strode next to him. They skirted the guards and made a beeline for the crowd. More guards appeared ahead, making a total of twelve. Their leader shouted expletives and raised his gun threateningly, but Bodie kept his eyes to the front and kept walking.

A guard stepped in front of Cassidy and reached out to make her stop. She grabbed his wrist, dropped her shoulder, and planted him on his back, then continued walking as if nothing had happened. The guard groaned in her wake, and the rest backed off.

"What's the plan, Flash?" she asked out of the corner of her mouth.

"Stay alive for one more second," he answered. "And then one more."

"Been there, done that," the ex–cage fighter said. "Didn't enjoy it."

The guards gathered, trying to create a barrier between them and the crowd, which was now only ten yards away. Bodie saw a man stalking through the throng, men and women making way for him, and wondered if it might be Ritter himself.

This is getting riskier by the second.

Some of the guests were fleeing the main building. Panicked screams filled the air. Car headlights were igniting up and down the long row of vehicles. It was only when twin beams flashed across Bodie's eyeline that he realized someone was speeding straight at them.

"Hey!"

He grabbed Jemma and prepared to leap to the side. The guards whirled around, most of them now venting their anger at the oncoming vehicle. In the last few moments, the car's hood dipped violently under braking, and then the whole left side slewed around as it went into a broad skid.

A groundswell of soil and stones flew from under its wheels, drowning the guards in a surge of earth. They tried to hide their faces but ended up flinching or falling to their knees. Bodie had already seen Heidi at the wheel and turned his head. The moment the upsurge passed, he was running for doors that had fallen open in the wild slide. With Cassidy and Jemma, he ran past several men with bloody faces and others trying to spit earth from their mouths. Heidi revved the engine. Cassidy dived headlong into the back seat. Jemma lunged right behind her.

Bodie spun at the last moment, aware that one of the guards was too close for comfort. He was no great fighter, but he ducked his head and lunged hard, smashing his shoulder into the guard's sternum and heaving him backward. The man was lifted off his feet and came down hard onto his spine. Bodie leapt the last few feet toward the car. He jumped into the front passenger seat just as Heidi slammed her foot down on the gas pedal.

He hit the seat hard and fell forward against the dash. Heidi performed a slow power slide, guiding the car gracefully until it pointed in the direction in which it had come. Earth was spat out from under the back wheels. Then she let the car shoot forward. Bodie found himself thrown back into the seat once more, thankful for the plush black leather but smacking his head so hard on the headrest that tears filled his eyes.

Cassidy struggled to sit up in the back as Jemma lost her grip and sprawled into the footwell.

Heidi kept the momentum up, moving rapidly along the lawn. She threaded the car through the gap where it had been parked and slewed it around so that it faced the far gate, then accelerated again.

Behind them the crowd divided, men and women running away from the shocking scene. The guards were left staring. Bodie tried to grab hold of the seat to steady himself.

"Are we done turning for now?" he mumbled into the leather.

"Strap in, kids. You've got ten to fifteen seconds before we hit the gate and then the main road."

Bodie just held on tight. "Please, please, don't flip us."

CHAPTER SIX

A short while later, Bodie sipped coffee and stood near the front window of the safe house, wanting to sit down but unwilling to put pressure on the bruised parts of his anatomy. Heidi's driving had been reckless, but she had saved their lives.

"I'm bruised all over," he'd said when they'd raced clear of the Ritter estate.

"But you're alive." Heidi had grinned at him. "And we have the statue."

A good feeling washed through him now. The first part of their plan to get the Bratva off their backs had been accomplished.

Barely. And now comes the most dangerous part.

They had contacted Gunn, Lucie, and Yasmine, who had been back at the safe house, and driven back without stopping. Once again secure, they'd arranged to contact the Russian brotherhood. Heidi had suggested they call Jack Pantera and bring him in for his input. Bodie had agreed. Despite retirement, Jack was still one of the best in the business.

Bodie saw his old mentor park a street away and start walking toward the safe house. "Jack's on his way," he said. "Hey, Cass, come here. We can watch and see if he's lost any of his old talents."

Cassidy joined him, and together they followed his progress, discussing aloud what they thought he would do next, when he would check for a tail or study a suspicious passing car, how he checked the progress of a sauntering dog walker. Pantera walked by the property twice and then turned down the path and continued around the back on the third pass. A buzzer sounded. Gunn pressed a button to let him inside.

Heidi's phone rang. She checked the screen and then sighed. "I'm gonna have to take this. Someone at the office needs me."

Bodie tried not to let any concern enter his expression. The office usually called when they had a new relic to chase. This wasn't a good time for a new relic. He looked over as Pantera entered the room and offered Bodie a hand.

"How's married life, pal?"

Pantera rubbed anxiously at his bald head. "Don't even get me started. It seems I'm to blame for everything. From the refrigerator that buzzes too loudly to the mere trickle that is the air-conditioning and the pool that smells of mold . . ." He sighed.

"You got a pool?" Cassidy feigned indignation. "Hey, Frizzy, I want to lodge a complaint."

Pantera hadn't finished. After the sigh, he put a hand on Bodie's shoulder. "Haven't seen you since Eli died, mate. I'm sorry."

Bodie swallowed dryly, caught off guard. His mind was still buzzing from the heist. "Ah, thanks, I . . ."

"Anything you need," Pantera said. "I'm here."

Heidi looked over, but then her speakerphone stopped ringing as her return call was answered. "Someone left a message?" she said.

"Oh yeah, that was Scottie. I'll pass you through," an agent replied.

As they waited, the rest of the team greeted Jack. Their old boss looked like he wanted to get right down to business, but then Heidi began to speak.

"Hey, Scottie. What's the problem? You know I'm with an asset right now."

"Sorry, boss, this can't wait. Something big has come in . . ." He paused.

The rest of the team focused, listening intently to the call.

"Ah, crap, that's bad timing," Heidi said. "Again. What have you got?"

"We have a man living in Italy by the name of Dante Caruso. He's a bit of a relic hunter—nothing on your scale, just a loner picking up scraps to help feed his family. He's a dreamer, a man who boasts to everyone who will listen that he's just biding his time, waiting for the 'big one.'"

"Oh yeah?" Cassidy chortled. "Aren't we all?"

Heidi frowned as Scottie continued. "Caruso's a well-known figure in his hometown of Siena. He travels far and wide and returns with baubles, trinkets. Three days ago, he came back to Siena following a two-month absence. He returned with no relics but tried desperately to gather a team together—a team he could lead in search of what he called the greatest treasure of them all. He's not far wrong . . ." Scottie paused for breath.

Bodie kept moving to counter bruised and stiffening limbs. The urge to devise a plan that would finally rid them of the Bratva menace was incredibly strong. It roiled through his gut like a tubful of hot sauce. And if he knew his team, they would be feeling the same. Cassidy was always eager, chomping at the bit to bring her prowess to bear. Jemma's active mind would be sorting through scenario after scenario, separating the wheat from the chaff. Gunn's deft computer expertise was always ready to go. Only Lucie and Yasmine were outsiders in Bodie's team, Lucie being the historian and Yasmine . . . well, they didn't know much about Cross's old flame yet. They had little idea of what she could bring to the table beyond her combat skills and Interpol connections.

Heidi spoke for everyone in the room. "Get on with it, Scottie. What treasure?"

"Well, Caruso hit the forums when he failed to muster a team. He put the word out, asking for help, and gave a couple of vague references alluding to his discovery. He mentioned World War Two and something that 'began in 1701.' Now any relic hunter worth their salt should recognize these not-so-subtle references?"

"Is that a question?" Heidi asked, turning to Bodie. "Do you know what he's talking about?"

Bodie shrugged. "Haven't a clue, sorry. We have much more important—"

"Oh, but I think he does have a clue," Scottie said. "If you know your relics, you will know that these two references point straight toward one of World War Two's greatest mysteries. Which is what happened to the Amber Room."

Heidi stared hard at Bodie, but the thief appeared suddenly interested in his coffee mug. The last thing he wanted right now was another confrontation with Heidi when they needed the CIA to help deal with the Bratva.

"Go on, Scottie," Heidi said.

"Several people sent direct messages to Caruso. He answered them with even more candor, telling of a long route through Poland, a train or a plane; he couldn't remember which. He appears to have some kind of memory issue, though that could be feigned. He also gave them a final, indisputable clue: Catherine Palace, which was the Amber Room's original location."

"So did they form a new relic hunting team?" Jemma asked, rustling sheets of paper with well-laid plans around the table before her.

"No, no. Nobody took Caruso up on his offer. Most of his personal interactions fizzled out, with some calling him a crackpot, others a charlatan just wasting their time. Mostly because the man's memory is a little fuzzy. I don't know why."

Bodie tried to hide his annoyance. "I hope you don't want us to travel to Siena just to see this man."

"You couldn't even if you wanted to. He's gone missing."

Heidi grew attentive. "Missing? Or wandered off?"

"Missing," Scottie affirmed. "His family has vanished too. A wife and son. Their house shows signs of a struggle, and . . . his mother-in-law was found dead at the scene. Murdered. Caruso, his wife, and his son were taken just hours after he used the forums."

"It's not our job to find missing persons," Cassidy said.

"No, but it is your job to find missing relics. And this is one of the biggest."

"Bigger than Atlantis?"

"They're still digging Atlantis out of the ocean. The Amber Room, if it exists, would be sitting right in front of you. Ready to reveal to the world."

"Any leads on where this Dante Caruso may have been taken?" Heidi asked.

"We're working on it."

"Of course," Bodie said, "Caruso might have perpetrated this himself. Taken his family. Forced them to go with him."

He watched carefully as Heidi palmed the phone and turned to address the room. "This new development is directly relevant to the relic hunters, as it concerns the famous Amber Room. And Bodie, stop acting coy; I know you've heard of it. The question is, Does Caruso's disappearance substantiate his claims?"

Lucie Boom moved to the center of the room as if addressing a class. "Most importantly, it doesn't disprove them. This entire event needs investigating."

"And I guess you can help with some background on the Amber Room?" Gunn asked.

"Of course. That's my job."

"Look." Bodie stepped in. "I'm sorry to do this again. I know we caused issues during the last mission when Cass and I focused on rescuing Jack whilst the rest of you struggled in Brazil, but—"

"You work for the CIA," Heidi said bluntly. "Who are the only people in the world able to safely facilitate for you a face-to-face with the Bratva. You know the deal, Guy, and last time—when you ignored my orders—you said that would never happen again."

"I'm pretty much impartial here." Lucie was still standing ramrod straight. "But I do remember the Bratva caused hell on the last mission. Nearly killed us all. We don't want that happening again."

Bodie placed his cup on a coffee table. "They almost scuppered it," he said. "Literally, at the end. And how long would it take to arrange a meet as important as this?"

"Not long," Heidi admitted.

Yasmine cleared her throat. "I understand I am not part of this team," she said, using both hands to smooth the front of her yellow dress. "As you know, I worked undercover for Interpol inside the Moroccan Bratva. Bodie and his team were high on their priority list, and you too, Agent Moneymaker. I suggest dealing with one significant enemy before crossing swords with what might become another."

Bodie smiled but then looked away. He was grateful for her input but at odds with her presence. He imagined she'd be feeling the same way and searching for a way to become a part of the team. She remained a kind of personification of Cross's death and a reminder that he was gone forever. Bodie wasn't sure he'd ever be able to work directly with Yasmine. He wasn't sure he even wanted to speak to her.

Jemma spoke up. "We need to stop feeling hunted and having to hide out in safe houses. I feel nervy, on edge, every second of every day. I don't even want to risk heading to the store to grab breakfast. My mind is befuddled, and that's not good for any of us."

Heidi placed her cell on the table and sat down heavily. "By rights," she said, "we should already be headed back to the office. But the odd thing is . . . I agree. We're here in Florida and not set up in DC for a reason—the Bratva. We just risked our lives to grab that statue for the Bratva. Let's see what it takes to end this."

Bodie wanted to cheer as she reached for her phone. Pantera gave him a thumbs-up, and Jemma breathed a sigh of relief. They weren't out of the woods yet, but this was a good sign.

While they waited for Heidi to complete her call, Bodie reflected briefly on Cross's funeral. He hadn't had much of a chance earlier, because they hadn't had a moment to rest. It had been a dismal day in every sense of the word: rain trickling from the sky as if it couldn't quite make up its mind, the grass damp underfoot, the entire area surrounded by a security cordon as Eli Cross had been laid to rest. The man's family had been there, but Bodie had barely gotten a chance to talk to them. It had been rushed. Not the kind of ending such a good friend deserved. Bodie still did his best to keep Cross alive, though—carrying every memory in his heart and reliving one each day. To Bodie's mind, the only time a person really died was when there was nobody left to remember them.

Lately, as a direct result of Cross's death, he'd become more introspective. He'd never forgotten his first family of friends, the Forever Gang, and he'd been recalling some of the great moments of his youth, before the death of his parents. It helped keep him optimistic against all of life's current conflicts and reminded him that the team he'd assembled now harked back to the team he used to run with.

The best days had always been unplanned back then, like a trip to the park that had become a quest through Highgate Wood as they'd searched for the monster that, according to local fables, lived there, preying on everything from rabbits to children by day and night. Brian, Scott, Jim, and Darcey had been his friends, all eight years old and on the cusp of perfection. When he thought back, Scott, the slow, deliberate one, reminded him of Cross. Brian, the adventurous one and the ringleader, reminded him of Cassidy. Jim, the quiet, introspective one, reminded him of Gunn. And Darcey, small for her age but a feisty thrill seeker who pushed all the boys to their limits . . . she reminded him of Jemma because of her spirit.

They had searched the woods for hours, enlisting the help of any friends they'd fortuitously come across, mapping out their route with care, stopping to eat sandwiches their mothers had wrapped in plastic film. They'd sat and eaten and talked and laughed without fear before resuming their monster quest an hour later. Comrades together, they'd taken each step with wonder, with fresh eyes and an unrestrained future. The sun and the summer and being together had been all they cared about.

But where are they now?

Bodie forced himself back to the present. Once the old memories of the Forever Gang had grabbed him, he found it hard to tear himself away from that happy place.

Because it reminded him of the tragedy that had come after but that had then, conversely, brought him full circle back to the family he loved now.

Heidi ended her call. "All right, well, that's three more people in the Bratva loop." She sighed heavily. "I don't like it, but it has to be. I spoke to two detectives who are as close to the Bratva as police can get. They know the main players and can get messages to the right people. They're willing to facilitate a meet and mentioned that the Bratva definitely have the hots for a certain group of relic hunters."

"Hey, we're famous," Cassidy said.

"Not in a good way," Heidi assured her.

"When's the meet?" Bodie asked.

"Nine a.m. tomorrow morning," Heidi said with a catch of nerves in her voice. "In some abandoned boat graveyard outside Miami."

"Do you think there are too many people involved in this now?" Bodie tried to identify her worry.

"Well, I just spoke to three men, who will have to tell at least two more cops and an unknown number of Russians. And then *they* will tell . . ." She spread her arms. "Who knows? But I'm happy that the meet is soon. The less time that passes between now and the handover, the better I feel."

"Did they sound amenable?" Gunn asked. "To the return of the statue, I mean?"

"That," Heidi said, "is the life-or-death question, my friend. I guess we'll find out tomorrow."

CHAPTER SEVEN

Bodie studied the abandoned boat graveyard suspiciously as he picked his way along a path between several rusting hulks.

Accessed off a side road that cut through an industrial park north of Miami, the boatyard was bordered by a tall black iron fence. There were several unofficial entrances cut through the fence, but the team walked through the only legitimate one—a wide, dusty gap once protected by a large black gate that now hung to the side, broken, askew, its paint flaking away.

Beyond the gate were boats of every shape and size. Some sat on timbers, splintered holes in their sides; others sagged, their wooden supports crushed by time. They were arranged so that a path cut through them, traveling arrow straight toward a ramshackle office building. It too was made of wood, Bodie noted with a little irony.

But the truth was the mold-caked hulks that lined their way only registered in the peripheries of their vision. To a person, Bodie and his crew were utterly focused on one thing only: the Bratva.

Bodie felt a fresh breeze play around his face. He glanced back at the others, who were mostly walking in a group. When one of the decaying boats shifted, probably through age and in response to the rising morning sun heating its timbers, Gunn jumped on the spot, and Jemma flinched.

"I wish they hadn't insisted we bring the whole team," he muttered to Heidi, who was walking at his side. "I hate it."

"The Bratva are pretty transparent in that respect," Heidi said. "It's all about honor. Their issue is with the whole team, so they want to resolve it with all of us."

"Or kill us," Bodie pointed out.

"I don't think so. Our contact reported that the brotherhood's leaders were amenable. Even impressed. The Bratva won't want to prolong a blood feud. If they can solve the issue today and save face, I'm sure they will want it behind them."

"And by the leaders, I assume you mean the old man's sons," Bodie said.

"Two of them," Heidi said. "The third is out of the country."

"This code of honor," Cassidy said. "What do you know of it?"

Heidi slowed her pace as she explained. "Well, it's complex. Their code translates to something like 'thieves in law' and has many obligations, including one that states they will not cooperate with the law in any way. But another states that if an enemy has honor and respect enough to pay his debts, then he must be taken seriously. That's where the statue comes in."

All this time, Pantera and Yasmine had stayed quiet, intent on spotting any hidden surveillance. Cassidy pointed out one man, Pantera another, but the team walked up to the timbered office without challenge.

Bodie and his friends stopped when the door opened inward. Dust plumed around the team as the morning sun beat down.

"Wait there," a man wearing a black leather jacket and reflector sunglasses told him. He turned back toward the room and barked out two words: "Check them."

Bodie waited patiently as they were patted down by four men. This was what they had expected to happen. *So far, so good?*

Maybe, but he'd told everyone to prepare for an uncertain, stressful morning.

"I hope there's coffee inside," Cassidy said, seeking to ease the tension with a bit of levity. "I forgot second breakfast."

The man wearing the reflector sunglasses regarded them without expression. Bodie noted that everyone wore shoulder holsters with Ruger handguns nestled inside. The handles were dull and pitted, no doubt through regular use.

"They're clean, Aslan," one of the four men said, stepping away from Pantera.

Aslan, the man with the sunglasses, glanced into the darkness of the room behind him. Bodie heard him mutter a few words before he turned back around.

"Come now," Aslan said. "But heed my warnings. Do not move quickly. Do not ignore orders. Know that you are always standing in the crosshairs of a high-powered rifle. Be respectful. And I would advise you to show remorse."

Bodie understood the reason for the warnings. The two men they were here to meet ran the Floridian Bratva. Important figures, with a great deal of power. But he also knew that this scenario wouldn't be unusual for them. Through his years of being a thief, of living amid the darker underbelly of society, he knew deals between organized crime and government agencies happened almost daily.

Bodie led the way, prepared to take the brunt of the blame from the Bratva. He carried the guilt of everything that had transpired since the team had crossed them. Stealing the old man's statue had been his idea. It didn't matter that he couldn't have anticipated the theft resulting in a fatal heart attack.

Inside, the building smelled dank. It was riddled with decay, timbers rotting on the walls, allowing daylight to leak through. Sunlight dappled the floor—random spotlights falling on heaps of old papers, a battered desk, and a broken filing cabinet. Two men sat on folding chairs at the center of the room, which Bodie guessed measured about twenty feet across and twice that in length. He counted four men standing in the half shadows, weapons raised. Three guards stood behind the two seated men. If he counted Aslan and the four outside, that made fourteen Bratva soldiers visible.

He had to assume there were more. Cautiously, hands held by his sides, palms out, he approached the center of the room.

"Stop," Aslan barked, and Bodie stopped nine feet away from the seated men. "Come no closer."

Bodie determined their features easily from this distance. Both were middle aged, probably in their late forties, and looked bulky under their designer Italian suits. They stared expectantly, saying nothing, offering no outward emotion, so he assumed they wanted him to make the first inroad.

The silence was so profound Bodie heard his friends breathing at his back.

"I'm Guy Bodie," he said. "I wish to say here and now that my team and I utterly regret the death of your father. We didn't appreciate the sentimental value the statue held for him, and if you know anything of our reputation, you will know that we only execute victimless crimes. I *do* understand your wish for vengeance, and it's with that in mind that we stole the statue back from its new owners and are returning it to you."

He paused to take a breath.

The man to his left looked down and started inspecting his cuffs. "It is good that you get straight to the point, Mr. Bodie. It is good that you come here—this way—to make peace. I respect your effort. Where is the statue?"

Bodie gleaned nothing from the expressionless faces. It was like trying to gauge the reaction of a brick wall. He watched the room as best he could, allowing Cassidy to step forward, unhook the rucksack from her back, and carefully bend down and reach inside with one hand. He felt the tension inside the building suddenly double.

"Careful with that," Aslan said. "We will shoot all of you if we suspect any treachery."

Cassidy took her time, eventually lifting the statue clear of the bag. She straightened with it clasped in her right hand.

"Crap, I really hope it's the right one," she said, half-jokingly, but received nothing in reply. The entire Russian contingent just stared.

Bodie sought to break the spell. "Do you want to examine it?"

"I am Carl," the man to Bodie's left said. "And this is Nikolay. Our father suffered much through his life. This statue that you stole many years ago was our mother's favorite, cherished by her until the day *she* died. It is old Russian. It is a part of the motherland"—he held one fist to his chest—"and part of my family."

"The way you have returned it," Nikolay said, speaking for the first time, "is honorable. Everything you have done to make amends shows respect. And on most occasions, it would be enough . . ." He left the sentence hanging as his face twisted in thought.

Bodie tried to quell an upsurge of trepidation. The Russian brothers knew what they were doing. This was being played out to punish the relic hunters even more. "'On most occasions'?" he repeated carefully.

Around the room guns that had been held loosely were now raised and concentrated carefully upon the center of the room. Bodie saw they were in a kill box. *We misread the bastards.*

"Good will," Carl said emotionlessly. "Our father would have killed you all where you stand. But we . . . we think the statue and some good will should be enough. We are honorable men."

Bodie breathed through clenched teeth. The words this man was speaking didn't match the atmosphere in the room, the raised guns, the vicious expressions, the flexing trigger fingers. Briefly, he looked away from the brothers and regarded his team. Cassidy was glaring at Carl with a severe expression. Heidi looked unsure, her normally calm outward demeanor pierced. Gunn, Jemma, and Lucie looked scared, eyes flitting left and right, arms held unconsciously across their chests in a defensive manner. Yasmine and Pantera stared back at Bodie with something that might have been resignation.

Bodie turned to the brothers and didn't hesitate. "If by 'good will' you mean to take a life, then take mine."

Surprisingly, it was Heidi who spoke up first, voicing her objections and jerking Bodie around to face her. "You can't," she shouted point-blank into his face.

"Heidi, I—"

"You can't!"

Then he was surrounded; Cassidy, Pantera, and Jemma grabbed his shoulders and shook them. Bodie was bewildered, unsure who to appease first. Even Yasmine looked like she wanted to say something, her mouth moving uncertainly but no words coming out.

Nikolay laughed coldly, cutting through their emotional scene. "You are assuming we are asking for volunteers? No. We want the life of Guy Bodie. He will honor our father's death by offering his life."

"I already did," Bodie growled, tired of being reverential to men who clearly wanted him dead.

"You did, and now we shall take it." Carl raised an arm. Bodie saw the sleeves fall back, revealing a gold watch. He saw Carl's fingers unfold. He saw everything—from Nikolay's cold glare to all those bodies that suddenly crowded around them.

His friends surrounded him, shielding his body.

Bodie's heart leapt to see their courage. It reminded him of the old days with the Forever Gang, who always had his back. Even Jemma, Gunn, and Lucie were there, terrified but standing alongside Heidi and Cassidy, standing between him and a bullet.

"You can't . . . ," Bodie started to say anxiously. "I won't let you." He fought to get clear, constrained by bodies. "Wait!" he shouted over toward Carl and Nikolay. "Please wait."

"Mr. Bodie." Carl was chuckling, this time with real mirth. "We did not say we wanted to kill you. We said we wanted your life."

Bodie scowled, thinking through the connotations. Did they mean servitude? Well, they'd have to fight the bloody CIA for that.

Nikolay saved him the trouble of asking. "Your service," he said. "When we need it. Just once. Anytime. Anyplace, and for anything. That is what we want. And we expect you to die for that service, if need be. That, and the statue, will clear your debt."

Bodie stared at them. "Surely the Bratva already have everything they will ever need . . ."

Carl shrugged and then waved his hands. "We may not need you," he said. "But we are careful men who enjoy options. Your friends can let you through now. Bring the statue."

Both Heidi and Cassidy held their ground, reluctant to trust the Russians, but Bodie pulled the statue from the redhead's grip. He shouldered his way through the group into open space, feeling as if the weight of worlds had been lifted from his shoulders—the burden of worry for his friends, for himself, coupled with a new feeling of freedom.

"Agreed." He handed Aslan the statue, who then passed it along to Carl. "Are we done here?"

"We are." Nikolay spoke for his brother, who was lost in the statue and the memories it represented. "You may go."

Bodie let out a huge sigh of relief, turned, and smiled at Heidi, Cassidy, and the rest of the team. Finally, they could move forward.

And that was when gunfire exploded inside the building, the sound of dozens of automatic weapons destroying the stillness both inside and out. Bodie felt the terrifying sense of betrayal just as the Bratva opened fire on an unseen enemy. Someone else had crashed the party.

CHAPTER EIGHT

Cassidy collapsed to the floor. Bodie dived down alongside her.

"Are you okay?"

"Yeah, you fool. I'm just ducking."

Bodie rolled away. Gunn and Jemma were on their knees. Yasmine was crouched down but staring at the entrance door, the sunlight that streamed through it, and the shadows that bordered it. *Not the Bratva.* Bodie knew that. Even distracted he'd registered that the Russians hadn't started the firefight. Two Bratva soldiers had already fallen, and the rest were returning fire. Aslan was shouting at the top of his voice, ordering his men to guard the brothers. The heads of the Bratva were to be saved at all costs.

Bodie already knew the best cover inside lay to the left side of the building. He'd noted it on arrival. A collection of old desks, filing cabinets, collapsed timbers, and two old outboards lay scattered across an area of twenty square feet. Bodie had also spied a pile of tools that might yield at least one makeshift weapon.

"Move," he cried out.

The Bratva retreated toward the rear of the building, firing constantly to cover their bosses' escape. Another soldier had collapsed under fire, making three in total, but the remaining men stayed in control, backing away. The new figures at the building's front door fanned out, slipping through shadows. Bodie rolled again and then crab walked as fast as he was able, approaching the left side. The gunfire was unrelenting, echoing from wall to wall, riddling the already-spoiled timbers with ragged holes.

The interlopers were closing in. Only a minute had passed since the attack had started. Miraculously, none of Bodie's team had been hurt. But they were bunched up, defenseless. They were ideal target practice.

"Who the hell are these guys?" he asked.

"No clue," Heidi said. "But they haven't hit us yet, so we might as well run."

Bodie cast a last glance at the Bratva—Carl and Nikolay were being bundled through an opening in the back wall—and then they ran, heads down, toward the meager cover. Everyone arrived together. Bodie rooted out a hammer and a crowbar from the mass of detritus, shaking his head.

"I don't fancy our chances."

"We've faced worse," Cassidy grunted.

Bodie hefted the crowbar. "You're mistaking us for SEAL Team Seven, love."

He counted four enemies closing in and another four still at the front doorway. Four more had pursued the Bratva. Bodie was aware his team was outflanked, outgunned, and outnumbered, but he retained hope simply because they hadn't been shot yet.

"Time to get the hell outa here."

Using the clutter of upturned desks and filing cabinets as cover, Bodie yelled at his team and charged headlong toward the nearest wall. It was an all-or-nothing gamble, but their situation was desperate. It felt like they were being hunted for sport by men who knew they had no weapons and nowhere to go. He picked the weakest spot he could see in the rotting timber wall and hurled himself at it.

The timbers broke under impact, snapping off and falling away. Bodie plunged through into daylight, hit the dirt, and then rolled, ending up on his knees, facing the way he had come.

The hole he'd created was barely large enough for him to fit through, but then Pantera crashed through, widening it, tearing timbers away to left and right. He staggered and fell as he came through, ending faceup on the ground. Bodie rose to his feet, still holding on to the crowbar, feeling the sharp pain of splinters and light cuts on the backs of his hands and arms. In another moment both Heidi and Gunn came through, leapt over Pantera, and rushed toward him.

Bodie cast around. The boatyard was enormous, but the path to the exit was clearly delineated. *Problem is,* he thought, *it's undoubtedly guarded too.* He saw a narrow track between two enormous hulking wrecks and directed Heidi toward it. "Go, go, I'll watch your back."

Bodie helped Pantera along and then watched Lucie and Jemma leap through the rough gap. More timbers fell away. He saw Cassidy on the other side, practically shoving Yasmine through before following so closely she might as well have ridden piggyback.

"Move your ass, Flash!" she cried. "They're not handing out toothpaste."

Bodie backpedaled, staring grimly as an odd-looking weapon was thrust out of the hole. It had all the appearances of a rifle, but the barrel was different. A man's head came next, and then Bodie turned his back on the gun and chased after Cassidy.

To the left, a shout went up.

More assailants, he saw, who, judging by the weapons they held, were part of the same crew. He counted five, stumbled on an unseen rock, and then turned his head forward. The boatyard was in chaos, but he had to concentrate on putting one foot in front of the other. The roar of two motorbike engines cut through the air.

Bodie heard a shout from behind, someone yelling at them to stop. He ran even harder, gaining the narrow trail between large boats a second after Cassidy.

The gap was so constricting it felt a little claustrophobic. The boats towered high, one on top of another, all the way ahead. The path was overgrown and strewed with garbage. Bodie saw the top of an abandoned crane to the right, a boat hanging from its rusting jaws.

At the front of the pack, Heidi suddenly shouted, "They're coming this way too!"

Bodie swore. When he focused, he could see quite far ahead. Two attackers were motoring up the path on small dirt bikes. They wore black helmets and motorcycle jackets and carried standard handguns.

Heidi turned tail. There was nowhere to go; the boats were too closely crowded. Bodie was very aware there were over half a dozen men closing in from behind.

"You have to take them down in front," he shouted.

He saw Heidi nod, her face grim. The motorcyclists swerved to a stop in front of her. Their tires kicked up a surge of dirt toward her. Before the man could leave his seat, Heidi had grabbed hold of his shoulders and used every ounce of strength to shove him against the hull of the nearest boat. The noise of his spine striking wood was dull but satisfying. The bike toppled, and the man cursed heavily. The second man leapt clear of his bike, but then Bodie's attention was diverted entirely away from the fight.

What the hell was that?

Timbers were snapping again, but this was a sound far deeper and more ominous than any smashed wall. It was the sound of something incredibly heavy shifting, coming apart. Bodie saw the big boat that the biker had hit; the timbers that held it in place had shattered, years and years of decay exposed by the impact, and now the entire boat was listing to the side. Not only that, but the one resting on top was moving too, transferring weight as the one beneath it collapsed.

The process would only gain speed. Bodie cried out a warning, then shoved Yasmine and Lucie past him, locking eyes with Cassidy.

Nowhere to go.

To make matters worse, the insecure boats were sliding into those beside them. The entire area around the relic hunters was shifting, turning more treacherous by the second. Bodie backpedaled as a chunk of rotted hull crashed down near Heidi, cutting her off from the second biker. Fear crossed her features, and she started to run toward Bodie, urging on those in front of her.

Bodie ran. Menacing groans and creaks came from his right, where decomposed wood and rusted metal warped and buckled. He reached the last boats and dashed out into space, again coming face-to-face with their attackers. The breath he heard so close to his right ear belonged to Pantera, and Cassidy was close to his left. The rest crowded behind. A horrendous grinding sound split the air as four boats collapsed along the path they had just escaped. Two vessels that had been loaded on top came crashing down. Particles struck their backs, a debris-and-dust whirlwind. Gunn folded, struck by flying timber, but didn't collapse. Holding a hand in the air, he managed to say, "I'm okay."

Bodie paused behind half a boat and stared at their enemies, the same four men they had encountered inside the building. "Let's attack these bastards."

Lucie stared back in horror. "Are you crazy?"

"It's that or we let them get closer, and then we're at their mercy anyway."

"Fair point." Heidi grabbed a length of pipe just as Pantera picked up a thick, jagged piece of timber.

"Stay behind us," Bodie said, motioning at Gunn, Jemma, and Lucie. "We ready?"

They were. Bodie abandoned cover, buoyed by two things—only four men faced them, and despite their guns-up stance, none of them had opened fire. He waved the crowbar and charged, rapidly closing the gap to twelve and then eight feet. Heidi was at his side, Pantera a step behind.

It was then, as he came closer, that he overheard a few snatches of the attackers' comms chatter.

". . . in sight. Target clear. Should we engage?"

"Engage now. Take them down."

Fingers tightened on triggers. Bodie dived headlong and yelled out a warning. Even as he did, he realized that these weapons were not quite right. Something different . . .

Then he hit the ground and rolled into the legs of one man, toppling him. When he folded, Bodie swung with an elbow, catching him in the right cheek. The man flinched. Bodie saw Cassidy grab hold of another attacker, lifting him off his feet. He grabbed hold of his opponent's rifle, forcing the barrel down toward the ground, and delivered a headbutt. There was a grunt of pain and then a headbutt in sharp reply. Bodie reeled, head ringing. Fleetingly, he took in the surrounding scene. Jemma and Gunn and Lucie were down, crawling along the ground, but they were practically flat on their faces. Gunn held a yellow-feathered dart in one hand, regarding it with an accusatory glance. Pantera lay on his back, a similar yellow dart sticking out of his chest. Cassidy, still standing, heaved her opponent off his feet so that he fell back onto his spine, crying out in agony.

Then she whirled and half stumbled as a yellow dart struck her neck.

Bodie warded his attacker off with one raised hand, the other still clinging onto the rifle. Now he could see one of the men diverting his attention toward him as Heidi struggled with another, losing her grip on the man's gun and falling away. As she fell, she kicked out, but her blows weren't enough to fell him. Mercilessly, he aimed the barrel of his weapon down at her.

What happened here? How did they know about this meeting? What the hell do they want with us? Who . . .

The questions flashed through his brain a moment before the dart struck his heart. There was no pain, no shock, no sensation at all. Bodie wondered for a second if the man had missed, but then something warm and overwhelming swam up to his brain.

Bodie's vision clouded. The last thing he saw was two figures standing over him, one talking into a radio.

The last thing he heard was: "Sir, we have the relic hunters."

CHAPTER NINE

Bodie came to consciousness and was immediately aware of a thick odor. Engine oil and mold, with a dank, cloying undertone. His head throbbed so painfully that he closed his eyes again, searching his memory for a clue as to what had happened.

Then it hit him. He sat up too fast. The room swam. The heavy aroma continued to assault his senses, and he fought down nausea. Bodie tried to breathe and took a slow look around.

They had been dumped unceremoniously, it seemed, onto a dirty garage floor. Dark shapes stood to left and right, vehicles in a state of semirepair, mostly shadows under the dull glow of a single ceiling light. He took a moment to count the other figures that lay around him—oddly there was one too many.

Bodie wondered if he was still under the influence of whatever drug they'd used back at the boatyard. His head felt fuzzy; his vision swam. The others started stirring. Bodie gave them a few seconds before explaining what he could see.

A minute later, Cassidy was on her feet. "We should search this place. Find out where the hell we are."

Bodie nodded and then wished he hadn't. "First, though . . ." He indicated the extra figure in their midst. "Any guesses?"

The figure was dressed in dark clothes—old jeans and a heavy jacket. Even from a few feet away, Bodie smelled an unwashed stench emanating from him. His hair hung limply, speckled with dirt and dust. Jemma, who was closest, reached out to shake him but then flinched away. "Wow, he needs a bath."

"We're locked inside a small auto repair shop," Cassidy said, returning from her recce. "Windows are small and grubby, but I can see a few houses and other businesses out there. Their names are not written in English. I see a road. The sun's shining. And the door's heavy steel; I guess we could break a window—"

Pantera rose, rubbing his bald head. "I'll take a look at the door."

Bodie knew that if anyone could use their skills to escape this room, Pantera was up there with the best of them. He climbed to his feet and brushed himself off.

"I don't get it," Heidi was saying. "Why are we here? The Bratva were satisfied. Who were those other guys?"

Bodie didn't have the answers. All he knew was that his association with the Bratva had grown more complicated. He now owed them a debt for lifting the blood feud and worried that when the time came, he might not be able to deliver. In addition, he couldn't have arranged the meet without the CIA's help—which put the relic hunters in their debt, also. The team's lives were becoming more complex by the day.

"Give that guy a shove, Gunn," Bodie said, referring to the dusty stranger. "He might know what's going on."

The computer geek frowned in distaste but crawled over to the anonymous figure and reached out. Right then, the figure sat bolt upright. Gunn let out a small shriek and lurched away. Cassidy grinned at the youngest member of the team.

"Classic Gunn," she said. "Scared of everything that doesn't connect to a keyboard."

"Yeah?" Gunn replied. "Have you seen yourself lately?"

Bodie eyed the stranger closely. His face was, not surprisingly, dirty, his forehead streaked with soil. His eyes were the only bright thing about him—piercingly blue, like sapphires shining under a shroud.

"What . . . what happened to me?" he muttered in what sounded like an Italian accent. "Where am I?"

"We were hoping you might throw some light onto that," Heidi said, scraping straightened fingers through her curls to remove the loose grime.

"I don't . . . remember. I . . . but they have my family!"

Bodie shared a glance with Heidi. "Who has your family?"

"I don't know," the man admitted. "Men. Bad men from the internet. Wait—you could be working with them! Do not talk to me." Quickly, he shuffled farther away.

Bodie watched as Pantera evaluated the locked door. "If they have your family, mate, they don't need us to work on you."

The man considered that and then nodded, holding a palm to his temple. "Yes, yes, you are right. But it's so hard to remember everything. It all . . . clenches . . . right here." He tapped his head.

"Clenches? Like stress?"

"Wait." The man stared at Bodie. "Who are you? Why are you here?"

"That," Lucie said, sitting propped up against the wheel of a car, "is the best question yet."

"The people who messed with us took a huge risk," Heidi said, feeling around her pockets for credentials. Bodie knew she'd carried them to the Bratva meeting, staying as transparent as possible—the Russian soldiers had been aware of everything. Finally, she shook her head. *They're gone.*

Bodie was about to speak when the garage door rattled. At first, he thought Pantera was trying something, but then he saw the older man step back, still scratching his bald head. Bodie's senses came alert, and he stepped behind one of the cars. Cassidy grabbed a torque wrench as a weapon.

"Get ready," Bodie said.

Bodie waited as the door screeched outward, its bottom edge grinding on stones. A moment later he counted ten figures entering one by one. Five carried weapons and fanned out while the others waited in a group just inside the door. Bodie took careful note that this time, the guns were equipped to fire bullets, not darts.

One of the unarmed men waved a hand. "We want to talk now. You will have many questions, I am sure. Come forward."

Bodie saw no reason to remain hidden. The speaker was about six feet tall with a ponytail. A network of scars crisscrossed his face. He was slim, but the T-shirt he wore revealed an abundance of stringy arm muscle and several faded tattoos.

"Why are we here?" Heidi stepped in front of a car, facing the speaker. "Who are you?"

"I am Gurka. We"—he indicated the four unarmed figures at his side—"are known by the alias R24. Meet Belenko, Dudyk, Vash, and Nina."

Bodie saw by Heidi's face that she knew exactly who R24 was. It didn't appear to be a good thing. He joined her in the center of the garage, studying the members of R24 and the positions of the men with guns.

Pantera came alongside, closely followed by Cassidy. Gunn, Jemma, Lucie, and Yasmine waited behind two vehicles.

"And you are here," Gurka continued, "because of this man."

The pungent figure leaned on his knees, looking away from his captors. He shrank away from the words, saying nothing.

"This is Dante Caruso," Gurka said in what sounded to Bodie like a Russian accent. "What he lacks in bodily hygiene he makes up for in his abilities to ferret out the cheapest, nastiest treasures this side of Cairo. But recently, Caruso uncovered something he'd never dreamed of finding. Something incredible. Yes?" This last word was clearly directed at Caruso. The man nodded quickly, still staring at the floor.

Bodie spoke up. "Mr. Caruso says you took his family. Is that true?"

Gurka raised an eyebrow as the one called Dudyk laughed nastily. It was Dudyk who answered, top lip curling with an expression of hatred. "Yes, his child and wife. We will kill them if he fails us."

"Don't worry," Gurka said. "Dudyk here hates everyone. He is a good man to send into a fight, and, of course, he is right."

Bodie couldn't see a quick way out. If you were captured, the discipline was simple—live a minute more. Every passing moment, hour, and day might offer up a fresh chance of escape. Pantera had drilled that into him since day one.

"You've heard of us, Agent Moneymaker?" Gurka offered Heidi a malicious smile.

Heidi answered after a few seconds. "R24 is a group of relic smugglers preying mostly on eastern Europe. The reports I have seen say they are ruthless and savage. Barely above the level of wild animals."

Bodie blinked and threw Cassidy a warning glance; they might have to fight. He tensed, prepared in case Gurka reacted badly to the description, but the man just threw them a grin.

"Is that what they say?" He laughed. "I love it." He punched Dudyk on the shoulder and clapped the one called Vash on the back. "We're wild animals!"

Bodie noticed that Nina didn't look particularly impressed, and Belenko had no reaction whatsoever. They were an odd bunch, this group . . .

Of what?

"So you guys are *anti*–relic hunters," he said. "Well, I guess that explains why you kidnapped Caruso rather than asking nicely or pretending to help. But what do you want from us?"

"R24 is the brains," Gurka said. "But you are Guy Bodie, and this is your team. I have heard of you. Of the Zeus statue and Atlantis. And before that. Your prowess is what brought you to our attention, why I am . . . hiring you." Gurka laughed loudly at his own joke. "But we hire mercs for muscle, to get their hands dirty. Caruso . . . why don't you tell them what you found?"

Heidi held up a hand. "I already know—"

But Caruso was displaying the first sign of interest since they'd met him. His body was upright, his face animated. His fists were clenched.

"The Amber Room," he whispered in a low, reverential tone. "I found the Amber Room."

CHAPTER TEN

"Sounds like something gratuitous to me," Cassidy said. "The den of a madam. Do we really wanna hear more?"

Gunn looked like he wanted to jump on the web and start research. Lucie stepped forward, as if eager to explain.

Bodie saw the potential of engaging Caruso, who appeared to be the only other person who knew the stakes. He crouched beside the Italian. "The Amber Room was looted by the Nazis in World War Two, yes?"

Caruso met Bodie's stare. "Yes, and it's been sought by individuals and governments ever since."

Lucie spoke up now. "The Amber Room is one of modern history's great mysteries." She took a breath. "How did you . . . ?"

Caruso blinked as she paused. "How did I?" He scratched his head. "Well, that's the question, isn't it?"

Gurka leaned against the front wing of a half-repaired car. "We asked around about Caruso. Seems he's always this way. His friends call him addlebrained. In truth, he's in the early stages of dementia. So yes, perhaps he found the Amber Room. Perhaps he didn't. Perhaps he found it and can't remember where. And that's why you are here."

Heidi frowned. "What makes you believe him? I mean . . . you raided a CIA-Bratva meeting in the US. Kidnapped us. Abducted Caruso and his family. That's some hard faith, right there."

Gurka shrugged. "Whatever you think of us"—he threw icy looks at both Heidi and Bodie—"we know our relics and their history. When Caruso described what he'd found over the internet, we knew his descriptions were genuine."

Bodie winced. "You described your find on the web, mate? Bad move."

"Carvings of angels and children." Caruso appeared to be lost in memory but spoke lucidly as he related his thoughts. "I saw jade, onyx, and quartz, backed by gold. To see the Amber Room with your own eyes, even packed in crates and dulled by decades of dust . . . it is not something you . . . umm . . . *mescolare*?" He struggled with the English for a second. "I mean . . . muddle up."

Bodie wasn't convinced. Lucie interjected with, "It did contain six tons of amber. You can only imagine the stunning effect it would have."

Gurka coughed. "What he described so well was the brittle, crumbling nature of the amber. How, when he attempted to lift one panel to look closer, it broke away in his hands. This is exactly what would happen as the amber dried out. It gave his story a ring of truth. Plus, he also recited what he remembered of his travels. Everything fitted. And if I'm being honest, Miss CIA Agent, extracting you from America wasn't hard or risky for us. As I said, we pay other people to take the big risks. And do the killing."

"It's still a risk," Heidi insisted. "What you're doing now. All of this is."

"The Amber Room was the biggest-value item looted in World War Two," Dudyk hissed at her. "We play with probabilities all the time. Live. Die." He gestured with both hands. "Win. Lose. Run or be captured. This probability is worth the risk."

Bodie shrugged unhappily at Heidi. The savage Russian had a point. The blonde agent stared disconsolately back, her curls flecked with dirt, her mouth drawn into a tight line. Despite their dire situation, Bodie found himself wondering if they'd ever explore the unspoken questions between them.

Is it real attraction or mild fixation? Is there something worth the risk here?

He'd felt from the beginning that an occurrence might draw them closer together, but the velocity with which their lives had accelerated recently had put personal matters on hold. Heidi had helped rescue him from a Mexican prison . . . they had barely paused for breath since. But the way she'd offered her condolences after Cross's funeral had made him realize there might be something deeper between them than a working relationship.

"Why us?" Gunn asked in a quiet voice.

Bodie studied the youngest member of their team. Both Gunn and Jemma looked scared, unused to kidnap and confrontation. Bodie also saw how Lucie's lips were drawn pale and thin with the strain. This was no place for their historian. Yasmine and Pantera, on the other hand, both stood easily, radiating confidence, accustomed to perilous situations.

"Why you?" Gurka was looking straight at Gunn, much to the young man's discomfort. "Honestly? Is there anyone better known in the relic hunting game? Is there anyone better connected"—he glanced at Heidi—"or more experienced? We want you, and we want your resources."

"And what do we get out of it?" Cassidy asked.

"We won't shoot you in this room, and we won't hurt Caruso's family. Yet. Is that incentive enough?"

Bodie's survival instinct kicked in. He evaluated the preparedness and positions of the five armed men in the room. The situation did not look good for his team. Their enemies were ex-soldiers, trained fighters, and while Cassidy might be able to match them blow for blow, neither he nor Heidi was close to her league. No matter how he looked at it, they were in dire straits.

For now.

"Also," Gurka went on, "we will take this one"—he indicated Lucie—"as added collateral."

Two men hustled toward the historian. Bodie set off quickly on an intercept course. One of the men, a merc with yellow teeth, raised his weapon, so Bodie gave him the full-on grin. Though he wasn't entirely sure if it was the smile or the blinding white rack that slowed him, Bodie was able to grab the rifle's muzzle and wrench it up toward the ceiling. The second man turned, but Cassidy confronted him, leading with an elbow to the nose that sent him staggering back into the garage wall. When he started at her again, she held up a hand, warding him off.

Bodie didn't press his advantage, just gripped the gun with its muzzle up, holding on tightly and matching the merc for muscle power. The three remaining armed mercs had already leveled their guns.

Gurka laughed. "Don't worry; she'll be coming along with us. But she will be . . ." He paused, thinking. "Kept separate."

Bodie held on to the weapon, almost nose to nose with his enemy, the man's bad breath filling his nostrils. Heidi caught Gurka's attention. "What the hell does that mean?"

"It means that we will all go together, but the blonde will travel with one of my men, under guard. That way, if you try to double-cross us, we can kill her quickly."

"Extra security," Dudyk added with a sneer.

"Then take me." Yasmine spoke from behind Bodie's back. "She is a historian, nothing more. If you take me, I will not fight you."

Bodie felt a surge of emotion. He warmed to Yasmine silently for trying, but then he remembered she was partly responsible for

Cross's death. And the Lucie he knew would have challenged the phrase "only a historian, nothing more," but Bodie doubted she'd heard anything beyond her own pounding heart at that moment.

Grimly, he held on to the gun, sweating and betraying no emotion. At his side, Cassidy tried not to get involved with her opponent.

"You seem to think you have a say?" Gurka put on a confused voice. "A vote, even? This is not a democracy. You will do as you're told, or one of you dies. In any case"—he shrugged—"a historian is valuable to us. I hanged our last one recently after he failed to deliver what he promised. Perhaps we will keep her permanently."

"Fuck you," Heidi said defiantly. "If we're going to help you, it will be on our terms."

Nina, the female member of R24, spoke up. She too had a Russian accent, and she fastened her gaze on Heidi. "Do not forget," she said, "that we have Caruso's family too, which we will not hesitate to execute. You are not just fighting for your own lives."

Bodie eased the pressure slightly. The merc pushed him away. It occurred to him right then—and he understood that Heidi would have considered it earlier—that the Bratva meeting had taken place without any outside surveillance. It had been set up by the CIA, but the Bratva had insisted on secrecy.

Nobody knew what had happened to them.

Except for the Bratva. But Bodie wasn't counting on the Russian brotherhood tracking and saving them.

"We will start tomorrow," Gurka said. "Get some rest. You will need it for the days ahead."

Bodie watched their new enemy start to file out, thinking: *So as usual, we're working with people we can't bloody trust.*

CHAPTER ELEVEN

Bodie had fought the urge to jam both hands over his ears all through the night. Caruso had kept everyone awake with his incessant jabbering, and he was still blathering now, as R24's mercenary team watched them leave the garage. Bodie was glad to escape the dank, oily smell and the lack of fresh air, though the bright, crisp day they walked into was anything but promising. Caruso still hadn't stopped talking, but Bodie understood. The man was worried for his family. He'd told them tales about his wife and son for hours, and most of the stories had ended in anxious tears.

"It all starts at Königsberg," Caruso reminded them for the thousandth time. "Königsberg is where we begin."

"Why Königsberg?" Lucie pushed through the group so that she could walk next to Caruso. "Because it's the last place the Amber Room was ever seen?"

Caruso frowned, and Bodie thought he might zone out for a moment as if to consider a long reply. They couldn't have the man losing his memory now. Lucie's question was crucial, given the circumstances. The entire group was headed toward three nondescript Ford Transit vans. Bodie counted carefully as the five members of R24 separated between the gray and white vans. The fifteen mercenaries divided between all three, six taking the driver and passenger seats up front. His own crew was divided between the black and white vans, except for Lucie, who was shoved into the gray one. It was a big group, but he expected Königsberg Castle was used to large parties showing up unexpectedly. Bodie stepped up into the black van, boots grating across the metal floor, and took a seat on a wooden bench affixed to the side. Others jumped in and shuffled up or took the bench opposite. There was an uncomfortable silence as the relic hunters eyed the mercs, who eyed them in return. When the van was full, the driver slammed the back door shut and climbed into the front. Bodie heard the engine start.

"In 1945, Hitler ordered the removal of all stolen possessions from Königsberg," Gunn said. "This order empowered the Reich minister of armaments to move national and cultural items, and none were so significant as the Amber Room. The enormous undertaking was begun and well underway, but then key figures fled the city and the Red Army attacked prior to the new occupation in April 1945."

"And the Amber Room?" Heidi asked, helping to divert Bodie's attention from the edgy van ride.

"Nowhere to be found," Gunn said. "Some believe it was actually destroyed in August of 1944, when the city was bombed by the Royal Air Force. Now, that's possible, but it doesn't explain why hardly any part of it was ever found. Even badly damaged, the amber would have been worth a fortune. It was the Soviets who declared the Amber Room was destroyed by shelling, from their own men, but why did they then start conducting extensive quiet investigations into its disappearance? Their own senior researcher was quoted as saying, 'It is impossible to see the Red Army being so careless that they let the Amber Room be destroyed.' And that"—he took a long breath—"was the start of the mystery."

"Königsberg was its last known resting place," Caruso said, lucid on this subject. "And the occupants of Königsberg Castle did have about three months to spirit it away. Somebody made plans to safely remove it. Probably several somebodies. It would have taken a lot of man power. Also, don't forget that those who remained had years to leave their clues." He shrugged then and glared up at the van's roof, as if seeking an errant thought.

"But how did you know where to look?" Gunn asked.

Caruso cocked his head at him. "Me? I don't know where to look. Why do you ask?"

"You found a clue at Königsberg Castle?" Heidi pressed gently.

"Well, 1968 is the problem," the Italian said.

Bodie was lost. "Why a problem?"

"That's when President Brezhnev of Russia ordered the castle destroyed."

Bodie's face slipped into shock, sharing the same confused expression as everyone else in the van, even the mercs. "Are you kidding me? You say this castle where you found the clue, this castle we're headed to now, no longer exists?"

"Yeah," Heidi said. "Did you time travel?"

Bodie saw an intent behind the flippant comment. Caruso's head was a mushy place, hard to navigate even for Caruso himself. Heidi was looking for clarification that his assertions weren't the wild ramblings of a befuddled mind.

"The cellars are *intatto*," Caruso said, again struggling with the English translation. "Umm, not damaged. Once, it was believed that the Amber Room itself was down there, packaged away. Many researchers visited. It was a great lure, but as time passed and nothing was found, people stopped coming. The area *rifiutato* . . . declined. Now, I don't believe anybody recalls those cellars very well. But I . . ." He tapped the side of his head. "I do."

Bodie stared, trying to figure this man out. "But you can't recall your entire journey? Or its end?"

"They have my family." Caruso pleaded with his eyes. "And when they find the treasure, who are we but witnesses?"

Bodie sat back, thinking that was a very interesting answer.

The side of the van jolted his spine as it bounced over the uneven road. Was Caruso following Bodie's own creed? Was he surviving for just one more minute, and then a minute after that, hoping for a lucky break? Did he know more than he was letting on, or did his moments of lucidity only come with talk of relics?

"We start with the cellars," Heidi said. "And then?"

Caruso couldn't veil the fear. "It is a long, dangerous road. My memory is fuzzy . . . but there are many pitfalls. Many predators."

As he spoke the final word, his eyes turned hard, staring straight at Bodie and then Heidi. Bodie got the message. It was kill or be killed from here on out. What they really needed was to get Caruso alone and learn what he knew. The guard who'd stayed with them last night had stopped all attempts at personal interaction.

But Caruso was right. The relic hunters, Caruso, and his family would be eyewitnesses to the greatest treasure find in centuries. *Expendable eyewitnesses.*

The members of R24 would ensure they were terminated, their bodies ground to dust and then scattered in the high winds. Nothing would remain.

As Bodie climbed out of the van, he stopped in surprise. When Caruso had said they were visiting a castle, even ruins, Bodie had expected a hillside and maybe some grassland or a forest. The remains of Königsberg Castle occupied a small, flat stretch of ground between old urban developments, blocks of flats, and busy roads. The parking area was large and faced the square where, once, the great castle had stood. Bright-red and yellow canopies stood to the left, a traveling circus. Bodie took a moment to stretch his limbs and then walked around to the front of the van.

Gurka stopped beside his left elbow. "You run, or you try anything—your blondie and the Italian's family die badly. Got it?"

Bodie nodded and cast around for Lucie. She was nowhere to be seen, probably still inside the gray van. The other visible members of R24, Nina and Vash, ordered mercs to check the surrounding area. Bodie saw them hide their weapons away and saunter off, trying to look casual in the bright morning light.

"Expecting trouble?" Heidi asked, a natural instinct for the CIA agent.

"My whole life," Gurka answered. "Now move, Caruso. Where are these cellars?"

The Italian moved off without a word, followed by the relic hunters, R24, and six mercs. Nobody spoke. The mercenaries broke away, pretending to be separate from the group, holding small handguns beneath their coats. Bodie found a moment to walk alongside his old boss, Jack Pantera.

"Thoughts?" Bodie knew they wouldn't get much time to speak.

"Follow the trail. A chance will come."

"The big issue is Caruso's family."

"Agreed."

Even if they fought and defeated the mercs, even if they freed Lucie, even if they beat R24—nobody knew where the Italian's family was being kept.

"Gotta extract that information from them," Bodie said.

"Or trade . . ." Pantera smoothed his bald head, where sweat was already starting to glisten as the sun rose higher. Bodie saw his nod toward the general area where the members of R24 were gathered around Caruso. Pantera meant to capture one of the group members. Not a terrible idea.

"You okay?" Bodie glanced at some of the cuts and bruises that studded Pantera's scalp.

"Yeah, it's all superficial. I know it's hard, mate, but you gotta let Cross go for now. We can talk and mourn later."

Bodie knew his old mentor wanted to help him, to ease his way through the pain. "I know. I'm trying."

Right then, they reached Caruso's side. Heidi and the others were listening to the Italian.

"Before its destruction, all the castle's works of art, from simple ornaments to great masterpieces, were removed and relocated. Once that task was complete, it left only the structure and items considered worthless. Of course, what is worth little today may be worth a great deal tomorrow, so rather than raze it all, the curators moved what they could to the cellars. It's a vast space down there and full of unwanted, humdrum old junk for the most part. But if you take your time . . ."

"What?" Gurka betrayed impatience. Bodie gathered that he didn't like being this exposed.

It was Heidi, though, who voiced the man's fears. "Scared of someone recognizing that ugly face from a wanted list?"

Gurka peered at her. "Careful, Miss CIA. We don't need all of you."

Cassidy took a step to his side. "Same goes for you, Ponytail. You hurt one of us, you'd best be ready to take down all of us."

Bodie gave Gurka the eye until the scar-faced leader deliberately turned his back on them. To Caruso, he said, "Get on with it."

"Every sconce, every fixture, every engraved floor tile was removed and packaged. Also," Caruso said, "every stained glass window."

"That makes sense," Pantera said. "No point destroying the glass if they didn't have to. Plus, they could use it elsewhere."

Caruso nodded. "They did, some of it. The rest is still here. I think I spent a day and a half combing through it."

"You remember your history very well," Gurka growled. "But real life is a problem for you?"

"Sometimes," Yasmine said, "real life isn't all it's cracked up to be."

"We don't have a day and a half to look," Nina pointed out, coming up from another direction, looking broad shouldered and well muscled in her tight-fitting coat. She and Cassidy could have been sisters. "Can you remember anything?"

"Get me down there," Caruso said. "It might come back."

Bodie noticed that Nina had the key to a padlock clasped in her hand. Now, as he stared harder, he saw Dudyk behind her, a twisted smile on his lips. He tracked the direction from which they'd come and saw a low building with a white facade at the far end of the open area.

What had they done?

Before he could ask, Nina unlocked a door and pushed Caruso through the opening. It took a few moments for everyone to file inside. Bodie followed Gurka into a wide, low room, where Caruso flicked a switch.

"This"—he indicated a door—"takes us to the storage areas." Caruso seemed entirely coherent now that they were following the treasure trail.

The Italian led the way. The cellars were cool, smelling of damp and old things. Uncounted footsteps echoed from wall to wall. Bodie saw a wide-open space stretching into the darkness and a ceiling about eight feet in height, lending the area a claustrophobic atmosphere.

Countless crates stood near the center, away from the walls, many covered with decades-old sheets, mildewed and partly eaten; others were exposed and with their lids ajar. Still more, Bodie noticed, had their sides burst open or their lids hanging askew, smashed. Caruso passed through the wooden boxes carefully, threading his way to the back of the stacks.

"I remember this." He kicked an empty bottle of Southern Cross vodka to one side and eyed the closest crate. "This one looks promising."

Bodie shared a glance with Heidi. Could they really trust this guy? Dudyk and Vash removed the crate's lid, which was already awry, and shone a flashlight inside.

"Stained glass," they reported.

"Told you," Caruso said, apparently pleased with himself. "Didn't I tell you? Take me to the scene, and everything returns. The glass pane you're looking for is in the pile to the left. I placed it third down and wrapped the whole pile carefully in a sheet."

Bodie watched as all five members of R24 worked together, lifting the glass out of the crate and placing it gently on the floor. It was Nina who unwrapped it and Gurka who removed the top two panes.

Then Caruso knelt at the man's side as though they were old friends. "Look," he said. "Just look at the picture and tell me what you see."

CHAPTER TWELVE

"See the date?" Caruso pointed a grubby finger at the edge of the pane. "That's when the panel was fitted. Twentieth April 1945. That's weeks or maybe months after the Amber Room left Königsberg. Do you see now? *This is the start of the journey.* The Amber Room's journey. And now we can follow."

Bodie squinted at the pane of glass, craning his neck so that reflections didn't ruin his view. The image itself covered about two-thirds of the pane. It was mostly black with deep-red highlights and depicted the Amber Room in situ at the castle itself.

"See?" Caruso said. "This is the last authentic representation of the room. Maybe this alone would be worth my family to you?" He looked hopefully at Gurka.

"Don't be foolish. Anything else and I'll bring you one of your wife's fingers."

Bodie knew Caruso was clutching at straws but didn't blame him. "Above the room is a separate picture depicting a mountain range," Caruso went on. "The word written above it in Russian translates to 'Tatra.' The third image, the church at the side, is very striking. Do you see how the steeple is shaped? The oblong windows? The door? All of these features are picked out in red because, I assume, they define a particular church in the Tatras." He broke off, suddenly staring around as if seeking a lost friend.

Bodie watched, still unsure if the man was acting. It now occurred to Bodie that Caruso became lucid whenever the mission required it or a choice presented itself. Relic hunting made him come alive; it made all the rusty, decaying synapses in his brain start to sing. In a way, that reminded Bodie of himself. It was the job and the promise of the job that made Bodie come alive too.

"The Tatra Mountains," Nina was saying as she squinted at the glass, "are some distance from here. They form a natural border between Slovakia and Poland. It's certainly not impossible that a train could have made its way there between January and September 1945, when the war ended. But are you sure about this, Caruso?"

"It is the clue I found and followed," the Italian said simply. "I remember."

"He's re-creating his journey," Yasmine said. "It's actually a good technique for those in search of answers to feelings of hatred, love, and grief. It's also a coping mechanism. He's remembering the journey when he reaches the start."

Bodie wondered if she'd attempted that internally to deal with her emotions regarding Cross. He wondered if he should try, but when he tried to recall the good times he'd had with the master thief, he kept coming back around to the Forever Gang. Somehow, he related Cross to them, and Bodie thought it was all about losing family.

"We will need provisions," Gurka said. "And much more equipment. If we're headed into those mountains, we will need everything we can carry."

"You know them?" Nina asked him, her Russian accent thick.

"No, but I have heard stories." Gurka shook his head slightly as if warning her to leave it alone. "Of death. Of beasts. Even monsters. Of ghosts and unexplained disappearances. I have always tried to avoid them."

"Sounds like my kind of fun fair," Dudyk said, grinning.

"It is not a place to be at night," Gurka said.

Bodie tried to catch Caruso's eye, seeking any sign, but the Italian only stared into space as if desperately trying to determine the future.

"Let's get started," Gurka said. "I want to be on the road today."

◆ ◆ ◆

The journey to the mountains was long and cramped. Again, they were separated and forced into three different vans. This time, the rear cargo holds were not only loaded with people—they were full of provisions too. Not just food, Bodie noticed. There were tents and sleeping bags, cold-weather gear, and a host of other items.

"Expecting a tough journey?" he asked Gurka as they set out.

"It won't be easy." The leader of R24 surprised Bodie by answering honestly. "If we are prepared"—the man spread his arms—"some of you may even live."

Bodie sat back, breaking eye contact, unsure now if the relic smuggler was being genuine. "That's right," Gurka told him. "Relax. Do nothing that will make me hurt you. This will be a long ride."

As the first hour yawned slowly into the second, Bodie shifted, stretching muscles and relieving tension. Pantera and Heidi were perched on the wooden bench to either side of him, their spines occasionally striking the van's metal side. Pantera looked queasy, and Bodie himself felt travel sickness coming on. With no recourse, he tried to take his mind off the journey.

The Forever Gang was the greatest part of Bodie's childhood, the glorious fragment before his parents had died and everything had changed. The first time he'd raised a fist in anger had been in defense of the Forever Gang. It had been one of those crisp but foggy, warm but rainy Southern England days, a day when good sense dictated that the five friends should have stayed indoors, but the day when their bond of comradeship had been cemented forever.

They found shelter from the frequent downpours under an old railway bridge, sitting on the rough slope beneath and listening to the trains thunder overhead, bound for some distant location in the north. It took a while to get dry, to shake and smooth the water out of clothes and hair, but nonstop excited conversation took their minds off any form of misery. Darcey was the feisty one, retelling a tale of a school incident and how she'd stood up to the resident bully. Bodie admired her for it, loved her for it, and only wished he'd been around to help. Darcey had taken a blow to the kidneys, but she hadn't backed down.

Brian started teaching her how to fight, how to punch, though he had no real clue. The constant drenching rain turned into an endless fine mist falling on either side of their timeworn shelter. A scraping of blue appeared overhead. The Forever Gang was so wrapped up in their friendship that the first they knew they weren't alone was when three large youths came sliding down the concrete slope to their right.

Bodie knew immediately that they were trouble.

You could see it in their expressions, in their body language. They were wet, miserable, and clearly in need of distraction. Bodie walked over to his friends, who had already crowded together as if sensing safety might lie in friendship and numbers.

"Look at this." One of the youths spat on the ground and puffed out his chest. "A toddler party in our lair. Which one of you arranged that?"

The other two laughed loudly and swore. Bodie detected the nastiness in their tones and suddenly felt a long way from home, from his parents. It was the first time in his life that he understood the incredible safety net they cast over him every day, every night, and craved it.

"They look scared." The ringleader sniggered. "Don't they look scared?"

"Like babies," one grunted.

"Like—" the third began.

He never finished. At that moment little Darcey took a step forward. "Go away!" she shouted. "Just go away and leave us alone!"

If her spirit had been a visceral force, the three youths would have started running and not stopped until they reached home. Darcey's face was heated, her voice strong. There was a fire in her eyes that both galvanized and scared Bodie. He was the first to step to her shoulder, backing her, closely followed by Brian, Jim, and Scott.

"Go away!" Darcey shouted again.

The lead youth stared for a few moments, clearly struggling with a decision. Bodie could easily guess what it was. This was one of those life-altering moments—either you backed away, took the hit, and lost the respect of your friends, or you ventured ahead and risked it all. For this youth, it was a hard decision.

"What you doing, Egzo?" one of his mates asked. "You scared of her?"

It was this prompt that pushed him into action, the challenge his friend laid down. The youth didn't hesitate. He stepped forward and pushed Darcey. She staggered backward, losing her balance. Bodie ran to her aid but failed to catch her before she landed on her tailbone and cried out in pain. Brian, Jim, and Scott closed ranks before Egzo, stopping him from advancing on her.

"Why would you do that?" Bodie cried out. "Why?"

Egzo looked unsure, but then one of his friends lashed out, slapping Brian across the face. Bodie reached out to help a shaken-looking Darcey to her feet. Scott backed away, unsure. The older youths saw that as a sign of weakness and came forward. They slapped and pushed the boys aside.

Only Bodie now stood between them and Darcey.

"Not so brave now," Egzo sneered at the small girl.

Bodie was vaguely aware that this was a life-changing moment. Before the three boys, he bunched his fists as he'd seen the bigger boys do. He stood up to them.

"Please leave us alone," he said.

They came at him. One punched him on the shoulder, giving him a dead arm. Another flicked out an open hand, connecting with his right temple. Egzo pushed out again, but Bodie was ready. He stood, put his head down to protect it, and flailed out. One punch caught Egzo in the face, making him yell. Another made one of the youths gasp. Bodie saw him holding his nose. Bodie was breathing heavily. Blood ran from his nose into his mouth, the metallic taste nauseating. He sensed a pause and stepped back. Darcey held on to his shoulder.

At that moment Brian, Jim, and Scott came in, using their considerably smaller bodies to push the youths aside. They surrounded Bodie and Darcey.

Egzo held up a bloody hand. At first, Bodie prepared for an all-out attack, but then he realized Egzo was trying to catch the attention of one of his friends.

"Stop," Egzo said. "Grimes. *Grimes!*"

And Bodie saw something for the first time. Back then, he didn't recognize it—just realized that this youth, this Grimes, looked "batshit crazy." Later, looking back, he would know that Grimes had murder in his eyes. Grimes wanted to mess them up badly. Only Egzo's voice stopped him.

"Grimes," Egzo said. "This is enough."

Blood had been spilled on both sides. Egzo gave all of them, but especially Darcey, a respectful salute and just walked away. After a moment, Grimes and the other youth walked after him.

The Forever Gang had used the rain to clean their faces as best they could; they'd talked continuously to allow pent-up emotion—anger, anxiety, and fear—to bleed away. They'd stayed close; they'd held each other; they'd used the whole nightmare experience to strengthen the bonds of their friendship.

There was nothing they couldn't face together.

Family is a sense of belonging. Bodie used the motto to this very day—but it had started right then. Bodie had gone home smiling that day, despite the blood. The union that the Forever Gang had made was worth the pain.

◆　◆　◆

"Where'd you go, pal?" Jack Pantera interrupted his thoughts. "Looked like you were dreaming awake for a while there."

"Old memories." Bodie cleared his throat. Not even Pantera knew about the best days of his childhood. He wondered briefly why his subconscious had plucked that particular memory from the past but then realized it was obvious. He'd stood up for Darcey against the bullies. He was doing the same thing now in a different way for his friends and especially for Lucie.

"I'm sorry." Pantera clearly misunderstood, assuming Bodie had been recollecting his days as an orphan.

"No, it . . . was before that," Bodie said shortly. "Before my parents died. I had an honest, tight, dependable group just like this one. To be perfectly honest, it spoiled me for what came next."

Pantera nodded, bald head glistening as sunlight came in through the van's rear windows. "And Cross?" he asked, wiping sweat away from his forehead.

"Trying not to think about that."

"I know it's raw right now, but I found in the past that reliving the good times helps heal the pain. You live again with them; you laugh and cry and see them as they used to be. As you used to be. It's the best therapy."

"It sounds worth trying. Thanks, Jack."

"Anytime, mate. Anytime."

"What about you?" Bodie asked. "Steph and Eric?"

He was referring to Jack's wife and child. Jack was divorced but had recently been placed with his family in a CIA safe house. Pantera lowered his voice. "Seriously, I told them I'd be back in a couple of days. They're gonna hate me all over again."

Bodie knew Jack's absences had caused the initial marital problems. "Surely they'll understand," he said. "You can explain when you get back."

Pantera eyed Gurka and Nina. "Our kidnappers have no intention of letting that happen."

"I know."

"We working on a plan? I've ignored two opportunities to escape already."

Bodie chewed his lower lip. "Escape isn't the issue. Keeping everyone alive is the issue."

"Too many enemies for that," Pantera said, telling him what he already knew. "Maybe the mountains will thin them out."

Bodie nodded. "Or whatever's *in* the mountains."

Both men fell silent, neither voicing the most obvious comment: *Let's hope they don't thin us out too.*

CHAPTER THIRTEEN

Cassidy felt like her bones were in knots. She slowly unfolded herself from the back of the van. It was early evening. A chill mountain breeze blew away any cobwebs she retained from long hours of monotonous travel. She took several moments to stretch and reconnoiter the scene.

The same three vans that had left Königsberg had arrived safely. Bodie and the others were climbing out of the black one. Lucie was already standing apart from the crew, guarded by two men. Cassidy examined the historian from afar and saw no signs of mistreatment.

She took a moment to untie her long red hair, shaking it out and running her fingers through the knots before retying it. Four guards turned to her, momentarily forgetting their charges. Cassidy was both the muscle and distraction for the relic hunter crew, and she never stopped evaluating her enemy.

A skill she'd first learned on the streets of Los Angeles, from the age of seventeen. All her life, Cassidy had known where she came from and exactly who she was.

Until Cross had died.

The loss of such a good friend, and how it had happened after they'd found Atlantis, had shaken her to the core. Before, she'd been the first into the breach, but she found herself more hesitant now, more vulnerable. She could still fight, still take lives to save her friends, but the assured part of her that used to know that was the right thing to do had started to raise questions recently.

Was combat necessary? What if the worst happened? What if she was responsible for the death of a friend?

Now, Cassidy checked behind her to make sure Jemma, Yasmine, and Gunn made it down from the van safely and to watch Belenko and Vash, their R24 sentries. Neither had spoken during the long journey. Cassidy had found the long, tedious hours challenging. She was a woman of action, unused to lethargy, always dynamic. She often stayed busy just to keep old nightmares at bay. Being stuck in a van for innumerable hours gave them time to feed, to grow more dangerous.

Cassidy pushed it aside now and strode over to Bodie. "Everyone okay here?"

"All good."

"What's next?"

"We just got here," Gunn moaned. "Give us a minute."

"You've been sitting on your ass for too long," Cassidy growled at them. "We gonna find this church or not?"

"She is right." Gurka looked as restless as she felt. "But first we should pack and equip ourselves for the long hike and the difficult days ahead."

Cassidy scanned their surroundings. R24 had brought them to a parking area nestled against the side of a mountain. The early-evening light was waning already, presenting the high, jagged peaks and rolling slopes ahead as mere suggestive shadows rather than the incredible vistas that they were. Other vehicles stood around, their occupants long gone. It appeared to be a staging area, where hikers and climbers left their transport to venture into the Tatras.

"You have the night to find the location of that church," Gurka told Bodie. "You'd better get on with it."

Cassidy watched as Gunn dragged out a laptop and sat it on a bench. He stretched, then started tapping. Cassidy thought for a moment and then went straight up to Gurka.

"We need Lucie," she said. "She's our historian and knows more about lost treasures than all of us combined."

Gurka looked skeptical. Nina, who Cassidy regarded as the brightest of R24's crew, looked up from the bag she was packing, matching the redhead stare for stare.

"Blondie is our insurance. Do you think we're stupid?" Nina rose, and Cassidy was struck by her fitness, her size, and her presence.

Cassidy didn't back down. "You've got fifteen armed mercs, plus you guys. Where can we go? We'd find this church a lot faster with her help."

She laid it on thick. She didn't know if Lucie could help. She just wanted Lucie to feel a little freedom and companionship for a while. But Nina walked right up so that she was in Cassidy's face.

"It is true," Gurka admitted. "This Lucie Boom is their researcher."

Nina held both hands up. "Okay, okay. But watch them."

Her last order was directed at the mercs milling around. Cassidy ignored them all, walked up to Lucie, and smiled.

"C'mon, girl. We've got a job for you."

Relief flooded the blonde woman's eyes. Cassidy led her back to the group, where Gunn was still tapping away on his keyboard.

"Thank you," Lucie whispered.

"No worries."

"Good move," Bodie said to her.

Cassidy shrugged. "Hey, it helps me too. The sooner we get moving, the better I'll feel."

Lucie crouched down beside Gunn. "What parameters are you using?"

"Parameters?" Gunn looked over tiredly. "Just Caruso here for descriptions. He says that the stained glass picture uses red highlights to define a specific church. The steeple is simple but bears two crosses and a round window. The windows are oblong and quite narrow. The door is wooden, with a brass handle, and is surrounded by a wide arch of stone, possibly flint mined from the mountains. I have already seen images on the internet where they call this a Devil's door. I am searching images inside the Tatras, but the friggin' service up here is a nightmare." He raised the laptop in the air as if searching for a signal.

Lucie huffed in her schoolmistress way and tapped Gunn's shoulder. "Move aside. We'll be here all night."

"This is my computer."

"Move anyway."

Cassidy smiled, happy to see the woman regaining her disposition—a disposition that grated occasionally, for sure, but one Cassidy was glad to see hadn't been cowed by her solo captivity.

"The Tatras are huge," Lucie explained. "Three hundred square miles, but only twelve miles wide. Of course, we know villages lie within, but many more are unknown. Off the map. Possibly abandoned. Did you know there's an unofficial registry of churches, compiled by everyone from priests to hikers across the world? It should provide a good starting point."

Cassidy watched her wait for the erratic signal to strengthen and then start to work, keeping track of the fifteen mercs and R24. She wanted to see their patterns, their interactions, and their competencies. Once Nina and Gurka were satisfied with their packs, they brought new, waterproof maps across and gave them to Bodie.

"Use these for reference," Nina said. "They will beat internet any day, and up here, it won't always work."

Cassidy nodded, agreeing with the black-haired woman. "Tell me again," she said, "why you need us. You guys seem capable of doing all this yourselves."

"R24 always uses others." Nina paused for a moment as she headed back to the vans, turning to Cassidy. "Lackeys. We do not do hands on. It is how we have survived so long in this cutthroat game and still prosper. Also, you found Zeus *and* Atlantis. You have the credentials. I myself have been fighting all my life, first on the streets of Kiev and then Moscow, where I tried to go straight, as you Americans say. The world didn't want me to go straight."

Cassidy was a little startled. Nina's early life sounded much like her own. Until she'd met Bodie, Cassidy herself had narrowly avoided jail and ended up in countless close scrapes. It scared her how easily she could have taken a different path and ended up like Nina.

"But . . ." She spoke her mind. "Using us, staying in the shadows, reveals something about you."

Nina raised her eyebrows. "Yes?"

"You have no intentions of letting us, Caruso, or his family walk away from this."

Nina's face betrayed no emotion as she shrugged and walked off. "We shall see. If you cooperate, we might not need to kill you."

Cassidy thought about how life had treated them so similarly and how they'd ended up so different. It was a conundrum she couldn't tackle right now, so she put it aside and turned to watch Lucie work her magic on the laptop. Nina returned five minutes later and placed a small pile of history books on the bench. Yasmine and Heidi started leafing through them without much purpose. Cassidy wanted to talk to Yasmine, wanted to draw her out a little and get her talking about her feelings for Cross, but this wasn't the time.

It was only after thirty minutes of intermittent signal had flown by that Lucie rested on her haunches, sighed, and said, "It's not there."

"What?" Gunn looked unhappy. "I thought you were certain."

"So was I. But it's not there."

"Are churches marked on the map?" Gunn asked Bodie.

The thief blinked back. "Why? Are you gonna check every one? We don't have months, mate; we have days."

Gunn bit his lower lip. "I was thinking we could cross-reference each one to the internet. Try to get an image up."

Cassidy wandered over to Heidi. "Hey, Moneymaker, what's with the books?"

"As haphazard a pile as I've ever seen. A history of the Tatras. An overview of the Carpathian mountain range. The illustrations and photographs inside are included purely at random, which means you're forced to check every page. Here . . . you can start with Slovakia and Poland's national parks."

"Wow, thanks."

The only light was two sparse pools thrown by tall lamps that barely illuminated the parking area. A cold wind started to whistle, making Cassidy shiver. It was a desolate plight they found themselves in, at an even more desolate place. Outside her circle of friends, Cassidy felt truly alone up here. The only sounds were the whispering of the mercenaries, the noises as they blew on their hands to keep warm, the tapping of Lucie's fingers, and the gentle whirring of the laptop. Cassidy checked constantly in the direction from which they had come but saw no signs of other vehicles along that lonely stretch of road.

Gurka came over, backed by Vash and Dudyk, threatening to drag Lucie back to the gray van. Bodie confronted them, promising it would take much longer without the historian's help.

Then Heidi Moneymaker spoke up. "Hey, what was the description?" Her question carried a note of urgency.

Cassidy leaned over, eyes locked on the picture she had found in the old history book. Gunn shouted it out as he walked across, closely followed by the others. Heidi tapped the page in question. "This looks pretty close."

"It's not close," Gunn said, staring. "It's an exact match to the stained glass image. We found it. That's the bloody church."

And then Dante Caruso leaned among them. "Ah, now I remember," he said with frustrating timing. "Bad news, I'm afraid. It's a ghost town."

CHAPTER FOURTEEN

Cassidy couldn't relax, ill at ease with the constant threat of death they toiled under. Once they'd located the church on a map, Lucie was taken from them and bundled into the back of the gray van. Dudyk followed, and they heard a shout and then a scream. Both Cassidy and Bodie were instantly on their feet, striding toward the van, but at a word from Gurka, eight rifles were suddenly leveled at them. Two barrels jabbed at their spines. Gurka held up a hand.

"She is our prisoner. You will not interfere."

"Then treat her well," Bodie said. "We've done everything you've asked so far."

"So far? That implies your obedience will end."

"It will, if you harm our friend. Or Caruso's family."

Nina, who to Cassidy's mind had been relatively rational until now, unexpectedly walked right up to Bodie. "Stop this bravado," she hissed. "You think we need all of you? No. You think we won't break bones and force you on? No. You think we won't leave you buried to your neck for the night animals to eat? No. We own your life now. Your pain. Your friends' pain. Get used to it."

Cassidy felt her fists bunch involuntarily. Nobody threatened her friends like that. The urge to punch Nina was strong but tempered by her new vulnerability. It took Bodie stepping across her to hold her back. He knew her so well.

"Get in the vans," Gurka said. "Get some rest. We will go into the mountains at first light."

Cassidy gritted her teeth, turned away, and climbed into the black van. She struck the side openhanded, because she wanted her enemy to know they weren't dealing with submissive captives here, and because she wanted them to know what kind of real anger they would provoke if they hurt Lucie.

The night passed slowly, uneventfully, and with little rest. Before dawn Gurka slammed the side of their van, ordering them out. Thick coats and backpacks were thrust at them, not heavy for Cassidy, but she noticed Gunn straining. Jemma too. Physically, this would be harder on them.

Of course, the worst affected would be Lucie. Not only was she unused to harsh exertion and to any form of combat, she was also under duress.

Gurka sent two mercs ahead. From what Cassidy overheard, they were the pathfinders, men with top-notch navigational skills. They would range afar and watch for predators of any kind. Gurka and Vash then arranged everyone in a line, warned the mercs to be vigilant, and set off.

Cassidy followed a level, winding path at first, which took them away from the parking area and out onto the lower slopes. In daylight, the vastness of the mountain range expanded to left and right, developing endless contours: flower-strewed slopes and green hills, high passes and low, verdant valleys. The air was clear, and she breathed deeply. She stretched as she walked, warming dormant muscles up for the day ahead. Gurka shouted out information, primarily to his mercenaries but essentially to anyone who wanted to listen.

"We're headed for the ghost town of Dydiowa. Abandoned over fifty years ago, it was small back then, home to around fifty residents. Who knows what we'll find now?" He shrugged. "Even before yesterday I have heard tales of these mountains. Be wary. Be careful. There are things here that don't belong."

Cassidy didn't sweat it. She would deal with whatever came to her. She didn't need some idiot brandishing warnings. She dropped back so that she walked between Jemma and Gunn. They would need someone with experience alongside them, even if they didn't know it yet.

"How far's this place?" she muttered.

Gunn adjusted his pack. "A solid five-hour walk."

"I thought the Amber Room was transported by train."

"It was. Some of the tracks are long gone, just like the villages they once ran to. It's the same all over the world, Cass."

"Yeah, yeah, I know that."

Cassidy felt the deep cold seeping through her jacket. Up here, there was no escape from it. Gurka and the mercenaries kept them on track. They stopped occasionally for breaks and to eat. The mountains were lofty, dark shapes at first, outlined by the sun rising behind them, but as morning turned into afternoon, Cassidy saw the beauty of their peaks and crags. For long stretches there was little sign of life, but then the occasional tourist stumbled past, or a seasoned hiker turned a searching glance over them. No weapons were in evidence, but almost to a man, the mercenaries looked like soldiers, and Bodie and Pantera didn't exactly come across as Boy Scouts. Still, they made progress, and shortly after midday, the trackers returned.

"Village ahead," one of them reported. "About two miles."

"Is it Dydiowa?" Belenko blustered at them. Cassidy had decided he was the least bright of the R24 group.

"Well, it doesn't have a signpost, man," one of the trackers drawled. "But there is a church matching the description."

"Perfect, well done," Nina said. "Now get back in front and keep leaving signs."

They nodded and departed. Cassidy prepared herself. Something told her that their best chances of escape would come when they found these waypoints that Caruso had trouble remembering. R24 would be distracted. The mercs would have their hands full. One fact made sense to her—if *everyone* escaped, their enemies wouldn't hurt Caruso's family. They would be forced to come after them.

Which was just what she wanted.

CHAPTER FIFTEEN

Their trek ended at the ghost town of Dydiowa, a minor village made up of perhaps thirty random dwellings and dissected by many overgrown paths and a central square that, even now, resisted the advance of nature. The square was barren, just brown earth. Cassidy watched several mercs fan out to explore the various paths, which was good. She caught Bodie's eye and nodded.

That's eight out of the reckoning in one go.

There were a lot of assumptions to be made. They had to assume that in the event of an escape attempt, the mercs had been ordered to capture, not shoot. They had to assume R24 expected to be tested. They had to assume they could rescue Lucie and that they would be hunted down rather than left to their own devices in the mountains.

The ghost town spooked her. At first she felt like she was being watched, but then she looked more closely and saw that the abandoned dwellings rustled with unkempt greenery. Bushes swayed and parted as small animals passed by. A branch had the appearance of a face. A door, ajar, creaked suddenly as the wind disturbed it. Cassidy clearly saw the church ahead—it was the biggest structure in the village—but then something happened that brought her up short.

One of the mercenaries dragged an old man out of the bushes. Without consideration he threw the flailing old-timer onto the ground, watched him roll helplessly, and quickly pursued. He kicked the old man, eliciting a cry of pain.

"Hey, what the fuck are you—" Cassidy started toward the scene.

Four guns turned on her, but Cassidy ignored them, overcome by fury. She reached the abusive merc and shoved him away. She bent down and helped the old man sit upright. "Are you okay?"

A deeply wrinkled face stared back at her. His teeth were yellowed and now stained with blood. He didn't understand her.

"Caught him spying," the merc explained to Gurka.

"So you thought you'd teach him a lesson?" Bodie's voice came from behind. "Big man."

"No," the merc said. "I'm a big man . . . with a gun." Cassidy turned as he pointed the weapon at Bodie.

"Stop," Gurka snapped. "Where did you find this man? Were there any others?"

"Others?" the merc repeated inanely.

Gurka cursed. "Look," he shouted. "Look for more of them."

"But what harm can they do?" Cassidy asked. "It doesn't matter if people still live here. We get what we need and leave."

"I want to see them," Gurka said with clear paranoia. "I want to see all of them."

She recalled Nina saying R24's long-term success relied on invisibility. Gurka's actions made sense—at least to him. Very soon, six mercenaries dragged eight others out of the foliage, ranging from a young girl of fifteen or so to men and women in their thirties and forties to a female senior. They threw the people onto the ground near the old man.

Guns were aimed at the villagers.

Cassidy watched the mercs, not the villagers. She wanted to gauge what kind of monsters she was dealing with. It didn't look good. Smirks and smiles twisted across every face. Sick excitement lit every pair of eyes. These were the worst of the worst. She felt that old fire rising that made her want to attack these men . . . these *monsters*.

Gurka didn't stop it; he just watched. Nina held up a hand. "Wait, wait," she said. "We have questions." She beckoned forth one of the mercenaries. "Tell them what I said."

An exchange of words followed, from which Cassidy learned that the villagers lived in Dydiowa and would not leave; that the church had been there since the old man could remember; and that, even in their distress, the villagers warned the mercenaries repeatedly of the dangers of the mountains.

Not the elements, nor the terrain, Cassidy understood. They were warned, specifically, of *beasts*.

"Beasts that should not be here," the merc translated.

"Night terrors in the mountains," Gurka said, shielding his eyes and gazing at the misty heights to their right. "It is as I've heard before. All who visit these mountains speak of this. I hear it from the drunk and the sober alike."

"They are of no help," Nina said dismissively.

"We should kill them," Gurka said flatly.

Nina waved at the church. "Let's see it for ourselves. Caruso, what do you remember of this place?"

The Italian regarded the church as if it were an old friend. "I—"

"Wait," one of the mercenaries said. "Do you want us to kill these people or not?"

It was a loaded moment, one in which Cassidy expected Nina or Gurka to give the order to set them free.

In the end, Gurka said, "We don't need them."

Ambiguous words, but Cassidy was watching the mercs very closely and saw a feral light jump into their eyes. One raised his gun and clubbed a man around thirty over the back of the head, sending him to his knees.

Cassidy was already in motion. She rushed the merc who'd just knocked down the man, took hold of his elbow, and rammed it upward, smashing his own gun barrel into his nose. Cassidy flung him down next to the man he'd floored.

Bodie overcame the man beside Cassidy, moving in close and elbowing him in the face. As he staggered backward, Bodie tripped him. The merc landed on his spine, but Bodie kept his gun. To the right, Heidi and Pantera tackled two more mercs as Yasmine confronted one to the left, proving her worth to the team as she took him out in just a few seconds before turning to the next man. Cassidy kicked her own opponent hard in the ribs, spun, and caught hold of the barrel of another gun aimed at her.

Its owner bellowed, ordering her to stand down.

"You would kill these people?" Cassidy snarled. "Hurt them? I don't think so."

She pushed the weapon away, grabbing the man's wrist at the same time and wrenching it hard. At the very least she wanted these men injured for their onward trek through the mountains. She was evaluating her every move, as she knew Bodie would be. And the other fighters in their group.

Caruso was crying, kneeling in the dirt, clearly thinking about his wife and son. Cassidy fought down a rush of guilt.

Heidi struggled to keep an opponent's gun barrel pointed at the skies, trapping the gun between them and using her left hand to deliver kidney punches. The merc fell over a boulder. His weapon went off accidentally. A bullet shot past Heidi's head and struck the church's steeple. Heidi jumped and landed on the man's stomach, knees first.

Pantera and Yasmine engaged two mercs, not in combat but with their dangerous presence alone. The mercs covered them as they circled, looking for an opening.

Cassidy saw Nina, Gurka, and the rest of R24 watching.

She let go of her opponent's wrist and jabbed at his eyes, then slipped past toward her actual goal. She now stood in front of the villagers.

"We can't beat you while you have those guns," she said. "But you are not gonna harm these people."

Heartfelt words, but also words designed to stimulate overconfidence in the mercs. She hoped they might reap the dividends later.

"Stand down," one man growled, finger flexing on his trigger.

Bodie took the chance to debilitate his own opponent even further, smashing a knee into his ribs, hoping to crack a few. Then he flung the man over his shoulder and saw the gun fall to the floor. But he made no move to pick it up.

Instead, he glared at Gurka. "I don't want this to escalate," he said. "But if it does, I'm coming straight for you."

Gurka grinned, stroking the shaft of a knife at his waist.

Cassidy evaluated the scene. The villagers stood in terror, protecting each other and their youngest. Lucie stood with Dudyk apart from everyone, watching in horror, fear etched into her face. The mercenaries looked unsure, which was a testament to the hold R24 had over them.

Gurka finally waved a hand. "Since you value them so much, the villagers can go. But do not test me again, or I will hurt one of you. Don't forget . . ." He waved in Lucie's direction. "One scream from her would have stopped you all."

Cassidy wasn't so sure but didn't push it. Bodie, beside her now, whispered, "That was risky, Cass."

"I had to stop them hurting innocent people. It's in my blood. You know it."

Bodie nodded. He knew almost everything about Cassidy's hard past, from leaving home at seventeen to living on the streets to meeting an older man named Brad at nineteen who'd become the love of her life, only to helplessly watch him die from a heart attack just before her twentieth birthday. Prior to Brad, Cassidy had never known love—her parents had never been abusive, but they'd never *wanted* her—and she'd barely learned how to give it back before Brad had passed. She couldn't return it, didn't recognize it. She was damaged, but she was loyal to her new family.

And she was viciously protective of those who couldn't help themselves.

"I understand," Bodie said. "And we learned a few things."

He gave her a brief smile, which she understood. They'd been testing weaknesses too, and they'd found several. Cassidy still worried about the way they kept Lucie apart and how close Dudyk stuck to her. They needed him closer to the fray—the man appeared to be a cruel piece of work. Cassidy expected he'd be happy to join a proper fight.

Gurka ordered the mercenaries to behave and the relic hunters to calm down. Cassidy would have checked her wounds then, but she didn't have any. A fact that she pointed out to the mercs she'd fought.

Get in their heads.

"We've wasted enough time," Nina said. "Now, get into that church."

108

CHAPTER SIXTEEN

Bodie walked into the church. The air inside was cold. No warmth existed in here, the building's brick walls and tiny oblong windows admitting and retaining very little heat. Heidi drifted closer to him and whispered with her head down, "Any plans?"

"We're in for the long haul, I think. There's no easy way out."

"Unfortunately, you're right. And it's worse than you think. When we got taken, during our Bratva meeting . . ."

She paused, so Bodie glanced at her. "Yes?"

"That night I had dinner plans with my daughter, Jessica."

Bodie closed his eyes. "Ah, crap, that's such bad timing. I'm sorry." Jessica was Heidi's eleven-year-old. She blamed Heidi's devotion to the job for her parents' breakup and divorce and had consistently refused to see and even talk to the CIA agent. Dinner plans were a significant breakthrough.

"Me too," Heidi said. "Back to square one, I guess."

"She'll understand if you explain it the right way."

"Unlikely," Heidi said. "But you know me—I'll try with all my heart."

They stopped in the middle of the church. Oblong in shape, it stood about twenty feet high in the nave. Several pews ran from side to side, dusty and chipped and damaged, some listing quite badly. Bodie spied an altar at the far end and two doors leading off the nave.

All eyes turned to Dante Caruso.

The Italian grumbled and shrugged. "Yes, I remember this place, but nothing else returns to my mushy brain. Maybe if I wait—"

"No waiting," Gurka said. "Everyone start searching now."

Bodie considered challenging that. It could take days to search this place properly, but again, maybe the activity would present escape opportunities. The members of R24 headed toward the oblong windows, hoping for more stained glass clues. Caruso didn't seem interested in them. Four mercs wandered up to the altar, and others started checking along the pews.

"Remember," Gurka called out, his voice loud inside the church. "Anything that represents the Amber Room, a train, the Germans. Anything."

Bodie eyed one of the two doors. Heidi and Pantera came alongside him. "Shall we?"

"Lead the way," Pantera said. "I notice they're keeping Lucie outside for this. Poor girl's gonna end up traumatized."

"She can take it," Heidi said. "She's a relic hunter."

"Well, I'm not sure I can take it." Pantera laughed at himself. "Tangling with that goon out there almost dislocated my bloody shoulder."

"Getting old," Bodie said, attention on the wooden door ahead.

"Oh, thanks, man. Thanks for that."

Bodie pushed the door inward. It led to a small room stuffed with papers and files, an untidy desk, and some old boxes. None of the items looked as if they'd been disturbed for years.

"I guess Caruso didn't explore this room," Heidi said, peering over his shoulder.

"At times like this, when we're at an impasse," Bodie said, "I like to ask, 'What would Cross do?'"

"Ah." Heidi nodded, still next to him. "I like how you keep him close."

"Close to all of us."

Heidi responded by laying a hand on his shoulder. Bodie took a slow, deep breath. He didn't like to admit that Heidi distracted him, that she constantly entered his thoughts, that having her so close wasn't easy. Even here.

"Let's look at the next door."

The second room was desolate. A couple of boxes stood near the right-hand wall. Bodie saw a single trail of footprints heading toward the boxes and another heading back. He crossed over and checked but found nothing of interest.

Back into the nave, and the mercs were standing around looking glum. They'd found nothing in the main area. Gurka and Nina were snapping photos of the windows and then blowing them up on their phones to study the artwork.

Caruso stared at the altar with his piercing blue eyes.

Vash, currently on his knees at the end of a pew, glared at the Italian. "It's not looking good for you or your family. This had better not be a fool's errand."

Bodie saw several mercs send hate-filled glares at Caruso and felt the tension in the church ramp up. "C'mon, Heidi."

They walked up to Caruso. "Any thoughts, mate?"

"I have no recollection of this place." Caruso squeezed his eyes tightly shut, as if trying to trawl through a slush of images. "But I remember that." He nodded at the altar. "And darkness. Pure darkness."

"You came at night?" Heidi said.

"I don't know. But I do remember one thing . . . I'd never been so scared in my life."

Bodie was trying to sideline thoughts of mountain terrors and so-called beasts. Truth be told, they were still in the foothills and had many dangerous days ahead of them.

They crossed to the altar. It stood on an upraised dais, dusty and leaf strewed like the rest of the church. Bodie saw several handprints and scrapes where boots had walked past.

Heidi scrutinized the exterior. Bodie got down on his knees and tried to heft the large slab. He checked for seams running nearby.

"Nothing," he said eventually, sitting back. "Dante—this isn't looking good."

Heidi was ahead of him. "I've been wondering where Lucie is. If this thing goes bad, one of us needs to save her."

Bodie drifted over to a nearby window. The mountain dust and glass staining made it hard to see outside, but he rubbed until it became clearer. Apart from mountain landscape and a few buildings, he saw nothing.

"I don't know where she is," he whispered.

Lucie Boom was trying to remain calm. Though she was only fifty feet from the members of her team, she felt isolated, which was R24's intention. The distance ensured cooperation. The man at her side—Dudyk—promised death with everything from the very flicker in his eyes to the hands that always rested on the hilt and barrel of his deadly weapons. He was a hard man, a vicious man. She could tell he enjoyed inflicting trauma, taking the terror as far as he could.

In normal situations, Lucie affected an outer calm. She spoke properly as she'd been taught, tried to command the room as she'd been taught. Engaged the audience as she'd . . .

It was all a lie, though, and she'd never tell. The closest she'd come was during a drunken party game in the quest to find Atlantis.

"My whole family is dead," she'd told the team. "Every one of them died from natural causes or accidents. Nothing sinister, and now, every day, every minute, I expect to go next."

Maybe at the hands of Dudyk? But no, that wouldn't fit. Dudyk, though, was a true monster, and she fully expected him to kill her, the theme of her fears aside.

He moved then, and she flinched. All he was doing was trying to find a better view through a church window, but he sensed her fear and slowly turned his head to give her an evil smirk. So far, she hadn't raised the courage to speak to him, but after watching her friends fight for the villagers, she decided that now was the time.

"Can you see anything?"

She'd noticed several times that he squinted. One thing she knew about captors was that the more you made yourself a person to them, the better your chances of survival were.

"Dudyk? What do you see?" She stood terrified, waiting for his reaction.

"I see nothing," he growled without turning. She saw him squint once more.

"Why is the Amber Room so important to you?"

Dudyk snapped his head around. "To me?"

"Yes." She studied the black tattoo that covered the right side of his face. He ran a hand over the stubble that covered his head.

"I do not care. They care. This bores me. Where is the fight? The combat? But you, why are you talking to me?"

Lucie shrank from his intense glare. "I . . . I've been alone for a while," she stammered. "And I'm a historian. You may need me." Proving her worth to them.

Dudyk caressed the hilt of his knife before drawing it slowly from its sheath. Lucie saw the glint of gleeful malevolence in his eyes.

"If we don't need you," he growled softly, "this will be the last thing you see."

He held the blade up before her eyes.

Lucie went white, stepping back, lost her balance, and fell on her tailbone. She cried out in pain, desperately trying to keep tears from her eyes. Dudyk only laughed. He turned away. She'd known a man like this before. Her uncle Jamie. On the surface he had been mean, hateful, full of insults. He'd pushed people away. She'd later found out that Jamie had been bullied mercilessly at school and at college. Pushing people away had been the only thing he'd known.

Was Dudyk like that? She saw no good in him, but she could relate to his severity because after a while she'd broken through to Jamie. They'd become friends. Somehow, though, she didn't see that happening with a member of R24 tasked with guarding and potentially killing her. This man had been around death all his life; she could see it in him, in every part of him. She found a spot to study far away, a dark, craggy mountain where, she thought, accidents were bound to happen.

Caruso wasn't studying the altar. He was standing as though using it as a reference point. He was staring back into the nave.

At the floor.

Bodie followed his gaze and saw several narrow tracks in the dirt.

"Total darkness," Caruso said, "down there."

"A cellar," Bodie said.

"A crypt." Caruso shivered. "I don't want to go down there again."

By now, a few mercs, Vash, and Gurka were watching. Yasmine waved at them. "Break out the flashlights and the spider spray. Looks like we're heading underground." She stooped and started tracing the tracks.

Within five minutes they had the trapdoor up and were staring at a wooden staircase that led into the ground. Gurka illuminated the space with a powerful flashlight, then unsurprisingly sent Bodie down first. Soon, Heidi, Pantera, Caruso, and Yasmine were following him, along with Gurka, Nina, Vash, and six mercs. It was interesting to Bodie that they left Cassidy up top—no doubt seeing her as the biggest threat.

Bodie climbed down the rickety stairs, testing every step. Once, the wood cracked but didn't break. A good thing, since he ended up descending thirty feet into what could only be described as an underground cave. The air was dank and musty. Cobwebs hung from the ceiling and hindered further progress. Slowly, as the others crowded down behind, he swept the flashlight around.

"See that?" he whispered to Heidi, waving the flashlight at the rocky walls. "Alcoves. And I do believe that's a coffin right there."

His words were eaten up by the oppressive cave. He felt like a trespasser, seeing many alcoves cut into the walls of the cave. From some of them empty eye sockets glared back: long-buried skulls. Bones were piled on the floor, some scattered. Even as he watched, a rib cage shifted as something slithered through a heap of old bones.

"Did you . . . did you disturb the dead?" Yasmine asked Caruso.

"No. They were already like this. Somebody ransacked this crypt, I think, a long time ago."

"Then the dead will not be happy."

"You!" Gurka shouted into the uncomfortable stillness much too loudly. "You, Caruso! What did you find down here?"

"I'm standing right next to you."

"Yes, just answer me."

Bodie understood Gurka's anxiety. It was the atmosphere down here, the presence of old death and crawling things, the air full of bone decay and barely heard whisperings. Nobody wanted to move through the curtains of cobwebs that barred their way. Nobody wanted to touch them.

Then Nina remembered herself. "Get on with it, for fuck's sake."

Caruso pointed ahead. "It's through there."

Bodie shook his head. "It bloody well would be."

They started forward, swiping at the hanging webs and pulling them apart, then trying to remove the sticky substance from their hands. Twice, Bodie felt something land on the top of his head and then scurry away. Once, something hit his shoulder hard enough to make a slapping sound, and he caught his breath. Through the webs they went, taking several minutes, until the far end of the cave grew near.

Bodie stopped, seeing an altar not unlike the one upstairs. "What next?"

"It is on the altar," Caruso whispered. "These crypts around us, these coffins, they were cleared out by the Nazis. Do you know what lies down here now?"

Bodie couldn't suppress a shiver. "What?"

"The dead slaves of Poland and Czechoslovakia. They shoved them in here, herding them in while they were still alive, and left them."

"I thought you didn't know what happened?" Yasmine said.

"I remember when I am around my relics."

"But why would the Nazis do that?"

"Because they were fucking Nazis. They thought they were superior, untouchable. They thought they ruled the world. That every idea that occurred to them, no matter how trivial or horrific, was part of some master plan."

"How do you know this?" Gurka asked.

"There." Caruso pointed at the altar. "It's all there."

Bodie saw a leather-bound book lying on top of the altar. Carefully, he swiped the last cobweb aside, noting footsteps in the dirt that could only belong to Caruso on his previous visit, and reached out.

Nina slapped his hand aside. "I'll take that."

Bodie swiped dust and cobweb scraps off his hair and shoulders straight into her face. "Then take it. I don't know why the hell we're here."

"Yes, you do. Same reason as the mercs." Gurka appeared behind a spluttering Nina. "To do the grunt work while we stay unnoticed. To die first, if need be. What does it say?"

The last sentence was directed at Nina, who was busy aiming a murderous look at Bodie. She recovered quickly and pulled Caruso to her side.

"Tell us," she said. "Tell us what you found."

Caruso's face suddenly shut down. "It's . . . it's the book. I don't know."

Nina shook him hard. "Do not play games with me. Think of your family."

Caruso squeezed his eyes shut. Bodie stepped up. "Hey, hey, it's your pathetic aggression that's affecting his mind. Can't you bloody see that?"

Nina swung on him. "Pathetic aggression? Is that what it is?"

Bodie held out a calming hand, imagining Nina would call out some nasty reprisal on Caruso or even Lucie. "Psychological issues," he said, "won't be solved by threat. Give the man some space."

"Move." Gurka interceded. "Let's get out of this place. We'll read the book somewhere . . ." He looked around, shivering. "Healthier."

Caruso was first out of the crypt, bolting for the stairs.

117

CHAPTER SEVENTEEN

Nina placed the leather-bound book on the church's main altar. Bodie breathed deeply. The air up here in the nave was far sweeter than below. He'd finished brushing himself off almost a minute ago but still felt his skin crawl at the memory of the unseen things that scurried and crept down there.

Carefully, Nina opened the book. Gurka stood to her left, Vash to her right. Bodie made a move to look over her shoulder and was pleased that nobody tried to stop him. Cassidy, he saw, had walked to the windows to check on Lucie.

"It is not so old, this book," Nina said. "I am guessing that the Germans made it."

Bodie wished Lucie were inside. Their historian was well versed in the Amber Room but, so far, hadn't been allowed much involvement in their search for the treasure.

"Or an undercover agent," Jemma said. "Working for the Russians, maybe, to keep track of the Amber Room."

"Leaving a trail, a bread crumb at every waypoint. Every stop?" Gurka nodded at her. "That actually makes sense."

Bodie said nothing. Perhaps R24 wasn't as omniscient as its members thought, if they were surprised that Jemma would come up with a good idea. But Bodie knew that Jemma's mind was the sharpest of them all.

Nina picked up the book and blew several layers of dust from its edges. Motes spun, catching the sunlight that speared through the narrow windows. As the woman continued leafing through the book, Bodie saw exquisite hand-drawn pictures of Königsberg Castle, of the Tatra Mountains, of valleys and lakes and much more. Dates and even times were written at the bottom of each page.

"A picture diary?" he suggested. "Look, every day he draws something different. This is a record of the trip from Königsberg to . . ." He paused.

"That is the Amber Room," Jemma said as Nina stopped halfway through the book.

The black-and-white drawing showed the room in situ. The words "Berlin City Palace" were inscribed underneath; Bodie assumed that was the setting for the picture. Several intricately crafted panels made up the walls of a large room, reaching all the way to the ceiling. Bodie picked out many of the complex art forms even in the pencil drawing.

"It tells us nothing," Nina said dismissively and turned the page.

A minute later she paused again, at a page that had been divided by a thick pencil line. The top drawing was a depiction of the church they stood inside. The bottom drawing portrayed an overview of a train track, significant because of a specific series of bends. Bodie thought the whole sketch looked slightly different to the rest of the book.

It was the final page.

Nina slammed it down on top of the altar, displacing clouds of dust. "What is this? Caruso, what did you find here?"

Furiously, she stalked over, grabbed the Italian by the collar, and forced his head toward the floor. "Answer me. Answer me, or I will smash your head on the ground until something falls out."

Caruso was talking frantically. "It is in the book. I know it is in—"

"We keep your family alive for cooperation. You will be straight with us, or I *will* have them beaten."

Caruso fell to his knees, hands covering his ears, eyes scrunched up. Bodie grabbed Nina's shoulder and pulled her away. Instantly, three rifles were leveled at his face. Yasmine moved behind two of them. Nina spun and kneed Bodie straight in the groin.

Cassidy jumped in between them, holding out her hand. "Stop."

Bodie had folded. Pantera took up a combat stance, ready in case there was violence. Heidi was close to Gurka. Jemma was near the book. Bodie struggled through the pain.

Nina took out her radio and thumbed the mic button. "Hurt the blonde," she hissed, staring defiantly into Cassidy's eyes. "Make her scream."

"Wait!" Jemma cried out then. "Please wait; I know what we're looking for."

Nina strode right by Bodie without a second look. "Show me."

"Not until you belay that order."

Nina cursed but thumbed the radio again. "Hold off," she said. "For now."

"It's the train tracks," Jemma said. "They're unique. They must be. It's where this man"—she prodded the book—"hid the next clue."

Bodie rose gingerly, holding his groin. The pain was subsiding. His team was still in place, but the mercs were rattled, on edge. Any escape attempt at this point was going to prove costly. He nodded at Cassidy, surprised that the redhead had jumped in between Nina and him with nothing more than a raised hand. It wasn't a good sign. He needed the old Cass back.

"You're saying that the owner of this book knew the route?" Gurka was saying. "Knew they would stop at the tracks? Why wouldn't he just draw the Room's final destination?"

"Well, we can't ask him," Jemma said with a hint of exasperation. "There could be any number of reasons. Maybe he was an officer, privy to most of the route. Maybe the chosen few kept the destination to themselves, or maybe they just searched out the right place. Maybe he overheard chatter. I mean, they followed a train track, yes? Perhaps they were following it until something came up."

"The best hiding places, like the best plot twists," Pantera said, "are always the impromptu ones. Those not planned."

"Can you find these curves?" Gurka asked Jemma.

"Give me Google Earth and Lucie. The tracks will be abandoned, sure, but they'll still be there."

Bodie was pleased that Jemma had asked for Lucie's assistance. Anything to get the historian away from Dudyk.

"Google Earth may not be enough," Gunn said fretfully. "You might need satellite photos, or GPR, even."

Gurka eyed them both. "Ground-penetrating radar?"

"Yeah," Heidi said. "But don't get ahead of yourself, kid. All we need to do is find the train tracks anywhere along their route, then follow the natural path they would take around or through these mountains. This set of curves"—she pointed at the book—"can't be too far away."

"Why?"

"Mostly because Caruso here found it on foot, I'm guessing. And because the Tatras aren't comparatively large."

Bodie knelt beside Caruso. "Do you remember anything, Dante?"

"My family," the Italian cried. "Please don't hurt my family anymore."

Bodie rose quickly and sent a vicious look at Nina. "Now he's no bloody use at all. Well done, you fucking psycho."

"Hey." Cassidy spoke from her position near the door. "Sun's getting low. So unless you're planning on tackling the Tatras in the dark, I'd say we need to make camp."

Gurka stared at the window as if he'd forgotten the time. "It would be better to stay for the night," he said. "Use our computers to find the route and start out at first light."

With that, the mercs began ushering Bodie and his friends out of the church and into a chill early evening. The village was silent all around them, the encroaching foliage rustling gently. Darkness was already starting to press between buildings and shroud the pathways. Beyond, the undulating hills were in shadow, and the mountains were black shapes against a gray sky.

Mists were rolling across the hills, seeping in from every direction, starting to blanket the landscape.

"Not good," one of the mercs whispered. "I do not like the look of that."

"One of the villagers told me the mists brought the night terrors," another muttered. "Maybe we should go back inside the church."

Guns were prepped and raised. In the church, Bodie had heard several safety buttons switched on. Now he heard them flicked back off again.

"There are more than enough houses," Gurka pointed out. "Choose one. But I want a two-hour shift change and four men with me."

The relic hunters, Gurka, Nina, Vash, and Belenko found the largest sturdy-looking abode, followed by four mercenaries. Bodie saw everything as an opportunity to escape, but this looked very promising. He checked around for Lucie, but the descending dark hid all but the closest of faces.

"We'll need our historian," he said. "Amber Room information could be vital at this point."

"Let me think on that," Gurka said. "First, I want Miss Blunt to prove her findings. Or your historian pays the price."

Bodie was getting sick of all the threats, but he held his tongue as the entire group entered a single-room dwelling through a rickety wooden door. A low table and chairs stood at the far end, along with some locally made cupboards and shelves. Two camp beds covered by several woolen sheets sat to the right. Only two chairs were in evidence, also handcrafted, which both Nina and Gurka fell into.

Vash sat on the floor, rummaging through his pack. "Here." He handed Jemma an eight-inch Fire tablet and pressed the button to switch it on. "It's tethered to my cell phone, so you should be able to use it as a modem even out here. Try it."

Jemma knew that, short of stumbling over them, the best way to find abandoned train tracks was by using aerial view. She took her time locating the correct area and then started to zoom in. Bodie walked over to Cassidy, Heidi, and Yasmine, who were standing by a low window.

"Plans?" He knew they wouldn't have much time to talk alone.

"Overpower them; take Nina and Gurka hostage in exchange for Lucie and Caruso's family," Yasmine answered.

"That's a good idea. Risky, though. R24 don't strike me as the bargaining kind."

"They'd call our bluff," Heidi said. "But also, if we escape and take Caruso with us, they're not gonna hurt his family. They need him."

Bodie nodded. "Yeah, I figured that one out already. We can deflect any blame by dragging him away. Well . . . there's no time like the present."

Heidi and Cassidy nodded. Bodie turned to catch Pantera's eye. The older thief had been watching, expecting something. Bodie gave him a "be ready" signal, something from the old days when they'd worked together that he knew Pantera would remember.

Bodie readied himself.

Then, through the open door, came a noise that made all the hairs on his arms stand up and sent a deep chill through his bones.

Somewhere out there, around the village, something very large started to howl.

CHAPTER EIGHTEEN

Bodie's initial instinct was the same as everyone else's—to check the nearest window. Night had fallen fully, and the lack of light was menacing. There were no stars or even a sliver of moon visible. Bodie had rarely seen such utter darkness.

Another howl split the night. Gurka thumbed a radio and asked the watchmen for a report.

"Can't see a thing, boss. Nothing threatening, at least."

Gurka swore. "I think it's wise to—"

A scream cut him off. A high-pitched cry of terror that gave everyone in the room, friend or foe, the same sudden jolt. Gurka thumbed the radio once more but heard only static. There was a second scream and then two quieter shouts, both full of pain. The howling began in earnest then, several throats crying out for blood.

Then a second voice came on the radio.

"Holy fuck, help me. I'm coming in fast. Look out for me. *Oh, shit, they're fucking terri—*"

Gurka winced as the sound of grunting and yelling filled the airwaves, along with something else: a feral snarl, a snorting bark. Bodie closed his eyes briefly as he heard the mercenary whimpering, begging for mercy, and then nothing.

No sound at all.

And then crunching, ripping, tearing.

Bodie saw that the house door was wide open, darkness pressing inside.

"Close that fucking door!" he cried. "Whatever that is—we don't want it getting in here."

"The villagers warned us," Gunn said. "Monsters."

Nobody challenged him. Two mercs moved to close the door. Pantera leapt over to assist them. Caruso had pressed himself against the far wall, eyes wide.

"What are they?" Cassidy asked him. "Do you remember?"

"Teeth," the Italian whimpered. "Claws. Eyes of fire. You don't walk these mountains at night."

More howls sent them back to the windows. Bodie found himself alongside Cassidy. "Seems we're fighting more than just other people this time," he said quietly.

The redhead took a deep breath. "Yeah, nature and the environment too."

They squinted into the darkness, knowing it would be practically impossible to see anything creeping around outside but compelled to try nevertheless.

Pantera motioned at the merc nearest the door. "You forgot to lock it."

The man's face acquired another layer of fear. "You think . . . it . . . could open a door?"

"Better to be safe than sorry, pal."

The merc jumped at the door and fumbled the lock until it clicked. Then he leveled his weapon at it.

Very quietly, he said, "Something's out there. I heard breathing."

Bodie saw a smear of darkness pass across the window. It was fast and low. Whatever was out there knew they were inside. "Can we shine the lights out the windows?" he said. "I have to know what we're dealing with."

"It'll give our position away," Nina barked.

"They have our position," Cassidy shot back in a sarcastic tone.

Nina bunched her fists. Cassidy stared back as if examining an interesting new species. Bodie took the flashlight one of the smarter mercs handed him and aimed it out the window.

"Ready?" he said. "One, two, three."

Then came the clawing at the door, not just a quick scratching but a long, deep tearing sound that lasted ten whole seconds. Bodie's heart leapt into his mouth as he imagined something taking long gouges from the external wood, starting at the top and working down to the bottom.

"God help us!" The merc stationed beside the door leapt back as if electrocuted. "Use the lights. I can't stand not knowing what's coming for us."

Bodie knew their initial anxieties were feeding off each other, enhancing everyone's trepidation. They were the ones holding the guns, yet primal fear was hard to overcome. It occurred to him right then that this was the perfect time to attack their enemy.

A heavy body slammed against the door, rattling its hinges. The merc closest squeezed his trigger and fired a volley of bullets. The lead pierced the wood and struck something outside. There was a heavy grunting sound.

Bodie saw that a bullet had also destroyed one of the hinges. The door skewed now and twisted to one side, held only by a single hinge.

"Fuck!" someone cried. Gunn scrambled away to the far side of the room. Jemma clicked on the laptop, trusting her friends and ignoring the commotion as best she could. Everyone backed away from the door.

It screeched as the remaining hinge threatened to give way.

Then a head appeared, a huge skull still shrouded by the dark. It crept out of the deeper darkness behind. Two glinting eyes shone, reflected by the room's lights. Bodie saw flared nostrils and sharp fangs that gleamed yellow and dripped with blood.

The thing snorted.

Mercs opened fire. Bodie's ears rang with the sound. The window right in front of him resounded as a heavy body struck it. Blood exploded from the shape outside the door, painting the walls and floor inside. The mercs paused, but then something huge hit the hanging door at speed, smashed it off its hinges, and came hurtling into the room.

It howled as it fell and then twisted upright, confronting them.

One merc fell to his knees before the thing, gun pointed at its head. Bodie wished he had a weapon, feeling exposed before this vision of pure hell. It was an enormous wolf, flesh ragged from fighting, muzzle stained with blood from feeding. Its teeth gnashed together as drool dripped to the floor. Its eyes were merciless, wild. Its claws rattled against the floor as it prepared to leap for the nearest throat.

A second huge shape filled the doorway.

The nightmare snarls were snuffed out by the sound of a dozen automatic weapons opening fire. The first wolf twisted and fell, parts of its skull and body torn away by bullets. The second wolf collapsed across the broken door, head lolling inside the house, blood pooling from its brain onto the floor.

Bodie shone the flashlight out the window. "Save your fucking bullets, boys. This is bad."

Countless shapes stalked the street, filled it so that all Bodie saw were the powerful, ragged bodies of wolves, their feral eyes and their nightmare heads swiveling left and right as they sought out their prey.

Something else rushed the door and hit the body of its dead fellow, making the entire frame shudder. Blood spurted from the dead wolf's numerous bullet holes, spattering the floor. Another reddened muzzle briefly appeared over the body, snorting and grinding its teeth before moving away a split second before shots were fired.

Again, it struck what remained of the frame, protected by the other's dead body.

The frame splintered. The door collapsed inward, the motionless wolf with it. Suddenly a wide space had been opened to the crawling night, and they were all exposed.

"Wait," Gurka said carefully. "Wait until you see the whites of its—"

The wolf came fast, leaping over the entranceway like a racehorse leapt a fence. It was in midair as the mercs started firing. Riddled with bullets, it came down hard, landing atop a man and snarling in its death throes, teeth still seeking the soft flesh of his throat. Luckily for the merc, it died a few seconds later, still fighting. Two mercs helped drag it off the fallen man.

Bodie listened as Gurka radioed those he'd sent to reconnoiter the area. One was already dead, but the others replied that they were okay, sheltering in houses. The villagers were nowhere to be found, it seemed, probably hiding in some safe area.

"So much for saving their lives," Gurka growled at Bodie when he'd finished. "They left us here to be massacred."

The thief shrugged. "So would I, if you threatened my family."

"We have threatened your family."

Bodie allowed himself a grim smile but said nothing.

Another snarl came from the blocked doorway. More gunfire made the wolf move off. Bodie wondered briefly how much ammo the mercs had brought but then saw one of them take out his dry mag and open a backpack that bulged with spares.

No chance that they'd run dry anytime soon.

Quickly, he checked outside again. The pack was thinning, but eyes still glared their way. Muzzles quivered with vicious snarls. The next thing Bodie saw was the wolf that blocked the doorway suddenly start to move, its carcass sliding backward.

"Bollocks," he said. "They're clearing the bloody doorway. Get ready!"

Very slowly, the dead wolf slithered back out into the darkness. For a moment there was complete silence. Nothing moved. Bodie heard only those breathing around him.

A merc turned to Gurka. "Maybe they're—"

And then they hit. Shapes streaked through the open door, silent as death and dripping hot blood from their fangs. Nightmare shapes. Monsters.

The lead wolf clamped its jaws onto the gun arm of the first merc to cross its path. He screamed. Gunfire erupted, the other mercs panicking as more wolves attacked. Gunfire rang out again. Wolves twisted and fell in midair, still snapping their jaws as they fell and died. One landed atop a merc and bore him to the floor, dug its great claws into his shoulders, and lowered its muzzle to tear out his throat.

Then its head exploded as another man pressed his gun to the wolf's head and fired.

Bodie and Cassidy were in front of Jemma and Gunn. Yasmine and Pantera were a step to the right. Caruso cowered at the rear of the house, behind everyone. Heidi looked ready to relieve one of the mercs of his gun and start firing herself.

Bodie could only hope that Lucie was okay.

The mercs bore the brunt of the attack, firing and falling and twisting to escape excruciating deaths. Wolves fell under the hail of bullets. More came, falling over their dead brethren. During all this the first merc who'd had his arm clamped wrenched free of the deadly jaws. He brought his gun up, only to find he didn't have the maneuverability to bring the weapon to bear. The wolf was faster, snapping down and tearing out the man's throat before he even knew what had happened.

The wolf leapt again through a fountain of blood, only to be shredded by bullets.

The wolves behind started backing away, seeing their dead and twitching brethren before them. Quickly, they turned and vanished back the way they had come, out into the night.

The house was left in chaos, mercs firing through the door into darkness, wolves dying on the floor, and the mercenary's body leaking pools of blood. Caruso was crying. Jemma and Gunn were whiter than bone.

Cassidy nudged Bodie. "You keeping count?"

"Course I bloody am," he replied. "Two dead. Thirteen left."

Pantera caught Gurka's attention. "What about Lucie?" he asked. "And your man, Dudyk?"

Gurka immediately checked on the radio, looking worried, but everyone outside the room was safe, hidden away inside a secure house they'd found.

"We're not even into the mountains proper yet," Heidi pointed out to Gurka. "Your tents aren't gonna be much use if we come across more of this."

"Yes." Caruso spoke into the silence, eyes focused past the walls of the house and toward the peaks. "Yes, it's much worse up there."

CHAPTER NINETEEN

A troubled night passed. It was cold enough to cause uncontrollable shivering. They moved out of the house and found another, crossing the pitch-black pathways in anxious silence. Guards were posted, but the wolves didn't return. The remainder of the dark hours passed with Gurka and the other members of R24 taking turns catnapping. Bodie and the relic hunters did the same, staying close. Jemma worked on the computer with Gunn. Bodie guessed it helped still the night terrors, both real and imagined. It took most of the night. Not because it was hard to spot the train track but because the signal was weak and erratic.

They shrugged on heavy coats, gloves, and hats and spent a miserable night in the ghost town, listening to distant, mournful howling, a chilling counterpoint to Jemma's and Gunn's quick-fire consultations.

Before dawn, Jemma caught Bodie's eye and nodded. She'd found the right area. Bodie saw no reason not to let Gurka know— he and his companions had been checking constantly anyway. Jemma proceeded to explain how she'd found the old train tracks that bypassed Dydiowa to the east and continued around one of the higher mountains. Gurka, Nina, and Vash checked the route, calculated distances and times, and sent three worried glances up through the house windows at the highest, darkest mountains and the treacherous passes that wound around them.

"The only way is over," Gurka said. "We can't spend a week going around it."

As a relic hunter, Bodie agreed with his thinking, but as a captive, he thought the opposite. But the mercs would take the risks, and from a callous perspective, that would almost certainly thin their numbers. The more hazardous their journey, the better. All he had to think about was protecting Jemma and Gunn.

And Lucie. But that was an entirely different problem.

For Lucie, the night had started as one of the loneliest of her life, which was saying something, since her closest family was all dead. She fought hard to keep up the prim-and-proper front, the reserved attitude, but she was ready to start blubbering in front of the hard-faced, violent Dudyk.

But her fatalistic belief had receded, for now. How could it not when Dudyk threatened to hurt her every few hours?

He was worse than she remembered Jamie being. Maybe there was no coming back for him. Maybe *he* had been the one bullying others.

The R24 psycho had crouched by a window all night, keeping one eye on the door he'd managed to wedge firmly closed. Most of the wolves' attention had been centered upon the other building, but occasionally, some snorting, snarling monster had come clawing at their door.

Dudyk had readied a rifle and two handguns. Always, he was ready. Always, he was watchful, in tune with his surroundings. Lucie had watched him for hours, taking her mind off the battle outside and the screams of the dying. Occasionally, every hour perhaps, he'd looked over to check on her. She'd barely moved, not wanting to alert the wolves or incite her captor's anger.

Near dawn, Dudyk spoke: "They are leaving now. So you can stop cowering like a frightened rabbit. Sleep, if you like. The next day will be hard."

Lucie scrunched her face up, confused by his words, both nasty and unselfish at the same time. So far she hadn't seen a scrap of goodness in Dudyk, only the desire to cause harm. She didn't trust him one bit, so she fought to stay awake even as her eyelids drooped. To keep from falling asleep, she tried conversation.

"Do you really hate everyone so much?"

She had given some thought to what she should say, but unsure how to talk to a homicidal relic hunter, she'd decided to keep it simple. And honest.

Dudyk seemed to notice her watching him. "What?"

"You heard me right. I used to have an uncle like you."

"I don't hate everyone," Dudyk said defensively. "Most people—like you and your friends—don't understand me."

Lucie coughed. "What is there to understand?"

"You see—this," he said, pointing out the guns, his harshly drawn face, the tattoos, and the scarred arms, "and you think you know me."

"No. I have always looked past the exterior. I value actions, morals, and respect."

"Just shut up," he said. "If they tell me to hurt you, I will hurt you."

She saw the truth of it in his eyes. Dudyk possessed no compassion. To him, she was a tool, useful in controlling Bodie and the others. A long, lonely night was about to turn into one more lonely day.

Dudyk took a radio call. "We will go up the mountain soon," he said. "It will not be easy."

Lucie met his eyes, saw the harshness there, and tried to keep her stiff upper lip from starting to tremble.

◆　◆　◆

It was a cold, dim, unwelcoming dawn. The entire group filed out of their houses to greet it, stretching, rubbing tired eyes, and making sure they were warmly wrapped up. They all wore thick coats over several layers, as well as thin insulated gloves, and they'd been given even more thermal coverings for the higher altitudes. The hope was that they would find a pass at a low elevation, but R24 had planned for the hardest outcome.

Without seeing or waiting for any sign of the villagers, the group set out. Bodie bent his head into an icy wind, keeping his eyes on the gravel-strewn path that meandered its way up to the higher foothills. The mountains were shadowed by the rising dawn, dark smudges at first, slowly emerging. The mists that had blanketed the land last night folded gently away, lingering only in the low valley and slopes they traversed. Bodie walked at the head of his own team, with Cassidy, Jemma, and Gunn behind; the rest were strung out along the path, sticking to the main route as they followed its many ups and downs.

Miles passed. The slopes grew steeper and rockier. The air became colder. Bodie could see his own breath steaming in front of him. Once, Gurka called a halt to allow everyone an energy bar snack. It felt odd at first, seeing their captors concerned for their welfare, but of course it was all personally motivated.

Two hours in, they stopped once more, perching wherever they could, on the edges of rocks or in the lee of a cliff. Bodie deliberately sank down next to Gurka.

"I have concerns," he said.

"About what?"

"First, Lucie. I don't trust that psycho you've got guarding her. And second, your hired help. Men who enjoy killing unarmed civilians aren't trustworthy."

Gurka finished unwrapping the skin from an orange before replying. "I do not answer to you, no matter how important you think you are. So you found Zeus and Atlantis—so what? That does not make you better than us."

"I never said—"

Gurka held a hand up to stop Bodie's words. "But you expect something."

"Sorry, I'm not sure what you mean."

"You expect *me* to give a fuck about you. I don't. So quit giving me the spiel, quit thinking you can make an ally of me, and understand this—you breathe only because *I* think we can use your experience. Now get the fuck out of my face."

Bodie backed off, unwilling to goad the man, thinking it better to keep a lower profile for now.

The mountains reared up around them as they climbed higher. The paths grew scarce, and they were forced to take some chances, climbing around outcroppings to gain new passes, scaling a good-size boulder that had fallen from above and blocked the way forward. But they looked after each other, Bodie concerned for everyone's plight and Gurka making sure the relic hunters and Caruso were as unexposed as conditions allowed.

The air grew even colder, the wind snapping at their faces as if it had teeth. The thought put Bodie once more in mind of last night's visitors. Twice, he heard distant howling and wondered if they were being tracked.

"I think we're coming around the side of this mountain," one of the mercs reported soon after midday. "The path falls, then rises across the next one, but then we're clear."

"Good progress," Nina said. "But it still means we'll have to spend the night out here."

Bodie forged ahead. The passes were rock strewed, with sides that crumbled away down sheer cliff faces. He guided Jemma and Gunn, telling them to follow exactly in his footsteps. Three times now, the mercenaries following them had almost fallen from the pass, two catching themselves on outcroppings and being hauled back to safety and a third saved by Belenko, the silent member of R24, who'd wrapped his bearlike arms around the merc before throwing him to safety without the merest hint of emotion crossing his face. The merc's gasp of thanks had gone unrecognized.

Bodie checked down the line as they crept along a four-foot-wide ledge with the high mountain at their back. They were side-stepping for safety. At the very rear Bodie saw Lucie and Dudyk. The historian looked okay for now, but Bodie knew she had to be suffering inside.

One chance, he thought. *Just give us one good chance.*

Sleet swept the mountains. Below, intermittently amid the driving rain, they could see swaths of green, flowers, trees, and blue lakes, and even Gurka had a wistful look on his face. It would be far easier to make the trek lower down but would take so much longer. Bodie lingered as long as he could on the ledge, making sure Jemma and Gunn made it, encouraging them with every step. Then he turned to face another pass made dark by the towering mountain above.

Ten more minutes, and they were out in the open again, negotiating a six-foot-wide path bordered by a rock face to the right and a sheer drop to the valley below on the left. The wind picked up, threatening to sweep one of them off the ledge. Bodie stood in the face of it, eyes narrowed. Ahead, Cassidy and Heidi followed Pantera step by cautious step, with the mercenaries in front of them.

Bodie paused for a moment to catch his breath.

And that was when he heard it. A distant roll of thunder, followed quickly by another. He looked up.

A large, irregular boulder had broken free from the lofty heights above. It had plummeted for fifty feet and then gotten caught between two ledges, but it was threatening even now to start falling again, and this time it would plunge straight down the vertical rock face into them.

"Lucie!" He saw immediately who it would strike. "Move! *Move!*"

It was rocking, rolling toward the edge.

"Lucie!" His shout was torn away by the cutting winds.

Bodie ran, head down. It was all he could do. The boulder was gaining momentum. Lucie was staring at him, Dudyk too, as if he'd lost his mind. Bodie smashed two mercenaries into the rock face on his way past as they tried to stop him, leapt past a shocked Yasmine, and screamed, "Look out!" as he ran straight at Lucie.

He calculated the boulder would be almost upon them.

He hit Lucie open armed, driving her back against the mountain. With only a split second to decide, he reached out and grabbed Dudyk too, unable to just let the man be crushed to death.

They struck the rock face hard.

The boulder smashed down just two seconds later, impacting the ledge with a resounding crash. To Bodie, it sounded like the whole mountain had collapsed upon them. Lucie screamed again, high pitched and right in his ear. Dudyk had been struggling in his grip but lost all his fight then, allowing Bodie to push him back against the rock.

The boulder took four feet of ledge with it as it crashed down and swept past. Luckily, it wasn't the four feet Bodie occupied.

Several moments passed, and the mountain grew quiet once more. All sound except the incessant wind stopped.

Then Cassidy's voice: "You all right, Guy? Luce?"

Bodie let out a long breath, let up his grip on Lucie and Dudyk, and tested limbs and muscles. "I think so."

Lucie fell to her knees, overwhelmed, the events of the last few days catching up with her. Bodie helped her gently to her feet, whispering, "It'll be okay. We'll find a way out of this. Trust me."

Dudyk heard him and regarded Bodie with utterly blank eyes. "You saved my life."

"I'll try not to let it happen again."

Bodie held the man's eyes a moment longer and thought he saw a glint of respect there—just a shimmer, but at this stage even a shimmer was better than nothing at all.

"We still have that gap to cross." Bodie stared at the new four-foot-long hazard. "Maybe you could lay down, mate, and we'll walk across your back."

Dudyk almost smiled.

CHAPTER TWENTY

The entire group—mercenaries, Russian relic hunters, and captives—worked together as a team to set up camp, in preparation for a lonely night out on the mountain. Heidi Moneymaker toiled alongside mercenaries and members of R24 to make their temporary shelter as secure as possible. She'd heard the wolves earlier, but nothing for a long time.

Were they being tracked?

After Bodie had saved Lucie and Dudyk, the group had navigated much more carefully, with lookouts to front and rear as well as spotters watching the slopes. Another rockfall had hindered them for thirty minutes, and then a dead-end pass had forced them to find another route.

Now, they were three-quarters of the way across the range. The sun was ebbing to the west, throwing lengthening shadows. One saving grace was they weren't as high now as they had been earlier, making the cold less bitter and the winds weaker. It was a good place to camp in the lee of the mountain, protected by a high overhang.

Heidi settled with her back to the wall, bone tired. Despite her situation it felt extraordinary just sitting there, in the quiet vastness, with endless, incredible vistas to all sides. The isolation itself was grand, the quietness overwhelming, the vault of the sky a wonder.

It had been a long, hard, rough day. She'd used muscles she hadn't known she had, and now those muscles were complaining. Slowly, she rolled her shoulders to ease away the stiffness.

"Want a massage?" Bodie dropped down next to her.

"I'm good for now, thanks."

"Maybe later?"

She looked at him. There had been this unspoken thing between them since they'd first met. A connection. An attachment that they hadn't explored. Still, it remained, and Heidi wondered if they'd ever get to exploring it.

"One more crazy adventure," Bodie laughed.

Which was something else causing tension and conflict between them. Bodie and his crew wanted out of CIA constraints. They mentioned it almost every chance they got. The entire scenario stupefied her. Heidi was caught in the middle of the conflict between the CIA and Bodie's bunch.

She already knew the outcome would cause chaos, which moved it far down her chain of thoughts.

Bodie interrupted. "You okay? Thinking about your daughter?"

She hadn't been, but she nodded. "I missed the first meeting she's agreed to in months."

"You can't deal with that right now. But you can handle it when we get back."

"I wish it was that easy."

Bodie shuffled into a more comfortable position. "Well, I'm here if you need me."

Heidi felt a moment's amusement. "You? What could you know about conversing with an eleven-year-old?"

Bodie shrugged. "I take care of Gunn every day."

Heidi smiled and cocked her head. "It's not the best résumé, is it?"

"I guess not."

"All this came at a bad time for you too, huh?"

Bodie sighed. "The world's a poorer place without Cross in it. I used to lean on him more than I realized."

"Well, lean on me now. I can take it." Heidi switched the subject to something that had been on her mind the last couple of days. "Have you spoken to Caruso? Do we know how much further we have to go before we reach the Amber Room?"

Bodie lowered his voice, staring at the ground. "I tried," he whispered. "But I think the guy genuinely can't remember. He has early dementia, but it's the excitement of being around relics that stimulates him enough to fire his memory again."

Heidi's suspicions were reinforced by her experience as a CIA agent. "I don't completely trust that opinion. The most likely scenario is he's terrified for his family and drawing this out, praying for some good fortune."

Bodie nodded, sitting back. Heidi closed her eyes, grateful for his close presence and the easy regard in which they held each other. Throughout the night they catnapped and chatted, keeping an eye on everyone else, including the mercs and R24. Gurka, Nina, and Vash sat side by side, chatting frequently. The mercs wandered to and fro, seeking out dangers along the pass in which they sat. Heidi watched Lucie at the far end of the line and saw her trying to engage Dudyk in conversation. It was a good strategy, though Heidi wasn't sure Lucie realized she was doing it for any tactical reason. It was just Lucie, trying to adapt and make the best of a bad situation.

The night passed slowly, a deep chill forcing them to huddle together. Heidi found peace in Bodie's warm body and fell asleep.

When she woke, it was to his gentle shaking. "Breakfast."

A tasteless bowl of camping rations later, the group broke camp and continued across the mountain, following a circuitous route and coming up against another dead end before finding a path that began to wind its way downward.

Heidi's spirits lifted when she saw foothills rolling between gaps in the rock faces. "A fine sight," she said aloud.

But then she began to worry about what came next.

Once the group was free of the mountains, Gurka called a brief halt for refreshments. It was clear from the spirited conversation that everyone was happier in the foothills. As she ate, Heidi saw Gurka walk over to Jemma. Bodie moved to back their researcher up, so Heidi walked over to lend her weight.

"Do you have coordinates for where you spotted the train track?" Gurka asked.

"I do."

"Enter them now. We can't be far away."

Jemma tapped numbers into a handheld GPS device and held it out to Gurka. The leader of R24 nodded. "Forty minutes." His face broke out into a rare grin. "Let's move out."

Heidi focused, concentrating on the position and well-being of the thirteen mercenaries still living. Two had collected injuries along the mountain paths, but nothing more than a twisted ankle and bruising. She herself had hurt the fingers of her right hand while grabbing a crumbling handhold. Nobody had escaped the mountains in great condition.

It helped her to think of their predicament as a mission, an operation where they had to extract themselves from a dangerous enemy. She'd received training for that dilemma at least. But no training during her time at the CIA had prepared her for the moral quandary she knew she would face if they ever escaped from this. The CIA would never willingly let the relic hunters go, but Bodie and his team were close to forcing the issue. She was their handler, but she felt for this team. She knew what they'd been through and what made them do what they did. She accepted it, even admired it in a way.

They were friends. Maybe, with Bodie, maybe more than that. Could she really turn them in? Could she effectively chase them down if they ran? The questions threatened to pull her mind apart, so she shelved them as best she could to focus on the upcoming threat.

As they reached the coordinates Jemma had given them, she became hyperaware. The distractions of the last few days, the journey, R24, the mercenaries, the wolves, and especially deliberations on how to approach her daughter—it all melted away.

They slowed beyond the foothills, approaching a rolling plain, a far more hospitable terrain. Heidi cast a glance back toward the mountains. They hadn't heard or seen anything to suppose the wolves were still tracking them, and if they were, hopefully the flat land would put them off.

Gurka walked alongside Jemma. "We should be able to see the tracks by now."

The mercs were kicking at the ground, which was a mix of green and brown. A dusty haze surrounded them. Heidi knew the tracks would have been overgrown by more than seventy years of neglect. Jemma started to walk in a pronounced curve before stopping and pointing at the ground.

"If you dig around here," she said, "you should find them."

"The next waypoint?" Gurka asked.

"No. We should make sure the tracks exist first, don't you think?"

Gurka threw a hard glance at Caruso. "Fair point."

Heidi walked over to the Italian. "Anything coming back, Dante?"

"It would be better if my family were here. Your Lucie is there—she is captive, but you see her every day. I have not seen my wife and son since . . . since . . ." He choked up a little.

Heidi still couldn't tell if the man was purposely deflecting or genuinely afflicted. Either way, the absence of his family had to be almost unbearable.

But this wasn't the time for kid gloves. "It's a shitty situation, for sure, but if you don't start producing the goods, it's gonna get a hell of a lot harder. For you *and* your family."

Mercenaries put their weapons down and broke out small shovels from their packs. Several started digging. It wasn't long before the first clang rang out. Gurka ran toward the noise, bent down, and helped clear soil and scrub away.

Heidi saw the brown, rusted train track less than six inches below the surface. Dante wasn't totally full of it, then. Hidden in plain sight, as Gunn commented. Jemma got her bearings from the track, pinned it on the GPS, and then pointed to where it ran.

"The curve begins over there," she said. "Not far now."

Heidi readied herself as they approached the specific series of curves that the picture diary had indicated. It was a large area, but they had a large crew with which to search. Gurka, Nina, and Vash shouted orders, and soon several groups were digging.

Nina ordered the relic hunters to spread out and stand guard.

Bodie confronted her. "Guard with no weapons? I don't think so."

"A guard will watch you. If you spot anything, use your tongues while you still have them. Try to run, and we'll shoot one of you in the leg. Then you'll see how much it hurts keeping up the rest of the way."

She turned away, as merciless as the mountains they'd just crossed.

Heidi ranged from the group, heading toward Lucie, who was sitting behind Dudyk on a low rock, but stopped when her bodyguard leveled a rifle. He didn't speak, just stared and waited. Heidi veered off in a different direction.

The mercenaries sweated. Most of the members of R24 joined the dig. Only Dudyk and one other mercenary watched the relic hunters, but it was enough. Heidi found herself staring at the mountains and the rolling plains, wondering how the hell they were going to find a way out of this.

They needed Caruso, a phone, a map, and an escape route. Preferably a weapon too.

Heidi watched the mercs curse and swelter into midafternoon. Today, the sun rode openly in the sky, not shielded by clouds. The whole area felt vast and humbling to her. It had stood for millennia and would stand for millennia more. She faced the sun and drank in the feel of it on her face, basking in the glow, if only for a moment.

"Got something!" one of the mercs shouted at last, half a day after they'd started digging.

Heidi started to walk back.

Two mercenaries knelt inside a coffin-shaped hole that sat beside dozens of other coffin-shaped holes their colleagues had been digging. The entire area now resembled a desecrated graveyard. Mounds of dirt marked the holes and the curving course of the tracks.

Bodie took it all in as he approached, from the stances of the mercenaries and positions of their weapons to the tired hunch in their bodies. Gurka was crouched down at the edge of the hole.

"What is it?" Bodie asked.

"A chest," someone said. "Heavy mother too. It's gonna take some lifting."

"It has been lifted before, though," a sharper man said. "It's loosely fitted down here with slack sand all around the edges, not the kind of compressed earth that seventy years would produce."

Bodie watched Gurka organize the mercs and his own team. They dug around the chest, exposed it, and looped a thick strap around it. Then a man started to heave. The chest rose steadily.

It came over the top amid a pile of sand and filth. Bodie saw a rusty metal chest with a black strap on each side. A lock drained sand onto the ground. Gurka ordered it dragged well clear of the holes and onto a patch of grass. Then he turned to Nina.

"Careful. Take your time."

Nina looked at him reproachfully. The expression on her face made him think of Cassidy. *The two women were definitely similar,* he thought. It gave him an odd reference that he tried to repress. At best, these people were cruel criminal counterparts to his team. He'd do better not to humanize them. He needed every ounce of focus right now.

Nina either picked or broke the lock; Bodie couldn't see, but soon it fell to the floor, where she started unstrapping the leather fastenings. Gurka stepped forward to open it.

Bodie craned his neck to see inside.

Shit, he thought. *That's really, really bad.*

CHAPTER
TWENTY-ONE

"It is a Sniper's Badge," Lucie said, and Nina nodded.

"I have seen them before, even in Russia," the woman said, peering at the object. "Though they *are* rare. Remember, Gurka? We traded one of these two, three years ago?"

Lucie, among them for the first time in days to lend her expertise to the find, ignored R24's conversation, speaking to Bodie and the other members of his team.

"A first-class Sniper's Badge was given exclusively to members of the SS. You see the gold sewing on the edges of the badge? Second class would be silver. These were awarded to a sniper with over sixty confirmed kills in the war and only to members of Aryan ancestry. Normally"—she rubbed the patch and turned it over in her hands—"they are plain on the back, but someone has taken the time to sew a man's name into this one."

"The owner," Gurka said. "Obviously. What is the name?"

"Klaus Meyer," Lucie said, handing the badge over.

"Is that everything?" Nina was glaring at the chest as if it might be hiding another treasure. "Could someone have taken the clue? Perhaps it was you?" She turned accusing eyes on Caruso and brought out a cell phone. "I need only press one button to send your family to Hell."

"I unearthed it," Caruso admitted. "And buried it again. The badge was on its own. It is the name you need."

"You realized you'd need to follow the clues again?" Bodie asked. "From start to finish?"

"I know my limitations." Caruso hung his head after a moment. "Through the years, I have done this kind of thing many times."

Bodie heard a distant howl and looked uneasily into the mountains. Many pairs of eyes followed suit. A pervasive air of fear existed amid the group that hadn't been dissipated by the new landscape or the bank of fog that was rolling in up there. It wasn't just the wolves either. The mountains themselves felt sinister. Several times Bodie had wondered if they were being watched. Was something else out here, tracking them, observing them?

Something worse than wolves?

"I hate this god-awful place," one of the mercs growled, and there were several accompanying curses.

Bodie agreed with them and studied his surroundings. There were a thousand places where someone—or something—could hide. And standing here, by the train tracks, they were totally exposed.

"Can we wind this up?" he said. "We're sitting ducks out here."

Gurka eyed him. "You're right," he said. "So Blondie, what does the name Klaus Meyer mean?"

"I may be a historian, but I don't know everyone from history, sir. Maybe Jemma can help you."

Bodie turned away to hide the grin. It was great to know Lucie's feistiness remained intact.

"Me," Gunn said quickly. "Pass me a computer, and I'll track the man down." After a minute he gazed speculatively at the clouds. "The big problem is . . . to get GPS, or any kind of signal out here, you need to be able to see enough of the sky for it to be able to *see* enough satellites. If there is a signal, it will be intermittent."

Gurka motioned for someone to hand Gunn an eight-inch tablet. Gunn explained as he worked.

"I'm searching the SS in 1945 for a Klaus Meyer . . ."

"Those records are online?" Vash asked.

"Some are plainly available," Gunn said, still waiting patiently. "World War Two researchers, academics, and professors compiled extensive lists from the time, especially members of the armies on all sides. Every country. Commendations, deaths, lists of regiments. That kind of thing. I'm diving deep now, to find the one that I need."

Ten minutes later, Gunn was still waiting. Gurka clenched his fists with frustration. "You'd better not be wasting my time, you fucking geek. I'll flay you alive and leave you here for the wolves."

"Hey." Bodie stepped forward. "There's no—"

"Wait." Gunn held up a hand. "Maybe there's another way. Do you have a satellite phone?"

Nina nodded at one of the mercs and then the backpacks. "Several. For emergencies."

"Let me see it. If it has Iridium internet access, we have a chance."

Bodie waited for Nina to hand over the phone, watching Gurka. The R24 leader was growing more and more hostile, edgier by the hour. Bodie doubted he even realized that, right now, his hand was gripping the haft of his military knife.

Gunn turned the sat phone on. "I can tether the sat phone's access to the tablet."

Bodie waited for Gunn to work his magic. He took a bottle of water from his backpack and washed down an energy bar with it. The minutes passed with little sound and movement, save for the still-panting mercs, Lucie's shuffling as she was led away, and Gunn's tapping at the plastic screen.

"All right, I have something. There were several Klaus Meyers, as you can imagine, but only one with membership to the SS in that year. And in addition, this Klaus Meyer was attached to the unit under control of the SS Führungshauptamt, which occupied Königsberg at the time of the Amber Room's disappearance."

Gurka still didn't look happy. In fact, the ruthless Russian only scratched one of the old scars that lined his face and gestured for Gunn to get on with it.

"I still find it impossible to understand that men and women adhered to the racist creed that certain kinds of people are *subhuman*," Yasmine said quietly, "or that it still continues, of course."

"Waffen-SS commanders and its members were judged to be a criminal organization within the Nazi Party," a female voice answered. Bodie was surprised to hear Nina answering Yasmine. "As you know, the atrocities they committed were numerous."

A somber silence followed, but then Gunn spoke again, this time without emotion. "We can see by the badge that this Nazi, Klaus Meyer, accompanied the Amber Room on its way out of Germany. He was on the train. Now, from the last clue, we've deduced that somebody on that train left a trail of bread crumbs for those who could follow. They either contrived a stop at this point or came back later. Possibly leaving the clues in reverse."

"Makes more sense," Gurka allowed. "Do you think it was Klaus Meyer?"

"Most definitely not," Gunn said. "The records say he was killed and buried in a village graveyard among the Tatras."

Now Bodie leaned forward, despite himself. "Buried here? Where?"

Gunn pointed at the screen. "Nica. A now-abandoned village."

"An abandoned graveyard?" one of the mercs moaned. "Out here? That's all we need."

"The danger is good for you," Cassidy said with a challenge in her voice. "I say, bring it on, and let's see which one of us handles it best."

The challenge went unanswered by the mercs, but Gurka turned to address them all. "Nica, then," he said. "Find it on the map, and let's go. The less time we spend in these blasted hills, the better I will feel."

It was only then that Vash let out a cry. "That mad Italian bastard. He's gone!"

"No." Nina pointed at a slope. "He's running. Get after him!"

Out of the blue, Bodie saw their chance to escape had come.

CHAPTER TWENTY-TWO

Lucie saw Caruso drift away. It was an odd sight. The Italian simply looked as if he'd decided to leave the group of his own volition. He turned his back and started walking, but everyone was so engrossed in whatever Gunn was attempting to do with the computer that nobody noticed.

Caruso picked his way among the foothills at a right angle to the mountains, disappearing down slopes and then reappearing as he ascended the next. He wasn't trying to hide. He wasn't running.

Lucie feared for him; she feared for his family more. The void a dead family member left in your life couldn't possibly be filled; their life experience could never be passed on. For Lucie, growing up as a teenager had been like starting all over again.

Then a shout went up: Where was Caruso? Dudyk heard and rose from the seated position he'd occupied for the last thirty minutes. Lucie saw the whole camp in disarray. Nina started shouting. Gurka held up both hands in an expression of anger. The mercs stared at each other and then at the disappearing Caruso.

Trust the mad Italian, Lucie thought, *to do the unexpected.*

Dudyk was concentrated solely on his R24 colleagues and their orders. Lucie saw Bodie staring at her and felt a sudden jolt of instinct.

Shit, they're gonna do something.

It was the first distraction they'd had. Lucie knew that the talent in their team—Heidi and Bodie, Yasmine and Cassidy—would attempt to escape.

And Dudyk appeared to have forgotten she existed.

Lucie watched Bodie. She rose to her feet and stretched her limbs. She looked for the easiest means of escape and for the closest cover. If she headed in Caruso's direction, there were several successive hills and a thick but small stand of trees. It was the best shelter available. The chances of the Italian picking it by random were extremely low.

Wolves howled in the mountains.

Not there for us, Lucie hoped. *And not now.*

Bodie nodded, a signal, and then the people around him sprang into action. Lucie didn't waste a second. She put her head down and sprinted away from Dudyk, aiming for the first hill. She ran up the slope, topped it, and then barreled down the other side. The wind whipped her hair, blew it around her face. Her panting was as loud as a train in her ears. She pounded up the next slope.

A shout came from behind, a vicious warning to stop. Lucie risked a glance back and almost tripped as her heart slammed into her mouth.

Dudyk was training a handgun on her. "Stop there," he cried. "Or I shoot your legs out from under you!"

Lucie knew he'd do it. Gurka had chosen Dudyk to guard her for a reason. He would do whatever he needed to ensure her compliance, from threats to severe bodily harm.

She ran down the next slope, temporarily out of sight. She had a fast and terrible decision to make. As she rose up the next incline, she was already looking back.

Bodie and the others were fighting and running. Caruso was gone. Dudyk was walking forward, still aiming his gun.

"Stop!"

Oddly, she knew he could have fired several times already. Why hadn't the Russian opened fire?

Lucie had always believed she would die suddenly, of natural causes, an accident, just like everyone else in her family. Gritting her teeth, forcing down the debilitating fear, she knew that right now, she had to test that theory.

Bodie saw every mercenary either watching Caruso or listening to Gurka. They were as distracted as they were ever going to get. Aware that the other members of his team were watching him, he nodded and sprang into action.

Grabbing the nearest mercenary's arm, he ripped the rifle from his hands and threw it onto the ground. Then he elbowed the merc in the face. His attack barely had an effect, but it did surprise the man. Bodie was able to push him backward and trip him up, sending him to the ground. As he fell, Bodie grabbed a handgun from the man's belt.

Pointing it at his face, Bodie grabbed two spare clips of ammo and a map. As he was about to open fire, someone clattered into his back. The bullet flew wide. He staggered, regained his balance. The merc tried to rise, but another man fell across him. There was no time. Bodie knew they only had seconds to make their escape.

Around him, his team fought wildly. Cassidy kicked and punched two mercs until they fell to their knees, winded. Gurka and Nina both shouted orders, the numerous distractions over-whelming them and confusing their men. Heidi grappled with a long-haired individual, pretended to stumble, and then hurled him over her right shoulder. He landed with a clatter and a deep grunt. Heidi was on him in less than a second. Quickly, she searched every pocket she could reach.

"We're good." She held up the greatest prize they could find—at this point even more valuable than the Amber Room.

A sat phone.

"Run!"

Bodie kicked his opponent in the ribs. They couldn't hope to outmatch the mercs, even if their numbers were equal, but they had the element of surprise, and all they needed was a weapon, a map, and a phone. Add to that the belief that R24 wouldn't just order them shot, that it needed Caruso too, and they had a chance. They had debated it several times already on their journey. Now they were testing their conclusions.

Bodie ran, pocketing the handgun and the map. He saw Cassidy relieve her opponent of a small pistol and then take off. Heidi and Yasmine caused disarray among the closest mercs, both women coordinating their attacks. Pantera had approached both Gurka and Nina, grabbing their attention, but had then smashed Vash across the skull and started to run.

Gurka shouted, "Don't let them escape."

Nina yelled, "Where's Caruso gone?"

But the mercs were in disarray, first headed for Caruso, then drawn into a fight with the relic hunters. R24 members screamed out conflicting orders. Dudyk was yelling at Lucie. Caruso, the focus of Gurka and Nina, had now vanished. Bodie and his friends gained thirty feet before the mercs picked themselves up off the ground. A weapon was fired, but Bodie gambled, thinking it would be a warning shot into the air. Jemma and Gunn were close by, running with their heads low and staying amid the pack. Cassidy was ahead, leading them over the hills and toward a huddle of trees.

"I've been scouting the terrain all along," she said. "At every rest point. Beyond the trees is a narrow but fast-running river, and beyond that, a group of mini peaks. Hopefully, we can get lost there."

Bodie eyed the mountains. Hopefully, they wouldn't have to venture back into those desolate, haunted reaches. He searched the hills for Caruso, kept an eye on Lucie, and watched the mercs mobilizing back by the train tracks.

"Run faster," he said. "They're coming."

And the shadows were lengthening as the Tatras prepared to welcome the setting sun.

CHAPTER TWENTY-THREE

Cassidy saw Bodie slow and check behind them again. Three mercenaries were chasing them like mountain runners, leaping from mound to mound, relishing the terrain and closing the gap at a rapid pace.

"That does not look good."

"No way can we outrun them," Pantera said.

Yasmine glanced at them. "Keep going. I will stop them."

Cassidy felt reluctant but nodded at the Interpol agent. "I'll help you."

Bodie alone knew what she was going through. "I'll do it."

"No." Cassidy didn't even look at him. "This is my job."

Yasmine looked relieved and, with Jemma, Gunn, and Heidi, moved away. Cassidy did the same, rolling into a fold of earth and coming up with the handgun she'd stolen. Yasmine grabbed a good-size rock and crouched two yards to her left. Guilt tore through Cassidy. She couldn't get Cross's death out of her mind and the vulnerability that it had left. She fought it, trying to find her old self, but doubt clouded everything. She wasn't scared of the approaching mercs; she was worried that another friend might die.

Soon, they heard the beat of boots striking the earth and readied themselves. Cassidy rose as a shadow reared over her, surprising her opponent. She fired instantly into his midriff, knowing that he wore Kevlar plates but also knowing the impact of the bullet would knock him off his feet. He fell, gasping, gun falling from nerveless fingers. Cassidy shot a quick glance over to Yasmine and then leapt to meet the third runner head-on.

Yasmine reached up and tackled her opponent around the ankles, sending him crashing face-first into the ground. His head hit soft grass and bounced, his yell barely heard. Before he could recover, she was on his back, punching the exposed ears and neck. In a few moments he was still.

Cassidy shoulder barged her second opponent as she rose. His momentum was enough to send her flying backward, but at the same time he flew sideways, completely losing his equilibrium. He landed in a heap. Cassidy staggered but caught herself, then reached the merc before he had a chance to react. She didn't waste a bullet this time, didn't want to kill the man in cold blood as he lay there wheezing. She struck him a blow across the temple with her gun and then one more for good measure.

Yasmine jumped to her side.

"Well done," Cassidy said.

"Thanks. How does it look back there?"

"R24 is leading the rest of the mercs at a steady pace. They're tracking us rather than chasing."

"Caruso?" Yasmine asked.

"No sign. But we're headed in the same direction."

"Let's go." But before Yasmine could move, Cassidy reached out a hand and placed it on her wrist, stopping her.

"You did well out there. Thank you for stepping up."

Yasmine smiled. "Anytime. I don't just want out of here; I want to fit in with you guys."

Together, they crawled through the terrain's deepest wrinkles until the ground started rising. Then they broke out into a run, following Bodie and the others into the thick stand of trees. The sudden darkness deceived their eyes at first, making Yasmine trip over a rotting branch. She caught herself, stumbling in Cassidy's wake for a few feet. Cassidy glanced back between the trees.

"I see them ahead. A few hundred yards to the northeast," Yasmine muttered.

"Yes, keep going."

Cassidy saw Bodie and the main team running at a pace that wouldn't rapidly deplete their energy. Bodie was angling their run to the east—the direction Caruso had gone. Cassidy caught up to the group.

"You seen that mad Italian yet?" she asked.

"No, but we have to find him. How'd it go back there?"

"Three temporarily disabled. The rest are coming more slowly."

She turned her attention to Lucie. "Are you okay? That bastard Dudyk didn't hurt you, did he?"

The blonde slowed a little as she answered. "He's a vicious man, but only with words. But it felt like he wanted to hurt me. You remember when Gurka ordered him to." She shivered. "He smiled."

"I'll teach him 'vicious' real soon," Cassidy spat.

"Asshole doesn't deserve to live," Heidi said. "So what does Bodie go and do? Saves his life."

The Londoner looked over. "I don't do cold-blooded murder, and neither should you. Self-defense, well, that's a different matter."

"I won't," Heidi said. "But if he hurts Lucie . . ."

Their historian's face became worried. "You implying he's gonna get another chance?"

Heidi pursed her lips. "It's touch and go. Unless we go back into the higher mountains, there's very little cover."

That spurred them on. The wood was thick and demanded concentration to avoid falling into a bough or tripping on a tangle of roots. Lucie waited a few moments before saying, "Dudyk did have a chance to fire on me. Had me lined up in his sights."

"You're saying he let you go?" Cassidy asked.

"No. But he could have stopped me. Opened fire. Maybe he's good enough to have nicked me; I don't know. But . . . he didn't even try."

"Probably worried he wasn't good enough, and they need you," Cassidy grunted. "R24, between them, don't have an ounce of empathy. They're ice-cold killers. They may think they're like us, but they're the complete opposite."

Lucie nodded. Bodie slowed and looked back, then gestured for the others to do the same. There were no sounds of pursuit. He wondered for a moment if those following them had decided to circumvent the stand of trees.

"C'mon," he said. "I don't want to get captured again."

Ahead, the trees seemed to be thinning. Bodie could see a gentle downhill slope leading to a fast-flowing stream and, beyond that, a series of rising peaks.

We need to get lost in there.

And it was going to be easier than he'd first thought. The sun was starting to set. Shadows were lengthening.

Another night in the Tatra Mountains beckoned.

CHAPTER
TWENTY-FOUR

Cassidy and Yasmine put their heads together and agreed that they could track Caruso. Bodie and Pantera watched their extremities as they broke from tree cover and raced toward the stream, confident that nobody was flanking them.

At the edge, Cassidy and Yasmine ranged left and right, looking for a sign of Caruso's passing. Heidi had borrowed the gun from Cassidy, and Bodie still held the other. Together, they watched the trees at their back, waiting for Cassidy and Yasmine.

Minutes passed.

"C'mon, c'mon," Gunn fretted. "They're gonna be here soon."

"Don't worry, kid," Heidi said. "We have firepower now. We'll hold them off."

"I'm pretty sure we don't have enough bullets."

Yasmine waved, then pointed at a patch of grass close to the edge of the running river. "Footprints," she said. "The right size and the right direction. Looks like he slipped into the river."

Cassidy waded across, fighting the current all the way. Bodie jumped in. The cold water came up to his waist, making him gasp.

"Bad idea," Gunn said at his side, "with night coming. We're gonna freeze our bloody bollocks off."

"Not my problem," Cassidy said, climbing out the other side.

Heidi followed, scrutinizing the way they'd come. "Hurry," she said. "They're here."

Bodie pulled himself up the far bank, dripping water, trying not to shiver. A look back revealed the mercenaries and R24 emerging from the thick tree line. Bodie didn't wait to hear them shouting threats across the river. He urged his team on, chasing Yasmine toward the peaks. Descending darkness was now their friend.

Yasmine took advantage of what little light they had left. Before the sun passed below the bulky mountain range, she rushed ahead, following Caruso's tracks as best she could. Cassidy tracked *her*, and the rest followed. Bodie counted the minutes as they hurried along. At least ten passed before Yasmine and Cassidy urged them to slow. For the first time, he found himself grateful that Yasmine was with them. She made a great counterpoint and backup for Cassidy and, in contradiction to what he'd initially thought, a positive reminder of Cross.

"It is inevitable that we will find Caruso," Cassidy said. "No need to break anything by chasing too hard."

"Why is it inevitable?" Jemma asked.

"He won't be moving as quickly as Yasmine. He's probably holed up for the night, since it's almost pitch black out here. The only issue is . . ."

"That she finds him before pitch black," Pantera said. "Our problem is precisely the same as R24's. We can't continue in the dark."

Bodie knew his old mentor was right. He hadn't thought to grab a flashlight earlier, and neither had anyone else. The mountains would be utterly dark, the kind of darkness people living close to towns and cities forgot. Those places always had reflected light, something shining up into the skies. It took a trip to a place

163

where light was totally absent but for the barest sliver of moon to remember what darkness was like.

A noise up ahead stopped them. Heidi raised her gun.

"Don't worry—it's me," Yasmine said.

"And me," Caruso whispered. "I didn't want to leave you."

"He found me," Yasmine said. "Saved me from a nasty fall, to be honest. Listen—I know you want to, but we can't keep going in this light."

Cassidy indicated their rear. "Those guys might."

"I hope they do. They will die."

"She's right," Heidi said. "I know this isn't the mountains, but the dangers are the same. A broken leg, even a twisted ankle, could be the end."

Bodie sought out a ledge from which they could keep watch. Yasmine and Cassidy found a wide niche where they could huddle and keep warm and defend their position if necessary. They left one gun with the group and another with the designated watcher.

The first hour passed in dark tension. After that, they allowed themselves a small margin of relaxation. The wind howled through the rocks, whipping up gravel and dust, blowing it around their hidey-hole. A mini squall swept through. They sat with their heads down, their eyes closed, not expecting sleep but at least trying to rest.

Two hours later, Cassidy gave up.

"Fuck it," she said. "This is depressing. Heidi, how about you pass me that map, and we figure out tomorrow's route."

Caruso laid a hand on the redhead's arm. "What is our next move? You must remember that my family will be killed."

"This is what we can do." Cassidy started to retie bootlaces that had come loose during the day. "Find the next clue; hide it so these bastards can never find it without our help. Then we negotiate."

"You mean to find the next clue *first*? Before R24?"

"Exactly. It's a race now."

"My wife," Caruso went on as if he hadn't heard her answer. "We met in Siena. I don't know what she saw in me then. I was a builder, a lazy builder." He smiled at the memory. "No money. No future. I earned what I earned and spent it the same night . . ."

Bodie didn't want to interrupt Caruso's recollections, particularly since the man appeared to find them incredibly difficult to find.

"She pursued me." Caruso gazed into the middle distance. "I used to say, 'Anna, I am not good enough for you.' She answered, 'Dante, I know, but luckily it is your heart that I love, not your brains.'" Caruso's eyes glimmered. "I can't lose her. I . . . can't. Not like this."

"We'll do everything we can," Bodie said. "For your wife and your son."

Heidi handed Gunn the map, angling it to reflect the feeble moonlight. "Nica," he said, remembering the name of the village. "Okay, it's not too far from here. Over the smaller peaks." He gestured with a hand. "It was abandoned in 1955, a few years after our friend Klaus Meyer was buried there."

Heidi waited, then, when Gunn was done, asked for the map back.

"What next?" Jemma asked.

"We have a sat phone," Heidi said, looking surprised at Jemma's question. "What the hell do you think I'm gonna do next?"

Bodie had been listening to the conversation, also attentive to anything their lookout might relay. Pantera was on guard right now but was unusually quiet. Bodie hoped he hadn't fallen asleep, then berated himself for being asinine. Pantera might have been out of the game a few years, but he was still one hell of an operator.

165

He watched Heidi, pretending to pay attention to the call but really just watching her face. No doubt he was attracted; no doubt he wanted more from the CIA agent.

But . . .

It was easier to let it lie. The future of the relic hunters, the team he cared for deeply, the family he belonged to, was not intertwined with the CIA. It couldn't be. So far, one mission had led to another, and now they couldn't abandon Caruso and his family. They would see this through to the end. But what came next? Would they run? And what would happen to Heidi if they did?

Another thought came to mind as he stared at Heidi. Yasmine's main goal, before they had been abducted by R24, had been to find Lucien, the man who had betrayed her and engineered her partner's and Eli Cross's deaths. Bodie wanted Lucien too. For Cross. Before they were done with the CIA, a side mission was in order.

Heidi's next words made him refocus. "Agent Moneymaker, yes. Abducted, and now we're in the Tatra mountain range. You can get a fix on this cell, but I will have to power down soon. I understand this is a multipurpose emergency number, but do as I've asked. We need urgent evac on this one."

As she continued, explaining enemy quantities and details and then the name of the village they were headed to, Bodie rehashed her words in his head. *Multipurpose number?* But he understood. Somebody had betrayed them to get them abducted in the first place. Heidi couldn't be sure she could get hold of the right person, so she had contacted the universal call unit. They would disseminate the message along the right paths. It would take longer but would be quicker and more productive than chancing individuals.

The point being—rescue was now a reality.

He shivered, clothes not fully dry and not likely to be as the temperature kept dropping. Thirty minutes passed, and then he started making his way to relieve Pantera of his watch.

"All good?" he asked as the bald man greeted him.

"No sign of pursuit," he said. "But something is out there."

Bodie frowned. "What do you mean—something?"

"I don't know. Shadows. Shapes. Barely seen. Not close. You sit here for ten minutes, Bodie, you'll see them."

"Hey," Bodie said as Pantera prepared to leave. "You've been quiet."

"Yeah, well." Pantera rubbed his bald head. "I'm not used to this, not anymore. And I'm trying to mend fences at home . . . you know."

Bodie nodded.

As Bodie turned to leave, Pantera nodded at him. "And you? I remember what you're like. I taught you all you know. Don't dwell too far in the past, Guy, because we need you in the present."

Bodie's watch passed in introspection. His thoughts were full of Heidi and what might happen, of the future of the relic hunters, and of the members of his team. They were closer to him than anyone in his life had ever been, save for his parents before he'd turned eight. One thing was certain—he wouldn't let them go easily.

Three times he thought he saw shapes in the dark, and once a light in the distance. The cloying blackness of the night hindered his senses and capabilities. Every time he tried to focus on what he thought might be a moving shadow, it vanished. Once, from above, he heard the pitter-patter of gravel falling down a rock surface as if disturbed.

Still, nothing happened.

I'll be bloody happy to see the dawn.

When Yasmine appeared to take her turn, Bodie stayed. Not because he didn't trust her, but because he was certain something was out there. Biding its time. And the two of them shared a great bond now, something they'd never spoken of. Something, even now, he didn't want to face with her.

167

To her credit, she didn't raise the issue of Cross at first. Instead, she listened to the sounds of the night.

"Wolves?" Yasmine asked after he whispered his fears.

"Too quiet. Whatever it is, this is far more careful. And meticulous."

Yasmine crouched. "And the light you mentioned?"

"Never saw it again, but it must be Gurka's men, right? Who else would be dumb enough to be out here?"

"I'm sorry," Yasmine whispered then.

Bodie's forehead creased. "What?"

"I know, in part, you blame me for Eli's death. I know he was your best friend. And I thank you for letting me work with you. I'm trying to find my place here. And . . ." She sighed. "I'm sorry."

Bodie was grateful for the sentiment, but now wasn't the time. "Cross was my greatest friend. But you're good, and you fit in well. Just keep doing what you're doing. I hope you stay with us until we find Lucien," he said. "After that, we'll see."

"I loved Cross, you know. Since I was eighteen. Interpol broke us apart back then; the job broke us apart. I loved him. I have been hollow since he died."

"I know." Bodie was becoming distracted by her. "So have I. They say it gets better, but I'm not sure that I want it to."

"Will you replace him?"

Bodie stared at her. "Cross? It hadn't even entered my mind. Listen." He made a decision. "You work for Interpol, right?"

"Worked. I don't know my position now."

"You're aware of our real issue? Compelled to help the CIA under threat of charges and imprisonment, with no clear exit date ever offered. What would Interpol do?"

Yasmine didn't answer straight away. Bodie thought she might be choosing her words carefully.

"They'll never let you leave," she said finally. "You keep performing like you have been, you keep showing success, and they'll never let you leave."

"You're saying we should run?"

"Where can you run to that the CIA wouldn't track you down?"

It was a good argument. One Bodie had been struggling with for months. There was no point showing their hand until they had something watertight in place. A solid, foolproof plan.

"When we get time," Bodie said with a hint of irony, "we're gonna start working on that question."

"I really hope you find an answer."

"We will."

He stayed alongside her for the rest of the night and, when the first signs of dawn showed, followed her back to camp. They roused the others, though nobody was truly asleep. Everyone stretched, groaning in low voices, watching the last vestiges of utter darkness fade away.

"Which way, Gunn?"

The young man led the way out of the narrow chasm, and they padded along a pass for the best part of twenty minutes. The day grew brighter and noticeably warmer. Every time a mini rockfall occurred around them, Bodie and the others stopped and aimed weapons. Those who had stood watch last night exchanged knowing looks.

Humans are not the only things tracking us out here.

But it was humans who first announced their presence. As Gunn and Jemma, leading the group along the only path, topped a rise, Bodie heard the sound of a gunshot as a bullet glanced off a nearby rock. He leapt on top of the leaders, bearing them to the ground. Cassidy ducked behind a rock and peered out.

"Up there," she said. "Not far as the crow flies but about an hour behind."

Bodie peered through clusters of small peaks. Standing atop a cliff were at least nine men, and Nina too, all staring their way, soundlessly, weapons raised. More shots rang out but glanced harmlessly away.

"Save your bullets," he told Heidi without thinking. "We'll need them."

She gave him an irritated look and then said, "More than that. We should move. All they need is a good vantage point to pin us down from while the rest of their crew sneak in closer."

A good point. Bodie watched as his group slipped away. Their pursuers didn't shoot again. The early dawn began to catch fire, sunlight rising and peering through the ragged rock faces. A narrow, rocky valley passed by a blue mountain lake, where they stopped and replenished the water from their packs. Bodie splashed the cold liquid onto his face, feeling new vitality enter his body. Caruso looked like he was preparing to remove several layers of clothing and jump in before Cassidy dragged him back, reminding him of their need to continue.

"I remember this," Caruso said with a hint of glee. "I remember this lake. I spent a day relaxing here. It was . . . a peaceful time."

Cassidy leaned in toward him. Bodie heard her whisper, "Last time you were here, did the wolves hunt you?"

"I don't know. I'm not good with bad memories."

Cassidy sighed. "I'm with you there, dude."

Bodie couldn't help but feel sorry for Caruso. To know your mind and memory weren't right. To know your family couldn't completely rely on you due to a medical condition. It had to be a heavy cross to bear.

Without wasting more time, they moved on, skirting the lake and following the map. Finally, Gunn stopped and pointed ahead.

"Nica is just through here," he said. "A small depression among the mountains with a path down to the hills and the lowlands."

Bodie stared ahead at the two fifty-foot-high peaks, their sides worn smooth by scouring winds, their peaks jagged and pointed toward each other, as if forming a natural gate.

What dreams or nightmares lay beyond?

"First things first," he said. "We take a look at the area and work out escape routes. R24 can't be more than an hour behind. It's imperative we find and hide that clue first."

CHAPTER TWENTY-FIVE

Nica nestled among small peaks that formed a natural fortress between the higher mountains beyond. It was a rudimentary cluster of small houses spreading from the rocks to the grassy plains, where, thirty feet to the east, it broadened into a rough circle. Bodie saw a church and pointed it out. Just like Dydiowa, the place was overgrown. Several roofs hung in disarray, and some walls had collapsed.

Unnerving, though, was the way the half-open doors shifted as he watched, the way old, tattered curtains twitched, the way a rusted, half-collapsed swing set creaked on ancient hinges, still moving as if propelled by ghosts long dead.

A breeze blustered through the place, moving a piece of wood here, a chunk of rock there, giving life to old relics. Bodie ignored it, preferring to focus on what he could see and what he feared physically rather than allow his imagination free rein.

"Church," Pantera said, "usually means graveyard. Move it."

"I'll stay with Yasmine," Cassidy said. "We can go to higher ground and watch for uninvited guests. Hand over the guns."

Bodie nodded and then started moving fast, picking his way down the rocky path and then among piles of earth and overgrown tangles of vegetation. Empty windows yawned as he passed the abandoned homes. Would there be possessions inside? Bones, perhaps? What had happened here in 1945?

The church was as sorry looking as the rest of Nica. The spire had crumpled at some point and now lay in ruins, just outside the front door. A fence ran, warped and bowed, around the rear. Bodie noticed all of the stained glass windows were still intact—seemingly more enduring than bricks and mortar. Back when he'd been a thief and a relic hunter, on the other side of the law, there'd been a thriving market in stained glass, the older the better. The fact that he noticed it now proved he hadn't changed all that much.

Pantera and Heidi moved steadily around the back of the building, surveying the small graveyard before shouting for the others. Bodie saw about forty gravestones, almost half of which were either leaning or fallen over. Pantera moved to the first and started scraping decades' worth of debris away.

"Not Klaus Meyer," he said and moved on to the next.

Bodie helped, starting on the second row. It was an odd atmosphere they worked in. The mountains to their right, their deep, majestic silence an almost overbearing presence; the knowledge that killers were coming; the terrifying certainty that something else was tracking them; the fear for Caruso's family; the uncertainty around the Amber Room. Bodie found it easier to dilute every sense and every emotion.

Together, he and Jemma moved on to the third row.

"Out of my depth here," she told him as they scraped at the grave markers.

"Hey, you wanted back in the field," he said with heavy irony.

"As a cat burglar," she said. "And only to refresh my skills. Years of sitting on your ass before and during missions don't keep you sharp. I'm finesse, Guy, not a blunt instrument."

"It'll end soon," he said, "if we find this clue first. The CIA are coming. R24 will get what they deserve."

"Assuming we survive that long, or if they don't capture us again."

"Hey." Bodie stopped for a moment. "Look at me, Jem. I'll keep you safe. We've been a team for five years. We look after each other. We fight for each other. Nothing will change."

"But everything has changed," Jemma said. "Since Heidi came into our lives. Since Eli died."

Bodie felt the weight of leadership weighing heavy. "Yeah, but mostly since Pantera got me thrown into that prison. But we'll find a way to break free. We always do."

Jemma's words made the protective side of him rear up and sent him back to the time he'd defended little Darcey from the bullies. So far, he'd done a shaky job of protecting Lucie and Caruso and the others. He'd been an integral part of the Forever Gang back then, a defender and a leader, which had possibly laid the groundwork for the man he would become. Bodie would never stop defending those around him.

It was Caruso and Heidi who found the gravestone they were searching for. After the shout went up, Bodie strode over and knelt on the soft grass. The half-century-old concrete was rough, showing signs that the elements hadn't been kind to it, but bore the name Klaus Meyer near the top. The plot it marked was weed strewed and covered with years of growth and rubble.

"Crap," Bodie said. "Anyone got a shovel?"

"Not in our packs," Heidi said. "The mercs had them."

"No." Caruso crouched close to the concrete marker. "This is the clue. It is as good a permanent marker as any stained glass window. Who would remove a headstone?"

Bodie studied it carefully. The concrete was thick, making it heavy. Meyer's name was deeply etched along the top lip. More writing filled the middle part—*In memory of our brother*—written in German that Pantera translated. Bodie wondered if the Nazis had buried more than one of their number here, men who had died during the train journey. Klaus Meyer could simply be a name on a gravestone, picked at random, entered into a journal.

"There's more writing across the bottom." Caruso pointed.

"It's sunk below the debris." Bodie struggled to twist the marker so they could see. Pantera bent with his eyes close to the ground.

"In English it says: 'At the peak of Draci, where the last standing stone awaits.'"

Bodie heaved the stone some more. "Is that it?"

"Yeah, pal, that's everything."

Cautiously, Bodie let go. He didn't want the marker to fall, despite the nature of the man it represented. Toppling it felt like desecration. Taking care, he stood back. "Anybody have a clue what that means?"

"Nope," Gunn said. "But give me the map, and I'll soon find out."

"You do that," Heidi said. "I'll switch the phone on briefly, but we're down to two bars."

Being able to switch the phone on occasionally would help mark their position for the incoming CIA.

Bodie handed Gunn the laminated map, then looked over to where Cassidy and Yasmine guarded their perimeter, but he saw nothing. The contrast between what he felt inside—the chaos, the anxiety—and their utterly silent surroundings was unnerving.

Then Jemma pointed. Cassidy came into sight, head down. A shot rang out. Yasmine, following her, fell to the floor, but it was an evasive dive. She rolled and came back up again, firing two shots in return.

Bodie saw the mercenaries now. They came over a peak that overlooked Nica, flanking the town at the same time as gaining a height advantage. Bodie jumped behind Meyer's gravestone as bullets began to pepper the ground all around. His team took cover behind other markers. Cassidy and Yasmine sheltered behind the crumbling walls of the old church.

Bodie knew their supply of bullets was low, not enough to allow a standoff here. R24 had enough men and ammo to outflank them. Ideally, they should escape as soon as possible.

But we can't take the bloody clue with us! They'll see it too.

Destroy it, then? That was still desecration, and besides, how could they destroy it with the meager tools at their disposal? Shoot it?

"Smash the stone," Pantera said, as if reading Bodie's mind. "So they can't follow."

Bodie frowned, hesitating a few moments more. That made him angry, since he was normally decisive, but his head was spinning with emotions. Cassidy and Yasmine returned fire at the mercs, warding them off. More bullets came slamming back down, spraying the side of the church and the paths of the graveyard.

Cassidy looked over. "Down to five bullets."

Yasmine looked grim. "Four. We can't sit here forever."

Bodie reached for a stone large enough to smash the marker. A bullet, by chance, slammed into the earth close to his hand, making him pull back and think again. The mercs were ranged along the peak now, just eight of them, along with three members of R24. Dudyk and Gurka were somewhere else.

Cassidy caught his attention and signaled a retreat. They had to leave quickly. There was no telling where their other enemies were. For safety's sake, an orderly withdrawal was better. Bodie gave her the signal to cover their backs and turned to the others.

"Move out," he said. "Stay low. We don't have time to smash the marker. We'll have to take our chances."

"Where to?" Gunn sounded a little panicked.

"There." Bodie pointed at the misshapen fence that bordered the rear of the property. "Over the fence and back into the peaks. Do you have a bead on Draci yet?"

"The mountain's that way." Gunn indicated a westerly direction. "Back into dangerous territory."

"Of course it is." Bodie threaded his way with the rest of them, from concrete stone to concrete stone, finally leaping over a decrepit fence and entering a rocky pass beyond. The pass led back up into the mountains.

Bodie saw a flash of clothing appear to the right of Cassidy and Yasmine, which was their blind side.

"Down!"

Thankfully, everyone heeded his shout, dropping to the floor. Just seconds later shots shredded the air they'd occupied. Bodie was in the best position and beckoned for a gun. Cassidy threw hers. Bodie watched it arc through the air, caught it, and fired once. The new mercs took cover, which gave Cassidy and Yasmine a few seconds to reach the pass.

"Run," Bodie yelled at their backs. "Just go!"

CHAPTER TWENTY-SIX

They hiked quickly up the pass and then the mountain, knowing that killers were at their backs. The mountain trek presented a new quandary. It wasn't a matter of allowing someone to fall back and cover their escape; it was the chance that that person—no matter how skilled—could get lost or fall prey to mountain terrors more easily if they were alone. It was a hundred other risks and missteps.

Up here, there would be no second chances.

Gunn led the way, following his map, closely supported by Cassidy and Pantera, who looked out for hazards. Jemma and Lucie walked together, trailed by the others, with Bodie at the back. He stopped regularly to listen, lingering until his companions almost disappeared from sight, but heard no signs of pursuit.

Bad news.

Unfortunately, R24 was being sensible about the chase. If it sent mercenaries out now, into the mountains, they might become lost and also wouldn't know Bodie's destination. Plus, they didn't have enough men to waste. Communications couldn't be completely relied upon. Nothing could. Better to wait and plan. Lose some time now to make it up later. But still, they wouldn't be far behind.

The entire morning passed, and the sun ducked behind a bank of thick black clouds. The cold mountain air began to bite. Bodie felt the cold in his bones as he continued to climb the steadily ascending path. They lost twenty minutes when the pass dead-ended and they had to climb across a rocky outcropping to access another. Once, Gunn stopped only three feet before a black hole in the ground, a cave that ran vertically downward. With utmost caution the group skirted it, but the dire warning of its existence served only to increase their concerns.

Up they went. It was midafternoon before Gunn announced they were climbing the slopes of Draci, with the peak towering above.

Shrubbery and patches of grass lined their way. A dip in the terrain led to a narrow lake, but they didn't venture down. They stopped to eat and drink, redistributing their weapons. Now, Bodie at the back and Cassidy at the front had control of the handguns.

"Why standing stones?" Jemma asked as they restarted their trek. "And why up there?" She stared at the peaks. "How did a train get so high?"

"It didn't," Lucie answered as if she'd been waiting for the question, which, Bodie guessed, she probably had. "At least, not from this direction. The ground on the other side of Draci is a long, gentle slope. The easiest and most cost-effective way to have laid the tracks would have been around the range back there"—she gestured back the way they had come—"and then around Draci itself, gradually descending to the flat plains on the other side. And that's no matter *who* laid them."

"You think the stones are a natural marker? Nothing significant?" Jemma asked.

"Standing stones, like grave markers and stained glass windows, are normally considered permanent markers," Lucie said. "Through history they have rarely been desecrated."

"Except in times of war," Gunn said.

"But they thought the war was practically over," Lucie said. "Whoever left these clues . . . they knew their history, they knew its patterns, and they knew their relics. I guess it goes without saying that the Amber Room has been considered a wonder since it was first unveiled. As for the standing stones . . ." She came around to Jemma's question. "They're worldwide and constructed for countless reasons. Outside Europe, some examples date back to 6300 BCE. I think they're such a recognizable part of our landscape that unless they're huge and famous like Stonehenge, nobody really notices the small ones anymore."

Bodie studied the way ahead. "Get a move on, guys. I'd like to reach the top of this bastard by nightfall."

The words muted them all. Nobody had forgotten the wolves or the predators that followed with guns. And nobody had forgotten the unknown nightmares that had plagued them the previous night.

They sped up as best they could. Two more cave entrances appeared along their route, running into the mountainside, black and deep and bristling with mystery. Too many pitfalls to count blotted their path and lay to either side. Despite their urgency, they had to take care. The sun had passed its zenith long ago and now marked midafternoon, waning toward the evening. A not-so-warm day started to grow really cold. Bodie joined the others as they stopped and buttoned every button, wrapping clothes as tightly around themselves as they could and fixing facial scarves. The rest of the journey passed in silence or angry grunts—the regular reaction of somebody slipping or knocking arms or legs against a projecting boulder.

Shadows stole among the rocks. Bodie had come to dread the dark among these peaks. Even now, it brought an unknown pattering among the heights above, the sudden shower of gravel, the sneaking of a shape that didn't quite fit.

All imagination.

But as they came over the crest of their final ascent, reaching the peak of Mount Draci, he realized that it really wasn't. In fact, imagination couldn't even come close to preparing him for the horror that waited.

CHAPTER TWENTY-SEVEN

Bodie froze as a blast of fear shot from his stomach to his brain. Judging from the body language of everyone around him, they all had experienced the same burst of fright.

Slinking before them, weaving among each other and around the middle of the bowl at the top of Mount Draci, were six pure black panthers, fully grown. Despite their pacing, their eyes never left their prey. The growls low in their throats conveyed terrible intent.

This was what had been tracking them? Bodie shuddered.

Nobody moved. Luckily, Cassidy was at the head of the group, holding her gun. Bodie had a line of sight to the left. But two guns with eight bullets between them weren't going to save them all.

"If they come," he whispered, "just scatter. Run. Split them up. Cass and I will do the rest."

He wished he felt as confident as he sounded. Minutes passed. The growls grew in intensity. The panthers crept closer. Gunn stepped unconsciously behind Cassidy as Lucie did the same behind Pantera. The entire group condensed, which was exactly what the panthers wanted.

"Remember," Bodie said, "there are flares and matches in your pack. You might need them."

Gunn turned a wild gaze toward him, but then the panthers attacked. Sprays of shale flew from underneath their paws. Snarls erupted from their throats. Cassidy knelt and lined them up in her sights. Pantera and Yasmine broke instantly from the pack, running left and right. Bodie adopted a wide-legged stance and aimed. Heidi sprinted after Pantera.

It was Jemma, Gunn, and Caruso who stood unmoving.

Lucie backed away slowly, heading for Bodie, interfering with his aim.

The seconds passed in a blur. Cassidy opened fire with the panthers less than eight feet away. Her first bullet took down the fastest of the six; her second entered the shoulder of the one to its right, sending it tumbling and bringing down two of its brethren. Bodie concentrated on the two to the left. His first bullet blew a head apart; his second winged an animal. His third shot almost killed Lucie as she stumbled into his sights, scared out of her wits by the attacking animals.

"Shit, move! I only have one bullet left!"

He rolled around Lucie, but then Gunn and Jemma were in his way. Caruso hit the floor. Cassidy was sidestepping. The panthers were incredibly fast, even the wounded ones. The two who'd tumbled quickly sorted their legs out. One fixed its sights on Heidi, the other on Pantera.

Cassidy fired again, putting her bullet count down to one and hitting Heidi's pursuer in the flank, bringing it down for good. That left three wounded panthers to deal with. But now those animals were almost on top of their prey, making it impossible for Cassidy or Bodie to risk shooting. Pantera fell as a powerful body slammed against his ribs, ripping his pack off and sending it crashing to the ground. Pantera stumbled and twisted, going down to one knee.

He came around with a wild swing but completely missed the panther. It crouched and then sprang at his throat. Pantera flung his body away to avoid it but ended up on his back, the beast poised above.

It panted heavily. It leaked blood. Its fangs glistened. It snapped down at his face. Pantera swung an arm up. Bodie heard his scream as fangs ripped at the material covering the man's arm. The jacket was thick, but it would only protect him for a second.

As Bodie ran, he saw Yasmine jump bravely onto the panther that was threatening Gunn and Jemma. He saw her punch it repeatedly where the bullet had entered. The animal screeched and squirmed.

Cassidy ran for the last wounded attacker as it leapt at Lucie and the prone Caruso.

Bodie saw Pantera wriggle out from under the panther and throw himself at the side of the mountain. The bowl they fought in was bordered by a low wall, a natural rock backdrop. When the wounded beast rose and leapt, Pantera threw himself around the wall, evading the attack. The animal hit the rock hard, bounced off, and then crouched, head close to the floor. Despite its labored breathing, it prepared to leap again.

Then Heidi came at it from the blind side. She had a flare—taken from Pantera's abandoned pack—in her hand and aimed it at the animal. She fired it immediately, giving the panther no chance. The flare smashed against the side of its body and sent it tumbling against the rock wall, now barely alive. Pantera staggered to his knees, and Heidi crawled to his side.

Bodie whirled. Lucie had fallen under a panther's attack. Even now it dipped its teeth toward her throat. Bodie saw blood spray high into the air. He heard Lucie scream. Her body writhed, flinging blood in all directions. The panther pulled away, went in again, jaws gnashing.

Cassidy reached it a moment later, pushed her gun close to its head, and pulled the trigger. It fell away in a cloud of blood and bone. Cassidy dropped her gun and reached down for Lucie. "No!"

Bodie had to concentrate on Yasmine. Though she had fallen atop her animal and punched it repeatedly, it had still gotten the better of her. Gunn and Jemma crouched nearby, both throwing rocks at the beast as it prepared to rip Yasmine's throat out.

The rocks hit, gifting Bodie a precious few moments. He breathed deeply, steadied his hands, and fired his last bullet—a shot that went through the animal's neck. It collapsed in a heap.

He turned to Cassidy and Lucie. "Cass?"

Lucie battered the redhead's attentions away, crying out in pain at the same time.

"It's her right arm that's wounded," Cassidy said with relief. "She got it across her throat just in time."

Bodie felt intense relief. Quickly, he checked on the others and then went over to Lucie. "Good job," he said. "How bad is it?"

Lucie showed him the wound. Where her jacket was torn, three deep slashes had punctured her skin. The blood flowed freely. Cassidy wasted no time cutting some material away and then washing the wounds with lake water.

"We have a first aid kit in our packs," she said. "Pass me the antiseptic and bandages."

"I'm amazed it didn't go for the sweater," Bodie commented, just able to see some black woolly material above her collar.

"Yeah." Cassidy smiled. "Let it see the sheep on the front next time."

"Just do it," Lucie said matter-of-factly. "I know you're trying to distract me."

As Cassidy worked, Bodie scanned the area for the first time. He saw standing stones, six of them in a row, running down the dead center of the bowl at the top of the mountain. He saw every member of his team dead tired, some with wounds, some bleeding, all sitting down except for Caruso, who still lay on his stomach.

And then he saw R24 creeping around the summit's perimeter. Thirteen mercenaries and five smugglers. All with guns trained on them.

"Fuck me," he said. "Can't we catch a bloody break."

CHAPTER
TWENTY-EIGHT

Gurka strode toward them with a livid expression.

"I should kill you," he shouted. "Or at least one of you. No, I should kill you all!"

Nina was a step behind. "Now you will learn the hard way who is in charge."

She came right up to Yasmine, unlucky enough to be her closest target, and punched her in the nose. Yasmine staggered and flung her hands up. Nina punched her in the gut. Yasmine twisted away and then came back with a side kick, quickly followed by a jab. Nina stepped back.

Two mercenaries fired just a few feet over Yasmine's head.

"You will not retaliate," Nina hissed. "What you will do is comply. *That* is what you will do."

This time she elbowed Yasmine in the face, drawing blood. When the Interpol agent didn't react, she moved on to Gunn, pushing him back hard so that he tripped and fell. Gurka smashed the barrel of his rifle across Bodie's temple, sending him to his knees. Vash joined them, and then Belenko, dealing out punishment to the relic hunters. Only Caruso and Lucie were spared.

But as Bodie stared up through a haze of pain, he saw Dudyk move in and drag the blonde away. He pulled her to the edge of the mountain to confront her.

Gurka stepped in the way. "You try that again. *Anything*. And I will personally end half of you. I will make the others watch. You think you can escape? You can't. Now, give me back the weapons you stole."

Three mercs had their weapons trained at Bodie's head. He offered up the empty handgun. Cassidy resisted until Nina had practically shoved a barrel in her mouth. Still, despite three hard punches, the redhead continued to give Nina a death glare.

Someone picked Caruso up and brought him before Gurka. The Italian looked shell shocked.

"You walked away from us," Gurka said slowly. "You *walked away*. For now, I must assume—because you know we can hurt your woman and child like we hurt your mother-in-law—that the fault lies with your addled mind. If I find out differently . . ."

He drew out his long military blade. "I will tell my men to slice their throats like this." Moving fast, he grabbed Caruso, spun him, and pressed the sharp blade to his jugular. Bodie saw a thin line of blood well up.

"Do you hear me, old man?" Gurka hissed.

"Yes, yes." Caruso had tears in his eyes. "I do. Please don't hurt them. Please."

Bodie had had enough of all the intimidation. His team was pretty well banged up as it was. "Hey, you've got us now. What are you gonna do?"

"Whatever we please," Gurka shot back. "Now, get out of my way."

Lucie was struggling with an endless succession of fears. First the mountains and the wolves, then the panthers and R24. The constant pressure of being hunted. She forced it all aside and returned Dudyk's stare.

His eyes were gray flint. "I've been told to hurt you. To teach you the wrong of what you did."

Lucie fought down excuses and entreaties, staying strong in the face of the monster. Dudyk snarled at her.

"You embarrassed me. Shamed me with your escape. I should have shot you. They think I am not their equal anymore."

Lucie backed away a step. Dudyk's eyes were as mean as his body language. But she'd seen it before, in her uncle Jamie. She was able to betray no signs of outward fear. He glared for another few seconds before stepping in, fists bunched.

"Pretend I hit you," he whispered. "For them."

He swung quickly. Lucie twisted to the side, crying out a little, then brought a hand up to her face. When she glanced over to the main group, both Gurka and Nina looked over with satisfaction. Dudyk grabbed her good arm and pulled her farther away.

As they walked, he said, "Do not think this makes me weak. I will still hurt you if I have to. Do not think to take any advantage."

But Lucie was wondering what the hell had just happened.

CHAPTER
TWENTY-NINE

Even as blackness threatened to steal the scene from their eyes, Gurka and Nina ordered everyone to spread out and start searching among the stones.

At the peak of Draci, where the last standing stone awaits.

Bodie recalled the wording they'd found on the gravestone. It pointed him to one of two stones. To look at, they were unremarkable in the world of monuments. Slabs of concrete about three feet high uplifted in the earth, marking a dead-straight line. To what purpose, Bodie didn't know, but it could have been many, from date lines to burial indicators. The stones themselves were plain, unadorned by any form of writing. He checked the earth around them first but found it hard packed and wondered if he'd be allowed a shovel.

Caruso's voice stopped him. "It is this one."

The Italian stood at the end of the line, looking down at the earth with fresh excitement. He turned an appealing face upon Gurka. "It is this stone," he repeated. "I remember now that I am here. Please don't hurt my family."

"Dig it up, old man."

The group drifted closer to Caruso as he fell to his knees and began scrabbling around in the earth. One of the mercs, to his credit, handed him a shovel. Soon, a mound of dirt had built up beside him. It grew so dark the mercs took flashlights from their packs to shine down the hole. Others built fires around and at the center of their camp. A good deal of illumination marked their position.

Good, Bodie thought. *Assuming someone trustworthy got Heidi's message, it will help the CIA to find us.*

Twenty-four hours had passed since the call. But now they'd lost the phone. When Gurka had taken the cell back and checked it for usage, Bodie had been relieved to hear there was no call history on the device: Heidi had remembered to get rid of everything. He'd stopped himself from offering her a relieved look, knowing she wouldn't appreciate it. But Gurka took few chances, and this was not one of them. He'd destroyed the phone immediately, leaving it buried in the earth.

Now, Caruso lifted a white cloth bag from the earth near the stone. It bulged at the bottom as though it was heavy. Setting it on the ground, he looked up at Gurka.

"Open it."

Caruso untied thick twine from the neck of the bag before reaching in and pulling out an object. It was a moment before Bodie understood the full import of what he was looking at, but Gurka saw it immediately.

"Oh, you beautiful, mad Italian bastard. That's the most stunning thing I've ever seen."

Nina cooed softly, the most natural human reaction Bodie had ever seen in her. It was now that he got a good look at the object in Caruso's hand. Under the artificial glow of the flashlights, it shone a particular color.

Amber.

Did Caruso bury a small piece of the Amber Room on his way home? Did he take a sample and decide to leave it as a marker? Bodie didn't want to think that the Italian had lost his marbles, but this act went some way toward confirming it. Wrapped around the piece was a note, which Caruso untied and read out:

"The monument at the Polish Black Pond," he said. "That's all."

Gurka almost leapt forward to take the piece of the Amber Room from Caruso's hand. It was a rectangular chunk, maybe eight inches by three, and it burned richly in the stark light. Its edges threw off beams of light that speared through the air and into the ground. Its surface depicted part of the wing of an angel.

"You didn't break this off?" Gurka asked.

"I wouldn't do that."

"But do you remember?"

Caruso looked adamant for the first time Bodie could remember. "I would never do that to a relic. Any relic. I don't recall burying it."

"All right." Gurka took the piece and the note and retreated to one of the campfires. Then he called Lucie over and asked her about the Polish Black Pond. The heat seemed to have gone out of their situation for now—even the mercs looked relaxed—so Bodie motioned his group to sit beside one of the slow-burning campfires near the center of the bowl. If they didn't look threatening, maybe they could get some rest tonight.

It would refresh them for tomorrow, when a new raft of opportunities would open up.

He nursed his hand wound, and the others tended whatever cuts, bumps, and scrapes they had. Lucie didn't appear to be struggling with her arm injury. Bodie listened as she described a well-known body of water on a nearby peak, just a lake like all the others around here.

Except this one was filled with black water.

Obviously, Bodie thought. As eerie as everything else that surrounded this op.

Nina came over to sit with them, saying nothing but shelving any plans they might have of discussing an exit strategy. Six of the thirteen remaining mercenaries took watch, disappearing into the dark. Bodie took note of how most of them limped or carried minor wounds. It was good for his team.

"Anyone know anything about this Black Pond?" Cassidy asked, mostly just to start a conversation.

"I know that it sounds bad," Nina answered her, which surprised Bodie. He'd been expecting a disinterested silence from the woman.

"How many more clues to go, mate?" he asked Caruso.

Predictably, the Italian frowned. "It is a haze now. Perhaps when I see the next relic—"

"Yeah, yeah," Cassidy interrupted. "When we get there."

"Why do you think the person who laid this trail chose a piece of the Amber Room this time?" Nina asked. "Assuming it wasn't the idiot Caruso."

Bodie blinked, unable to associate her with the woman he generally regarded as a murderous sociopath. "Maybe it was all they had left at this point," he said. "To be fair, it could have been buried on the way to its final resting place, or after somebody found it."

"Or it's a trophy," Jemma said. "Something they could come back to."

"My family," Caruso said, leaning forward, his face painted a lurid orange by the campfire flames. "Might I speak to them?"

Nina hesitated, which Bodie saw as a good sign. They had been on this trek for days now, and Caruso's family had been taken some time before that. It had been a while since he'd had contact with them.

Bodie opened his mouth, preparing to argue all this with Nina.

"Yes," she said, taking out her phone. She inputted a number, spoke softly to someone on the other end, and then looked at Caruso. "No more than a minute, and no details," she warned.

Bodie made a face at the others. Pantera spoke up. "Any chance I can call *my* wife?" he said with a smile, suggesting that he was joking. Heidi was quick to add, "I have a daughter," but her face was gravely serious.

Nina shrugged. "No more calls. We need his cooperation until the end. Not yours."

"Then tell me again—why the hell are we here?" Bodie asked.

"Do you not listen?" Nina counted the points off on her fingers. "One: due to your circumstances, we could acquire you quite easily. Two: you are the best at this, and if even once you prove useful, then we profit. Three: This is the Amber Room. Of course we need the best. Four: I like complete skill sets. Five: our motto has always been *Why the hell not?* And six: R24 thrives because it uses others. It always has and always will. The further removed we are from view, the better for us."

Bodie stared at the campfire as Caruso said a few words to his wife and daughter. The man's blue eyes shone with tears in the flickering light, but Bodie saw a smile and was happy for him.

At least for now.

Tomorrow, they could all be dead.

CHAPTER THIRTY

Lucie watched the others from her lonely place at the far side of the camp. Dudyk had built a small fire, but it didn't help her feel safe for a number of reasons. Firstly, they were situated close to a rocky ledge that was accessible from both above and below their position. Secondly, the flames didn't cast much of a glow.

And then there was Dudyk.

He watched her. He gazed as if studying something he might like to dissect. What was wrong with him?

He scratched at the scrub of bristle that passed as hair before throwing more wood on the fire.

"Why did you help me?" she asked in a small voice.

Dudyk glared. "I don't do everything they tell me. I am not the monster they think I am."

Again, he reminded her of Uncle Jamie. She hoped that the similarities were not too close, however. She didn't like where Jamie's demons had eventually taken him. She had realized early on that Jamie was suffering. Someone who'd terrorized him at school had gone on to the same college. It was personal, and it was wicked psychological intimidation. Jamie had presented all his pent-up emotions through anger to the outside world. The bully had eventually been caught and charged through evidence on social media.

But it hadn't stopped Uncle Jamie from being so overwhelmed by hateful emotion that he'd walked distractedly in front of a speeding bus.

Lucie gathered her errant emotions, concentrating on the man in front of her. "You spared me just to spite them?"

"Maybe." Dudyk stirred the flames with a long stick. "I don't know."

"What other reason could there be?"

"You should stop talking now."

"Dudyk." Lucie gathered her courage, ignoring the darkness that nestled around and the indeterminate noises coming from the mountains. "I am a simple girl from a simple background. A historian. I don't make conversation. You noticed my sweater before we put on all these coats?"

Dudyk grunted in a noncommittal manner.

"Woolly and usually embroidered with an animal. That's my talking point. That's how I get people to chat. I think that's sad. Don't you?"

Dudyk poked the fire strenuously, still saying nothing.

"Look, I'm a screwup. I don't show it, but I'm one big fucking catastrophe. My entire family died from natural causes. All of them. Now, I suffer every day—no, every *hour*—from intense paranoia that something similar will happen to me."

Dudyk had stopped poking the fire halfway through her revelation and now stared. "Through all this, you think you will die naturally? That is—"

"Insane? Yes. Welcome to the world of Lucie Boom."

"How will you die?" Dudyk suddenly grinned. "Eating a can of beans?"

Lucie was shocked to see his reaction but chose to go with it. "Your rations are pretty bad."

"If a rock fell and struck you, would that count?"

Lucie now saw he was mocking her. "I don't think my fears are funny." She spoke in her old clipped tone, happy to find it was still there.

"Oh, I am not meaning to insult," Dudyk said seriously. "I was trying to ease your fear."

"You were? Well, thanks."

It was an odd discussion, Lucie thought, and made stranger by the way they smiled at each other right at the end. The moment was broken when a branch snapped inside the fire, sounding like gunfire. Lucie jumped and wrapped her arms around her body.

"God, I hate this," she whispered.

Bodie kept an eye out for everyone. He saw Lucie's exchange with Dudyk. Nina staring from Gurka to Pantera and then to Yasmine and the others, evaluating them. He saw figures slipping by in the dark—mercenaries on guard. He heard the mountain noises, both the natural and unnatural ones. He assessed the members of his team, concluding that, apart from weariness, they were all in comparatively good shape. Of course, there were aches and pains, bruises inflicted by R24. There were fears running deep. But there was hope too.

Since Nina had proved to be genial tonight, Bodie moved close to Heidi.

"You okay?"

"Yeah, I guess." She held a thick stick in the flames, watching the end catch fire, before shaking it out and starting again.

"Can they track us?" he asked, meaning the CIA. To avoid anyone overhearing, he kept his voice as low as possible.

"Nope." Heidi threw a surreptitious glance at Nina. The woman was gazing in the other direction. "But they have a general

197

area. I also mentioned the train tracks. I hope the tech passed it through to the main office pretty quickly."

"When?" Bodie kept it short so that Nina wouldn't get suspicious, but the black-haired woman didn't seem interested.

"Another day?" Heidi guessed. "Maybe longer."

"Crap. We'll be at the Black Pond in the morning by all accounts."

"We survive," Heidi said. "Another minute. Another hour. Another day."

"They're bullies," Bodie said flatly. "I've dealt with bullies before. I've defended my friends against bullies. Believe me, we won't die here."

Heidi smiled fondly at him. "Well, that's really nice of you, Guy. I assume you have a plan?"

He shrugged. "Nah, but I get that you've been trained by people to whom plans are everything. I'll think of something. And when this is over—" Bodie began.

"Don't start."

"Uh, what?"

"I know what you were gonna say." She affected a deep voice. "'When this is over, we're leaving the CIA, dude.' Or something like that."

"I never say 'dude.'"

"What about the rest?"

"Yeah, something like that. You have to give us our lives back."

"Me? I'm not the Central Intelligence Agency, Bodie. I just work for them."

"You're saying your hands are tied? How can that be?"

"You wish. But I don't have the final say, which you know. If it were up to me . . . you'd have been cut free after the Zeus thing, let alone Atlantis."

Bodie wondered at the double entendre. Was there a way they could explore the unspoken lure that drew them? Should he mention it clearly, without ambiguity? Bodie couldn't see it going any further, but then he wondered if this was some kind of plan—a CIA trick, ensuring that they got close enough so he wouldn't try to escape her. He wouldn't put anything past the CIA.

"We ended the Bratva threat," he said. "With your help. With their help." He meant the CIA. "But we're free now."

"You think," Heidi said. "Don't forget R24 abducted us and attacked them at that final meet. They might blame you. We just don't know."

"My immediate thought," he said, "is what would Cross do?"

Heidi reached out. "He'd be happy that you think like that."

He stayed quiet, thinking that her point about the Bratva was a good one. Until they returned to reality, they just didn't know. The flames took his attention, and he stared into their burning heart, wondering if he could conjure up an old memory of the Forever Gang, a good one that could take him away, but all he could seem to think about was the time they'd saved Darcey from the bullies. If the Forever Gang reminded him of his relic hunter friends, then the members of R24 were the aggressors from that long-ago day. Thinking of them that way made his situation easier to deal with.

He settled down, deliberately wading through past memories to find better ones.

It took a while, but it was worth it. Those memories were the only stable reality of his life.

CHAPTER THIRTY-ONE

The morning trek was dismal, undertaken amid a cold mountain mist and full of treacherous pitfalls. The mist made the rocks slippery. They were forced to descend halfway down Mount Draci before they could start ascending its adjoining partner. While the heights weren't always dangerous in themselves—they were far lower than many other mountain ranges—threats still lurked at every turn.

Up here, Bodie could think of no way to escape. He considered his team at every step, every turn in the path, but found himself hoping that after the Polish Black Pond, they would start descending.

They moved steadily around the mountain, reaching its far side by midmorning. The mist still hung thick and low. Their vision was minimal. Mercenaries trudged alongside and in the middle of their group. There didn't seem to be any order among them. The members of R24 walked at the front and back. Bodie saw Lucie at Dudyk's side and wished for the thousandth time that he could help her.

They came around a jagged outcropping, ducking their heads to avoid a particularly sharp edge, and were forced to lean out over a two-hundred-foot precipice. After that they angled downward for a while, skirting a black hole in the ground. Another ten minutes of hiking, and then an enormous overhanging boulder had to be negotiated. Even as they crept under it, the granite mass shifted, as if the slightest sound might set it loose. Bodie held his breath all the way under and then again as each member of his team risked a nasty fate. When they were past, even Gurka gave a loud sigh of relief.

"Almost there," he said.

He sent the mercs ranging ahead. Bodie came around a gentle curve in the pass, emerging into a wide bowl with rock walls to two sides. The third side fell away into a steep canyon, while the fourth was open, a visible plateau leading down the mountain. Bodie assumed that was where the train tracks passed below.

At the center of the bowl was a deep lake, waves lapping over a smooth shore. Wreaths of mist swirled across its dark surface and sent gray tendrils questing, but even in the spooky half light, Bodie could see that the water was black.

"Why is that?" he wondered aloud.

"Something to do with the color of the volcanic stone that forms the lake bed," Lucie said from the back of the group.

"Either that or it's full of dead souls," Gunn said. "Evildoers trapped for eternity."

More than one merc and Dudyk gave him a hard look, but Gunn wasn't watching. He was staring at the lake.

"What the hell was that?"

Bodie stared hard at the rippling waters. "What?"

"Didn't you see? I thought I saw something break the surface. A curved spine or something."

Cassidy turned on him. "Fuck, man, are you fucking serious?"

Gunn shook it off. "Must be my imagination."

Despite this, the mercs arranged themselves warily, close to the water's edge, with guns ready.

Gurka spoke the last clue from memory: "The monument at the Polish Black Pond."

To their left stood a six-foot-tall slab of rock. It was light gray and shaped like an altar, with an apex on top. Light mists drifted around it, lending it indistinct form, but even from here Bodie could tell it stood right at the edge of the canyon.

"What are you all waiting for?" Gurka snapped. "Move."

Bodie acquiesced. He wanted down from these heights as much as R24 did. He, Yasmine, and Cassidy reached the monument first but deferred to Caruso.

"Any ideas?"

"It isn't easy. You should let them do it."

Bodie struggled to catch Caruso's answer. When he did, the clarity of it drove a splinter of suspicion into his brain. Was Caruso having a lucid moment? Was he warning them?

Or . . .

Probably the former. Bodie tried to hold the Italian's gaze, but the man turned away, head bobbing, now gawping at the undulating waters. When Gurka approached, Bodie turned to him.

"He doesn't know. I can't see anything."

"Look harder," Nina snapped, then turned to the three closest mercenaries. "Help them."

Bodie, Yasmine, and Cassidy moved to the safe side, leaving the perilous flank overhanging the canyon to the mercs. The drop at the verge of the monument was over eighty feet, but it was staggered. It would be a long, fast, slippery, unstoppable ride to the bottom.

Bodie pretended to scrutinize the slab of stone just below the apex.

"That Nina annoys me more than any of them," Cassidy whispered, "with her comments."

Yasmine bent down with them. "She reminds me of you."

"*What?*" Cassidy looked affronted, but Yasmine shook her head. "Not her actions. Her mannerisms. You know, if you guys had taken a different path, fallen in with someone other than Pantera and Cross, you might have become these people."

Cassidy didn't answer, and Bodie saw the truth of it. It didn't take much to follow the wrong turn on a path strewed with obstacles. "Hope you're not suggesting we feel sorry for them."

"Not after what they've done and what they're threatening to do. No."

"Losing Cross," Cassidy said softly, "made me see my own mortality. When you love your team, it's like loving your family. You never believe that sooner or later one of them is gonna die."

Yasmine touched her. "You have to believe that Cross loved you," she said, "just as you are. He wouldn't want you to change, the same as he wouldn't want me to change. That's why I still want Lucien. Why I'm following orders. I'm staying true to me."

Cassidy nodded at Yasmine gratefully. Before Bodie could say anything, something else took their attention.

One of the mercs had leaned out precariously while one of his colleagues held on to his waist. "It's clean," he reported now. "Nothing out here."

Bodie was wondering if Caruso had indeed confused this clue with another when the Italian, looking excited and engaged once more, said, "Can you see all of it out there?"

The merc stepped to safety. "No, the outer side of the apex is too high."

"Ahh," Caruso said.

"Check it," Nina barked. "Get on with it. What else are we paying you for?"

Bodie stood back and watched the unfortunate mercenary size up the slab. He asked for a boost from both colleagues and was

203

soon clinging to the apex with both arms spread, looking like he was giving the monument a hug.

Cautiously, he peered over the top of the weather-beaten peak. "I can see writing," he reported. "Looks quite fresh."

"I don't care how it looks," Gurka growled, shaking his head. "I want to know what it says."

"Give me a break, man. I'm reading it upside fucking down."

"Use your phone." Nina shook her head at his incompetence, then motioned two mercs to grab his legs and steady him. "Just take a photo and come down."

It took some dicey maneuvering, but the merc reached over with a hand to take several snaps of the writing that ran across the canyon side of the monument. Once done, he jumped down and handed over the phone. "You're welcome."

Gurka snatched it away, fingers flexing close to his gun. Bodie imagined if R24 hadn't needed all their mercs, one would be dying right now. The scarred man turned the screen upside down and shared it with Nina.

"Down into the Valley of Amber, beyond the great tributary, look for the tracks and the cave."

"It's quite legible," Nina commented suspiciously.

"It's on the leeward side," Lucie explained. "Away from the worst of the elements."

"Thoughts?" Gurka turned to Bodie.

Jemma answered quickly. "It's leading us back to the tracks and then a cave. 'Valley of Amber' has to be a metaphor."

"And I guess we follow a stream or a river," Yasmine added, but her last words were lost under an ominous noise from the direction of the lake. Everyone's head spun at the same time, examining the restless waters. At the center they were choppier than ever, waves undulating outward. Thick mists swung away from the area and reformed elsewhere. A large wave broke against the shore.

"Now *my* imagination's working overtime," Bodie said. "Shall we get the hell out of here?"

For once, R24 and the mercenaries were in unqualified agreement with him. The entire party moved as close to the sheer canyon as they dared and skirted the lake, keeping weapons trained on its black surface. Bodie knew their fears were impractical, but so far they'd come across wolves and panthers on this mission. Who knew what else might haunt the Tatras? And up here, rational thinking wasn't always advisable.

With his team around him and Lucie at the rear, he headed for what they now knew would be the final leg of their journey. The sloping plateau ahead led to the valley floor, where a cave was home to the Amber Room.

What happened when they got there, what decisions were made by every person present, would decide all their fates.

CHAPTER THIRTY-TWO

Their descent was quicker, but it was past midafternoon before they gained the valley floor. The plateau was steep, littered with rocks that they could rest against and gullies where they could ease the tension on their hamstrings. Bodie fell in next to Cassidy and Heidi.

"This is the end," he said. "You two ready?"

Cassidy adjusted her pack. "You know me, boss. Always ready. I've been saving myself for a final fight. And what Yasmine said earlier, about Cross, it makes sense."

Bodie nodded. "Yeah, it does. I'm starting to like her."

Heidi never stopped scanning the terrain. "There'll be no running this time," she said. "We have to finish it."

Bodie agreed. "When it happens, go for weapons first. I'll pass it along to Yasmine and Pantera."

A merc wandered close, momentarily ending the conversation. Bodie stopped to speak to everyone, preparing them for what was to come. As they descended, the mists receded, giving them the false impression that the day was just starting, brightening steadily. It was an odd sensation. Bodie watched the valley floor emerge through rolling hills.

It was a wide, oblong plain—a patchwork of random greens and browns, bordered by relatively low rock faces and dissected by a narrow, fast-flowing river. As far as Bodie could see, they were the only living souls for miles around, but he didn't take it for granted. On the plus side, it did become progressively warmer, easier on the feet, and far less dangerous.

They rested on level ground, which was in itself a relief. More than that—it was soft ground, a welcome change from recent days and nights. A decent meal and a full bottle of water, and forty minutes later they were headed across lush flatland toward the banks of the river. Gurka broke out a map.

"We're here," he said, pointing. "The largest tributary close by is there." He jabbed at the map.

"Spread out," Nina said. "Look for train tracks along the way. And look carefully, because they will be long overgrown."

It was unnecessary, and Bodie noticed lots of eye-rolling among the mercs, but R24 had been asserting its authority throughout the quest. He wasn't surprised.

They spread into a long line across the plain, several feet between each person. Walking forward, they started kicking at shrubbery and loose soil. Caruso professed to know nothing of their journey from here on out but did start talking about an old airplane, which just confused everyone. Dudyk and Lucie were on the far side, nearest the river. Several mercenaries walked between them and Bodie, thus continuing the historian's isolation. Gurka was not slackening his unyielding rule.

Bodie walked close to Heidi. "Did you get a look at the map? The tributary looked to be about six miles away. At this pace it'll be practically sundown when we reach it, never mind find the cave."

"Another night," Heidi said, "will give the CIA more time to find us. It's not a bad thing. You know why."

"It could be," Bodie said. "Look at the cliffs."

Heidi turned her head slightly, scanning to her right. She was surprised to see a group of men up there, perhaps twenty strong, standing and watching their progress. "Crap, that's not good."

"Could it be the Agency?"

"Not a chance. First, they *shouldn't* be here yet—it's statistically possible but realistically too soon—and second, they sure wouldn't reveal themselves like that." She shook her head warily. "Could be a local gang or drug runners or something?"

Gurka had spotted the newcomers too, but he gave no outward sign save to instruct the mercs to ensure their hardware was on show. At this stage, he wouldn't want a battle. Far better to avoid it.

"Do you think they know what we're up to?" Bodie asked Heidi.

"How could they?"

"Are you kidding? There are thirteen mercs here, plus five R24 assholes with all the morals of a half-starved snake. To a man—and woman—they're governed by profit."

"Again, why would they reveal themselves?" she said.

Bodie shrugged. "I don't know. It's one more obstacle. Did you think this would be easy?"

When she didn't answer, he looked over and caught her smiling. He said, "With you on board? Not for a minute."

"You're saying I'm trouble, then?" she asked.

"A magnet," he said. "For danger. Just look at my life since I met you."

"Since I saved your ass, you mean."

"You gonna keep holding that one over me forever?"

"Damn right. I haven't seen you saving *my* ass lately."

They passed the time with banter, easing the mounting tension that they both felt. They progressed slowly, periodically checking the cliff for the men lined up above them. The figures just stared down, weapons in hand but held loosely. They barely moved.

"Makes you wonder how these train tracks were never discovered," Heidi said as the hours wore on. "I mean, all the people who built them. The men and women on the train. Those who unloaded the treasures. Did they all just forget after the war?"

"I know a little of this"—Gunn was to Heidi's right and close enough to overhear—"from reading about the Amber Room. The tracks, most of them, will already have been in situ. The Germans would have diverted just the last few miles or so to suit their own route. In war, it's a normal scenario. Nothing is sacred to invaders. As for the people . . ." He made a sad face.

"They killed them." A new voice spoke from Bodie's side. "It is what happens when people become superfluous."

Bodie looked over to see one of the mercenaries with a slight smile on his face. The implication in his words was obvious.

"How can that be true?" Bodie asked. "When you're still alive?"

The man smirked, not lifting his eyes from the ground. More time passed, and the tributary could clearly be heard before it came into sight. Bodie dug hard at the earth as he walked, kicking with heel and toe, sometimes bending and scraping soil or grass aside to look below.

Inevitably, with almost thirty searching in a grid line, the tracks were found, and a merc caught Gurka's attention. It was all low key so that, Bodie assumed, Gurka could keep the find hidden from the watchers. Soon, they were gathered closely, as if pausing to take onboard refreshments.

Most took advantage of the stop to do just that.

"The tracks run dead straight right there." Gurka indicated a spot. "I do not know if our stalkers are aware, but this search is almost over."

Bodie didn't like the sound of that. "You have no clue what's inside the cave. You're still gonna need help."

209

"True." Gurka nodded. "Caruso—what will we find in the cave?"

The Italian bit his lower lip and answered with a question. "The Amber Room?"

Gurka snorted in disgust. "I don't know why we even brought you along. But we will put up with all of you for a little longer. And if we need you to fight"—he nodded toward the cliffs—"you will fight for us, to keep your loved ones safe."

"That wasn't part of the deal," Bodie said.

Gurka slid out his long blade. "Then I'll cut your throats now," he said, "with pleasure. Anyone who doesn't want to fight, stand up."

"Do the tracks follow the line of the river?" Pantera asked to grab the killer's attention.

"It appears so. Once we get past the tributary, they should run to the cave. The tributary will slow our new friends down, since it swings to the right, cutting across their path, not ours."

"The river narrows ahead, after the tributary." Nina was consulting the map. "But there are still mountains to both sides of the valley."

"The other problem," Bodie said, "is darkness. It's already close to sundown. It's not as dangerous down here, but we could still miss something vital."

"I do not intend to stumble along in the dark," Gurka grunted. "Nor do I intend to lead the watchers to our cave. We will make camp soon, and we will make ready."

The words were ominous. It was clear that Gurka expected an attack and appeared to be prepared to make camp and wait for it. But they couldn't run out here. They couldn't hide. And they couldn't lead these people to treasure.

Like it or not, Bodie and the relic hunters had a fight on their hands.

CHAPTER
THIRTY-THREE

Bodie stared out at the night, willing the shadows not to take on the shape of an enemy combatant. Their camp sat inside a rough circle of irregular stones with a mountain at their backs. For now, it was in darkness.

The mercs were at the outer perimeter, weapons ready. R24 formed the second circle. Bodie and his team sat at the camp's center, unarmed but with orders from Gurka to "get involved if the shit really hits the fan." Lucie, for once, was close by and free of Dudyk.

Bodie heard Cassidy checking that the blonde woman was okay. There was a quiet affirmative and then the clatter of two objects landing inside their camp.

"Fuck me!" a voice cried out. "That's a grenade!"

Bodie felt a moment of pure terror. They couldn't see the explosives. Couldn't deal with them. Were they to die here, so easily, after all they had been through? His heart thumped like a jackhammer as he turned to shield his friends.

The devices discharged. They weren't grenades after all but smoke bombs. Men began to cough and break rank. The smoke billowed out and then drifted upward.

"Shoot, you fools! Shoot!" Gurka's command ended in a violent fit of coughing.

Some mercs opened fire in the dark; others tried to stay low and stay under the rising smoke. Bodie heard grunts of pain, but then their camp was overrun.

Men jumped among them. The air reverberated with grunts of pain, the occasional gunshot, and falling bodies. Bodie saw a figure rear up before him. He didn't strike because he wasn't sure it was an enemy, but then he took a rifle barrel to the temple. He fell sideways, hitting the rocky floor. It was impossible to fight with any composure—the air full of smoke, the darkness impenetrable, the screams and cries and orders of men disorienting to the senses.

Four pairs of legs stomped around him, but who was the enemy? Nina's sharp voice pierced the dark.

"Do it!"

Bodie knew two fires had been prepared and was furious that it had taken R24 so long to light them. It showed a certain amateurishness. Instantly now, they flared to life. Shadows erupted all around him, frantic battling shadows. Bodie saw the enemies he knew struggling against over a dozen strangers, with more ranging around the battle. It was all close-quarter combat. Knives glinted and flashed. Two mercs lay dead already along with four of the newcomers. Dudyk, Vash, and Belenko were holding five at bay. The smoke had stopped billowing now, but Bodie's throat was dry, and his eyes were watering. His team lay or knelt all around him. Cassidy had a man by the throat. Heidi was dragging Lucie from another's hands.

The melee continued. The fire crackled and spat. Lurid, dancing flames painted the rock walls all around with nightmarish entwined shapes. It was a scene from the seventh circle of Hell, a demonic vision. An enemy's arm broke, his keening scream adding to the horrific spectacle.

It was then that he saw an incredible vision, a woman with jet-black hair and a powerful frame slipping in between mercenaries, hurting them, sending them falling to the ground. She carried two wicked, curved knives, which were mostly caught by stab vests, but what distinguished her was the way she moved, the incredible dancing, deadly ballet as she dodged between the bulkier fighters, helping her colleagues out, saving their lives, never stopping. Sweat flew off her in a fine mist; the dark strands of her hair clung to her forehead and cheeks. For one moment she saw Bodie, caught his eye, and nodded.

And then she was gone, throwing herself into the thick of the battle for her friends.

Bodie picked up a rock and smashed the first enemy he could find across the face. A cheek burst and blood sprayed as the man fell limply to the ground. Bodie leapt over him, struck a knee-high rock, and went sprawling.

He rolled onto his back and quickly assessed his plight. He was clear. He rose, but then someone stumbled across him, sending him back down. There was no skill here. Just luck. Bodie jumped onto the man's back and kidney punched him. An elbow connected with his temple. His vision clouded. The jumping, flitting shadows played havoc with his senses. He saw one, abnormally elongated by the fire, rise high and fall upon him. The fists hit a moment later, smashing his head into the ground.

He stared up into nightmare eyes.

It was the flame and the shadow again, catching reflections and distorting them. His attacker was pulled away, uttering a cry. Cassidy stood above him.

"No time for a nap, boss."

Bodie took a breath and rose. His head cleared. Around the camp and among the rocks, the eleven remaining mercs, R24, and the attackers fought together, struggling for space. His own team was dealing with just two men. Yasmine concentrated on one while Heidi and Pantera confronted the other.

"We need to pin one of these—"

They were swept apart as four battling men staggered between them, one sending Bodie sprawling once more. This was bloody madness. What could anyone hope to achieve? The enemy combatant with the broken arm was on his knees six feet to Bodie's right. Someone swung a knife down toward his neck, which he was unable to defend against, and he fell dead. The merc who'd killed him was suddenly hit by a beast of a man, a bearded giant. He went flying, head over heels. The giant turned to Bodie.

He had a Glock in his hand and time to use it.

Bodie pounced up from his heels, shooting forward at speed. The gun tracked him. He closed the gap. He wasn't going to make it. The Glock leveled. In the second or so it took to reach for the gun hand, he noticed two very clear things.

The large man had a welcoming smile on his face.

And familiar tattoos across his left cheek.

What . . . ?

The Glock didn't fire, but the man pulled him into a bear hug. "You know us?"

"I do now," Bodie grunted out, face crushed to a rough stab vest. "The bloody Bratva. What the hell are you doing here?"

"You thought we wouldn't hunt the ones who wronged us?" The man threw him around a little to imitate fighting moves.

"We handled that," Bodie gasped. "It was done. I met the bosses in Miami. It wasn't us—"

"We know," came the reply. "I don't mean you. I meant these R24 people and their mercenaries. That is who we hunt."

It suddenly made sense. The Bratva had justifiably taken offense when their meeting—and their hierarchy—had been raided, threatened, and attacked by mercenaries with guns. Now they were here for revenge.

"How did you find us?"

"You made a call to the CIA? We heard that."

Around them, the fight still raged. People struggled to win, or at least not to die, with every sinew, every ounce of will.

"You were listening? And you beat the CIA here? That figures."

"We were closer," the man allowed. "But they are closing in too. This will end by tomorrow."

"You have to go," Bodie said. "Leave now. They have Caruso's family. And one of them watches Lucie constantly. If they suspect anything, they will give the kill order."

"We are losing this fight anyway," the man said. "Be ready."

In moments, the man had thrown Bodie to the ground and given a command to his men. The attackers began to melt into the night. They fired high to warn their opponents to keep their own guns in check, but the mercs had no intentions of continuing the battle and soon sank into repose to check their wounds.

Bodie grabbed Cassidy and quickly explained before walking over to Heidi. The rest gathered around, sitting back on their haunches and taking stock. A sense of shock stole over the assembled figures. Several dead bodies lay around, surrounded by pools of blood. Gurka himself looked shell shocked. Dudyk made his way back to Lucie's side, though he had never been farther than two arm lengths away. It took Bodie and Cassidy ten halted minutes, but they explained the new Bratva revelations to the team.

Heidi shook her head with some irony. "Of course a criminal organization makes it here before my own government. That's a given."

"What are you talking about?" Gurka glanced at them suspiciously.

"Just happy to be alive," Cassidy said. "Glad they're gone."

"Then you are fools. All of you. They have gone, yes, but how do you think we enter the cave without being seen? How do you think we will do that?"

It was a fair question, one Bodie had thought of but hadn't voiced out loud. It put them in a corner. It would force R24 to make hard, definitive choices, none of which would be good for his team.

"You have the rest of the night," Heidi snapped. "Why not think on it?"

She didn't have to voice what they, and Caruso, already knew. None of them were going to make it out alive. None of them would be set free when the Amber Room was found. R24 would follow the Nazi example and get rid of everyone who knew about it. And that meant Caruso's family too.

Tomorrow was truly the endgame.

It was a telling moment when Gurka gathered his fellow R24 members together, all except Dudyk, and walked with them into the darkness—there to discuss and decide whatever twisted plan would work best for them.

CHAPTER THIRTY-FOUR

It was a hard night.

Bodie's initial thought was that R24 had decided to take the battle straight to the Bratva, because last night, its members hadn't returned at all. It was only an hour before dawn that Gurka led his rancorous crew back to the camp and sat staring into a fire for the next ten minutes.

Then, he made an announcement.

"All of you," he said, speaking directly to the mercenaries. "Hit those bastards hard. Hit them now, before dawn. Whoever walks back from the battle, I'll triple your fee."

Bodie tried reining in his emotions. Gurka had just passed a death sentence on the eleven mercenaries who remained, but to a man, they looked eager to earn their new reward. It was a risky scenario. Maybe Gurka was hoping they would weaken the Bratva enough in order that R24 could finish them both off. By his count, the Bratva were down to fifteen. It was possible.

He saw Dudyk readying Lucie. Nina was repacking her rucksack with care. Vash and Belenko were preparing weapons. Gurka was sitting quietly, eyeing the mercs as they made ready.

Heidi tapped Bodie's shoulder and leaned over to whisper. "They're sacrificing their own men," she said. "Using the battle as a distraction so they can find the cave without being seen."

Bodie thought she was guessing, but it felt right. "Sounds like a play they would make."

"It's good for us," Heidi went on. "Brings our enemies down to five."

But not good for the Bratva.

An odd thought. Here he was, anxious for a criminal gang that, until a few days ago, had been sworn mortal enemies.

He was surprised by Cassidy whispering in his other ear. "Keep it clean, you two. What's up?"

Bodie pulled away. There was something he didn't want to explore right now about having two women whispering in his ears. Before he could explain, though, the mercs started to leave. R24 members urged their captives to follow them. They walked steadily until they could see the valley floor ahead and the cliffs opposite, where the Bratva had been standing the day before.

Gurka pointed out a barely discernible route. "We scouted it last night. You can get right up to their camp that way." He proceeded to show the mercs another path that the Bratva were using. The black skies were already turning gray as he ordered them to move out.

"It'll be light in twenty," were his last words to them. "Good luck."

When the last man was out of earshot, he turned to Caruso, his face etched with anger. "Now, you Italian fuck, you will show me the entrance to that cave, or I'll order my men to break your wife's fingers."

Caruso stared, shocked. "I am . . . aren't you waiting to see . . . oh my . . ."

Bodie coughed. "What he means is—aren't you waiting to see how your men fare first?"

"Don't pretend to be stupid. We'll find that cave on our own and kill any men who survive. But I'm sure you already know that."

Gurka and his comrades had to act quickly, Bodie thought, if they were to find the cave while the mercenaries were distracted. "So you're threatening Caruso's wife again? The guy has mental problems. He can't tell you what you want to know!"

Caruso wrung his hands together. "Please don't hurt my family."

Gurka already had a phone in his hands. "Line's already open." He brandished the device like a weapon. "Last chance, Dante."

"Follow the tracks," Lucie said from the back. "Just follow the tracks, and the cave's at the end."

Dudyk shushed her quickly. Bodie was surprised at the lack of venom in his tone but realized the group was trying to stay quiet as dawn approached the vast, echoing mountains.

"It is," Caruso added immediately. "We follow the train. I remember following the train."

Gurka snarled at him. "How fucking far? It could be miles!" Then he brought the phone close to his mouth. "Hurt her."

Instantly, Caruso fell to his knees. "No, *please.*"

"Be quiet." Nina slapped him.

"Not my family. I am helping you. I am. If you have to hurt someone, hurt me."

Gurka watched him closely, as if evaluating an act. Without moving, he spoke once more into the phone. "Hold off. For now."

They started down the brief slope that would take them to the valley floor. All around, the darkness was tinged with a lighter gray, giving them just enough illumination to navigate by. The mercs had had enough time to cross the valley floor by now and start ascending the far cliff. Soon, they would be seen, or they would attack. Either way, a battle was imminent.

Finding the train tracks, Gurka and Vash started off at a fast pace, and within ten minutes, they were approaching the large tributary. It bent away to the right, not obstructing their path, the increasing roar of rushing water drowning all other sounds out for the next ten minutes. Gurka increased the pace. Bodie bowed his head as water spray filled the air. The eight relic hunters and Caruso walked between the four members of R24, with Lucie and Dudyk at the back. It was a hard slog. By the time they left the tributary behind, they could hear gunfire.

"Good," Nina said on hearing the brutal sound. "It is perfect timing for us."

"Men are dying," Yasmine said. "Even your men."

Bodie remembered she had been undercover inside the Bratva for a long time. It only occurred to him now that she might know some of the men on that cliff, or maybe their friends and brothers.

"Shut up and walk," was all Nina would say.

The tracks ran dead straight for a mile and then started curving to the left. Gurka, Vash, and Belenko toiled hard to ensure that they didn't stray. When the tracks bent away, it took the leaders many minutes to find them.

The bend ran toward a high mountain. The rails were totally buried beneath three feet of brown earth. They were rusted, pitted. No wonder they had lain here unnoticed for decades. And when Bodie studied the mountain they ran unerringly toward, he quickly voiced a thought.

"There's no cave."

Gurka cursed and told him to be quiet. The fact that the tracks ran toward the mountain was significant, Bodie thought, but at the end of the tracks he'd been expecting an opening, maybe a cave. He looked at the valley floor extending ahead toward the mountains. He saw the range beyond, peaks jutting up at the brightening sky. A chill wind scythed down through the passes, blasting into his face. *The mountain in question wasn't strictly a mountain,* Bodie thought. It was comparatively low, more of a craggy, rocky hill. It rose vertically for around five hundred feet, had steep, sloping sides and a peaked summit. But it was part of the Tatra range.

The foothills running up to the mountain were short, less than a hundred feet of terrain, dotted with large boulders, shrubs of grass, and a few small trees. They climbed through it, still hearing gunfire echoing across the valley. When they reached the foot of the mountain, Gurka stopped and turned.

"It is a good bend for a train," he commented. "And the tracks stop here." He uncovered a hard edge before turning to Caruso.

"This is your last chance."

From Gurka's tone, his countenance, and his body language, Bodie knew the Italian was out of time. That meant Bodie and his crew were also out of time. But they could still fight back.

"The end of the . . . *ferroviari* . . . the tracks." Caruso stared at the earth as if trying to claw through the wreckage that was his memory. "I know what that means . . ." He paused.

Bodie readied himself. He saw Cassidy and the others move closer to Gurka and his four teammates. Lucie was rapt with attention.

Dudyk stared Bodie in the eyes, an unreadable expression on his face.

"It means we have found the Amber Room," Caruso finished.

Gurka snapped, reaching out for their guide and grabbing him by the neck. He wrenched the older man so hard that he instantly fell to his knees; Gurka bent and allowed him to fall, staring straight into his terrified eyes. Bodie couldn't let him hurt the older man and took a step forward, but both Vash and Belenko aimed their guns at his chest. It was only Nina, thinking to check the rock face out, who averted bloodshed.

"The rocks aren't right."

Gurka looked over, keeping his hands around Caruso's neck. "What?"

221

"Look here. Put him down."

Bodie waited for Gurka to start walking and then followed the scarred man to the rugged rock face. He was past taking orders. Nina waved a hand. "Cracks. Lines. From below the foothills, even from the foothills themselves, they look like jagged mountain fissures. Fractures, actually. But up close, it's clear. Someone fitted the rocks across the entrance, not perfectly, but well enough to hide it. And the entrance was huge."

"No," Gurka whispered in horror. "Do you mean someone found the entrance later or that this was put in place by the Nazis?"

"Someone did find it." Bodie pointed behind a sprawling, bristly tree that hid a small separate entrance to the far left of the rock face. Small boulders lay on the ground all around it.

Nina stared. Caruso looked over their shoulders. "That might've been me."

Gurka whirled. "Was it? *Was it?*"

"No. Maybe. I don't think so."

"Fuck."

Quickly, Gurka shepherded everyone together. Bodie tried to reason with him. "You seriously don't think it would stay undiscovered for seven decades, do you, mate? The fitted rocks are a great disguise but not foolproof. Once you get up close, it's pretty obvious."

"I am not your mate. Now, move."

"Did you use this entrance?" Vash asked the Italian.

Bodie didn't have to hear to know the Italian muttered something noncommittal.

Slowly, the entire team worked their way inside the mountain through the small entrance. Tension ran high. Guns were held ready. Bodie dared not think about what they might find inside.

CHAPTER
THIRTY-FIVE

R24 members clicked their flashlights on as soon as they were inside. Bodie followed Nina, stooping under rocks and trying to avoid the questing branches of the prickly tree. Thick debris covered the ground, which he waded through. Slowly, the entire team entered the cave.

"Do you see it?" Caruso asked somewhat comically.

Gurka snarled at him. Everyone except Dudyk swept their flashlights around the cave, illuminating the interior. Bodie saw the scene through flashes of deep gloom, clouds of disturbed dust, and waving lights, but it was clear this cave did not run deep. It stood about fifty feet in length and one hundred high.

And it was empty.

A mushroom cloud of disturbed dust billowed up sluggishly, following the curve of the roof and swirling high above. Beams of light swooped left and right, crisscrossing and then shining on the floor. Gurka and his colleagues probed the cave as if they couldn't believe their eyes.

Caruso sat despondently down on a rock.

Nina turned on him. "This is all you've got? What did you do—find that small chunk of amber in here, then run back home bleating about finding one of the greatest treasures in history? Did you think your friends would love you? Respect you? And then it all backfired—"

"When we came along," Vash said. "You've been stringing us along all this time for fear of what we'd do to your wife and child."

Bodie was studying Caruso the whole time. Usually, when close to relics, the man's synapses started firing, and he became someone new. A changed man. But not now. Bodie's team was still in position, close enough to grapple each member of R24. Caruso looked entirely miserable. So miserable, in fact, that Bodie took another hard look at the cave.

"Where might you have found it?" he asked, his voice echoing. "The piece you think you buried?"

If Caruso had offered one more shrug, one more confused expression, Bodie was sure Gurka would have shot him. But the Italian seemed to possess a sixth sense. Deflecting Gurka's anger, he rose and walked deeper into the cave.

"Back here," he said.

Was it Caruso's way of giving Bodie and his team the option to act or wait? Did Caruso really know where he was going?

Bodie saw then that the rear wall of the cave was constructed in the same way as the outside, only this was a far superior job. Barely any cracks could be made out. It had been fabricated with large, square blocks that had been fitted together and then daubed with a mixture of cave dust and mortar. It looked authentic, like the back wall of a cave.

"Hey," Bodie said. "This wall is false as well." He saw no other choice but to point it out. Maybe something beyond this wall would give them their opportunity.

Gurka swore and stalked across. Nina ran up and made to slap Caruso around the head. Bodie caught her arm. The gentle tap of a gun barrel at the nape of his neck warned him to let go.

"You can't coerce him," Bodie tried to explain. "Especially not with violence. The memories are fleeting and brief. Please."

Gurka waved him back as he studied the rear wall. "Blow it," he said. "I'm tired of all this. Tired of waiting. Blow it up."

Caruso's eyes bulged. His arms started to flap, his face contorted, and his mouth fell open. Bodie grabbed him, dragging him away.

"Leave it," he whispered. "All we need is a good chance, and we can end this."

"But . . . the room."

"What about your wife? Your daughter?"

Caruso nodded quickly. "You are right. I want to see them again with all my heart. All these years searching for treasure, and it was right there all along. At home."

"Don't worry. Despite their crass methods, these relic hunters know what they're doing. They have experience, if not scruples. I'm sure they'll use less powerful explosives."

He found out five minutes later. As they took shelter at the front of the cave, Vash shouted the all clear, and Belenko pushed a button. A low rumble was heard, and then the crashing and tumbling of heavy rock. Bodie ducked under the thick unfurling cloud that rolled their way.

They waited until the hazy air had dissipated and then stood up, flashlights trained on the cave's rear wall. To start with, they couldn't penetrate the lingering screen of dust, but then Bodie saw a wide passage stretching back into the mountain. Gurka was there a moment later, playing his light around the ragged walls.

"This is more like it. Come on."

Bodie fell in line behind Yasmine and traversed the narrow section. Soon, he heard Gurka let out an exclamation of shock. A few seconds later the passage opened into a large chamber, vaulted a hundred feet above and several hundred feet wide. It was probably twice as long.

But that wasn't what had made Gurka shout.

It was the old, ruined German aircraft that lay ahead down the center of the chamber. The main wings had been torn off, but the body appeared largely intact, though smashed, dented, and ripped in many places.

Bodie shook his head. "Am I really seeing this, or is it exhaustion?"

"I see it," Pantera said. "How the hell . . . ?"

Everybody stopped when they saw the plane and fanned out, so now Lucie was relatively close by. She shifted uneasily.

"Even I can't explain this," she said.

Gurka started moving carefully, bypassing the rear wings, which, judging by the ragged pieces of steel that remained, had also been torn half off. The rudder and vertical stabilizer remained intact, attached to the rear. Gurka continued to the rearmost window and peered inside.

Using his sleeve, he rubbed the window, which was only partially cracked.

"It is a Junkers aircraft," Caruso said quietly. "The name is there." He pointed at a dirty serial number running down the rear left flank. "And registration number. It is from 1945." He let that sink in. "When it disappeared."

"Shit!" Gurka suddenly exclaimed.

They approached as he wiped the glass vigorously once more.

"What is it?" Nina asked.

"Skeletons," the scar-faced man said. "Six I can see, and probably more. I see old German uniforms."

"I remember this," Caruso said. "I researched it on the day I returned. The registration is logged as 'missing.' Its last flight was early 1945. I am sure this is where it ended up."

"Who was on board?" Heidi asked.

"That's the interesting part. About a dozen men—all of them part of the upper German echelons. Eight topflight leaders disappeared around that time. Of course, they might have been killed in battle, lost, or dead a hundred different ways, but they could also have been on board that plane."

"Flying here, you mean?" Gurka turned. "To view the Amber Room?"

Caruso flinched at the man's voice but nodded. "That was my thought."

"It makes sense," Nina said. "First the Nazis remove the treasure, transport it here, and then the hierarchy wanted to view it."

"All traces of the plane have been removed from outside this cave," Gurka said reflectively. "But how did it get inside?"

Caruso then gave Gurka the same look he'd been subjected to the entire trip. "Are you joking? It crashed, of course."

Bodie fought hard not to smile. "Probably crashed on landing," he said quickly to deflect Gurka's sudden annoyance. "The valley's wide and flat enough to be able to land a plane and then taxi here. They overshot, killing everyone on board. Or else—they overshot, crashed into the cave, and were then shot by their fellow assholes."

Cassidy eyed the plane as they moved to the front. "There are lots of bullet holes," she said. "In the main body of the plane, at least. You can't tell with the windows."

"Maybe it was shot down, then?" Gunn suggested.

Gurka barked orders at Vash and Belenko, speaking in Russian for the first time Bodie could remember. Both men dragged over a large rock that they could use to reach the plane's door, climbed up onto the body of the aircraft, and then started work with a crowbar. With one heave they wrenched the door open. Both men fell off the rock and onto the hard floor as metal screeched and tore. A moment later they were inside.

Gurka ordered those outside to the front of the plane. When he got there, Bodie saw a skeleton in one of the front seats, the long-dead pilot. His bare skull was lying forward, pressed against the cockpit glass.

Gurka studied what lay beyond the plane. "Caruso?"

The Italian stared as if entering a strange room for the first time. Bodie felt for his dilemma. In the glow of three flashlights, it now appeared that the rear of the cave had four different exits.

"It's definitely one of those," Caruso said.

CHAPTER
THIRTY-SIX

Lucie was kept separate by Dudyk, apart from the pack. They were farther away from the plane, but she could still see Vash and Belenko inside as they walked carefully along the aisle.

"What are they looking for?" she asked.

Dudyk shrugged. They had struck up an emotionless way of conversing since she'd revealed her deepest fears to the Russian. "Anything," he said. "And then they will return to guard the entrance."

She'd even been the recipient of two more smiles from him. Though neither had been particularly warm.

They walked very slowly, keeping their distance from the others. Bodie and Cassidy were approaching one of the new tunnels, guarded by Gurka. It looked like due to lack of manpower, they were checking one new cavern at a time.

Even Lucie, with her inexperience in captive situations, knew this was exactly what Bodie wanted.

"I'm surprised Gurka sent all his men to die," Lucie said.

Dudyk replied with a soldier's view. "It has weakened us."

"That's not really what I meant."

"Yes, yes, you are sentimental with all lives. You tried to save your uncle, only to see him die anyway. I have never had a choice. None of us have."

"A man like you could surely choose what you want to be."

"A man like me?" Dudyk shook his head. "Look at you. So naive. So wrapped up in your self-absorbed fears. You think I grew up with a home? You say everyone close to you died. I grew up with *nobody* close to me. Alone. A street rat. To end the nightly abuse, I joined a gang. The gang protected you, fed you, housed you, but in return you worked for them, doing everything they asked. I killed before I turned thirteen. I tore families apart to keep my place. It was the gang or the army."

Lucie had never heard so many words falling from his mouth. Was this his response to how she'd laid her heart bare? "I—"

"You think you know the world because you are a historian? You know nothing of life, death, and struggle. At least these others—these relic hunters—understand where I have been and what I have done. They know because they have been there too. You? You are an infant."

Lucie saw no malice in him right then, just a need to vent, to insult somebody. She didn't mind that it was her. Instead, she stopped so that he would look at her. She wanted to say, *I do know death,* but she kept it to herself.

Instead she said: "And your worst fear?"

"I face it every night," he said.

"Nightmares?"

"Sleep. Because in sleep I see the face of every innocent I have ever hurt."

His biggest fear was sleep? No wonder he was so out of sorts and quick to anger. "Redemption doesn't come through more brutality," she said. "I may be an infant, but even I know that."

Dudyk glared and then must have seen something in her eyes. A slight smile crossed his face. "You mock your captor? Is that wise?"

Before she knew what she was doing, Lucie reached out a hand and laid it on his wrist. The gesture was light and heartfelt. "I see good in you," she said. "I see it struggling to get out but failing."

"And what do you suggest?" For a shocking moment Dudyk covered her hand with his own.

"Fight," she said. "Fight for yourself this time, not for *them*."

Then Vash and Belenko jumped down from the plane, empty handed, and shouted that they would start guarding the entrance.

Dudyk turned and walked away without another word.

Heidi watched Bodie take the left-hand passage. Gurka pushed Cassidy after him and then followed closely, a handgun aimed at their spines. Only Nina remained to watch the rest of them, but the R24 female had pulled away to create a large void of space, enabling her to see everyone and maintain her threat.

If they rushed her, they could take her down, but some would die. Heidi studied the three remaining tunnels. Two clearly led to a single high cavern—she could see its shape in the light of the flashlights—while the other traveled farther into the mountain.

Soon, Bodie returned, looking despondent. Gurka waved his gun around. "Empty," he said. "Keep your flashlights." Then he turned to Heidi. "You, let's try the next passage." He took another flashlight from his pack and threw it to her.

She set off, flashlight held steady. The rear wall of the cave was wet, dotted here and there by clinging moss. She entered an archway carefully, checking for pitfalls along the ground and anomalies in the walls—anything from a dissecting passage to lurking predators. The passage was short, and the next cavern opened quickly around her. She saw an empty hollow with a small stream running down one side. The stream bubbled up from underground and disappeared through the far wall.

Gurka prodded her in the back with the gun. "Move."

"It's empty."

A sigh. "Fucking Caruso. I'm looking forward to flaying that man alive."

She retraced her steps, more worried than ever. She knew he could do it. She thought about her daughter and the office back in DC. She thought about her husband. They'd split, essentially, because she had a voice within her—a voice that compelled her to help people.

Look how she'd ended up. Was it all worth it?

They returned to the main cave then, just as Belenko came running up to Nina. "Three helicopters are approaching," he said. "High in the skies."

Gurka cursed. "That makes everything harder," he said. "Can you see who it is?"

"There are no markings."

"Return to the entrance and keep me informed."

But Heidi knew. The CIA were here at last. Even the appearance of the choppers changed Gurka's plans. He now had to include them. The CIA wouldn't be able to get a fix on their position, but it was now her hope that they would see the Bratva and the mercs fighting.

Even so, she had to draw their attention.

And then Gurka let out an irate shout. "Where the hell is Caruso?"

CHAPTER THIRTY-SEVEN

"I remember!" Caruso cried.

Bodie whipped his head around as the Italian suddenly vanished into the final tunnel. Without thinking, he raced after the man, Cassidy at his side. Everyone broke into a run, ignoring Gurka's shouts and Nina, who, at the back of the group, could barely be heard.

Bodie reached the tunnel seconds after Caruso and saw him running ahead. "Wait!"

The Italian grinned back at him. "Are you kidding? You'll die of *meraviglia* . . . of wonder . . . when you see this."

It was the lucid comment of a man driven by his passion. A moment of clarity, inspired by the nearness of the Amber Room.

Bodie sprinted behind Caruso, heedless of hazards. Despite his apprehension, he was at heart a treasure hunter—and this might be the greatest treasure of them all. The feeling in his heart was more than fear—it was passion, hope, and a rising sense of anticipation.

He figured Caruso would encounter any pitfalls first. The tunnel closed in, its roof brushing the top of his head, its sides reaching for his elbows. Caruso, ahead, seemed to bounce from wall to wall. Bodie chanced a glance back, saw the odd sight of a multitude of faces and flashlights bobbing behind him, and grunted as his right shoulder hit a nasty outcropping.

Finally, the tunnel ended in a vast cave. The walls were tiered from floor to ceiling—deep, wide ledges dug into the rock one above another.

Bodie slowed, jogging a few feet into the cave so that he wouldn't get trampled from behind. He found it hard to take in the sights that were suddenly presented to his gaze.

The chamber resounded with gasps of wonder.

Caruso had fallen to his knees. Bodie walked to his side and placed a hand on his shoulder. "Well done, Dante, well done, mate. You've done your family proud."

Gurka and his companions brought their flashlights to bear.

Wooden crates had been placed down the center of the cave, splitting it in half. Some had their lids askew, while others were as tightly closed as the day they'd been dragged there. The many ledges that lined the walls were overflowing with dusty treasures. Bodie saw strongboxes with cracked lids, full of coins. He saw piles of banknotes. He saw several framed paintings, covered loosely by frayed sheets that had once protected them but had decayed with time. Even now, the gilt frames flashed. It was all too much to take in. He was aware of figures moving past him: Yasmine approaching the right-hand series of ledges, Pantera stooping to rattle a handful of coins through his fingers, Gurka roughly pushing Heidi aside. Not a single ledge that lined the room was empty, and they rose over a dozen tiers high and ran around every wall. There were statues of brass and bronze and gold. Candelabras and chandeliers, drooping and cracked. Magnums of champagne sat amid thick debris on the ground.

Even without the Amber Room, Bodie thought, *this is a monumental find.*

"A hell of a cache," Jemma said sadly. "And a terrible cache."

"The Germans stole . . ." Bodie paused. "Countless treasures from Europe. The true cost can never be counted."

Caruso still knelt near the middle of the cave. Gurka walked up to him, grabbed his hair, and forced him to his feet. "Where is it?"

"Just lighten up, bud." Cassidy confronted Gurka. "You got what you wanted."

Gurka aimed the gun at her, finger twitching around the trigger. Cassidy didn't back down, staring him point-blank in the face, an act that reminded Bodie of the old Cassidy, someone they sorely needed right now.

Caruso waved his hands for attention. "This way," he told Gurka. "Look."

And he led them along the line of crates. Bodie studied the row carefully now. Each crate stood about five feet high and eight long, constructed of nailed planks of wood, bonded by thick metal straps that ran around the outside.

Caruso jumped up on a rock positioned beside the fourth crate. After reaching in and grabbing an unseen object, he turned to address all the people in the cave as they stared up at him.

"This," he said, "is the eighth wonder of the world."

CHAPTER
THIRTY-EIGHT

Eight flashlights illuminated the oblong amber panel that Caruso held up. The surface glowed as if it had recently been burnished. In addition, the amber was backed with gold leaf, lending the radiance an even richer luster. Bodie realized he was looking at the top edge of a picture frame, something that had been set permanently in the walls of the room.

"How many crates?" Gurka whispered.

"Eighteen," Caruso said. "The same amount in which it was originally shipped to Russia in 1716. Once reconstructed, it will measure one hundred eighty square feet and glow with six tons of amber and many priceless gems."

Caruso handed it down to Gurka, but the leader of R24 wanted more. He ordered the Italian down from the rock and climbed up himself. Then he shone his flashlight inside the box. After a moment he turned a crooked grin on Nina.

"Everything we've done has come to this. It was all worth it." He paused for a moment and then said, "Let's do this properly. Break out all the flashlights." R24 followed his directions, placing the lights all around the chamber, balancing them atop rocks and ledges and inside niches, so that the cavern glowed bright with illumination.

Gurka then lifted piece after piece from the crate, turning and angling them to show their splendor, before moving on to the next. Randomly, he checked and scrutinized the crates' contents, but it soon became clear that Caruso was correct, and the entire Amber Room was present.

"Nina," Gurka said suddenly, as he walked back toward the group from the farthest box. "I really don't think we need the relic hunters anymore."

His gun came up. Nina was already training hers on Cassidy and Yasmine. Bodie spread his arms. "Hey, wait, who's gonna help you drag these things out of here? You killed your merc pals already. You need us. What about transporting them?"

"That plan was already in place," Gurka scoffed. "You think our contacts are not waiting for our call? That we cannot arrange this? If so, you really are stupid."

Bodie positioned himself as prime target, standing in front of Gurka. "We had a deal."

"Yes, and it will end with your death."

Lucie spent the entire deadly conversation watching Dudyk, who only glanced at her before looking down. That gesture spoke volumes. She barely saw the Amber Room and the treasures arranged around the walls. When the opportunity had come to offer up some history to the group and thus calm her nerves, she'd stayed silent. Dudyk continued to give her fleeting looks, his face as hard as stone.

Earlier, he'd affirmed that he would carry out R24's demands. He would hurt her if he had to. But would he kill her?

She watched the gun in his hand. She saw both Gurka and Nina raise their guns and take aim. And then Bodie stepped in front of their weapons.

Dudyk moved to the right and raised his own gun. The tortured expression on his face told her that he didn't like what he was about to do, but he would most certainly do it.

◆ ◆ ◆

Bodie adhered to the old creed. *Live a moment more. Just one more . . .*

Hoping for a miracle.

Gurka made a final glance over at Nina, who nodded.

Bodie had a plan in mind. The crates would provide cover. Many of the treasures arrayed around the cave were potential weapons. There was a case of military knives on the second shelf to his right.

Cassidy would have seen it too.

The only issue was—he couldn't save everyone.

Which was why he tried one last time. "The knowledge we have." He tapped his temple. "The relics we've stolen for customers, some believed lost to history . . . we could lead you to a dozen almost as rare as this."

Gurka looked annoyed but visibly wavered. "I know, but why say this now?"

Heidi drew his attention. "What better time is there?"

Gurka looked between the two, finger still on the trigger. Bodie was coiled, ready to spring. He hoped Cassidy was just as prepared. Gurka cleared his throat. "It is an intriguing thought," he said. "But I fear—"

Vash then ran into the cave, pulled up sharply, and exclaimed, "Whoa . . . is that . . . ?"

"What do you want?" Gurka snapped.

"It's becoming worse out front. We keep trying but can't reach the mercenaries on the radios."

"It's become worse? In what way?"

"The choppers landed opposite the cave, near the middle of the valley floor. We counted twelve soldiers with weapons and three men wearing suits and body armor. Maybe they are reinforcements for the group that attacked us?"

"No, they'd have gone straight to their aid. We have to assume our men are dead." Gurka swore. "And now we are outnumbered. It is unfortunate that they landed so close."

"What shall we do?" Vash pressed.

"Do they know we are here?"

"They appear to have no knowledge of the cave."

While the two men were talking, Bodie was shifting, preparing. His friends were doing the same, attaining good positions from which to launch a final attack. But when Bodie heard the next shocking words leave Gurka's mouth, he froze on the spot.

"This has been a waste of time," the leader of R24 said. "Just blow the cave. We will use the drama as a cover for our escape. As for these *relic hunters*," he spat, "tie them up and leave them here. They will die in the blast. A fitting end for you all."

Bodie was staggered but fought to remain emotionless. "You're not serious? Destroy the Amber Room, all these treasures? And us too? You're fucking crazy."

"It's another example of why we have survived for so long. You think we haven't done this before?" Gurka laughed. "We are the imperative, the essential survivors. So we will kill the captives if we have to, blow the chamber, destroy the treasure, all in an effort to mask our escape."

"But you forgot something," Bodie said.

"Us," Cassidy said.

239

CHAPTER THIRTY-NINE

Bodie had no option but to concentrate on the weapon before him. He was close enough to grab it. Gurka was distracted by Vash and the situation's shifting dynamics. Bodie stepped in fast, grabbed Gurka's arm around the wrist, and jerked the weapon so that it pointed at the floor. Gurka's trigger finger tightened reflexively. The gun discharged, the sound filling the chamber. Bodie's head pounded. He kept hold of Gurka's wrist as the man tried to wrench it free. Keeping hold of that gun arm was life.

Cassidy leapt at Nina. Heidi whirled on Vash, whose gun was still tucked inside his waistband. Cassidy forced Nina's hand up toward the roof, propelling her backward. They staggered eight feet before crashing into a sidewall. Precariously balanced treasures toppled and spilled around their feet. Cassidy gripped Nina's wrist hard, finally able to unleash some of her pent-up feelings.

"Talk to me like a piece of shit, will you? Order me around? Not any fucking more, you won't."

Cassidy slammed Nina's arm into the rock again and again. With her free hand she struck at the woman's ribs and kidneys, landing blows hard enough to make her opponent puff and gasp and squeal. It was great therapy for Cassidy . . .

. . . but it was taking too long.

Heidi fought Vash. He might have been scrawny, unwashed, and reminiscent of a weasel, but he was strong, tough, and fast. She kept him occupied, giving him no chance to reach for a weapon. It took all her training. His blows made her flinch, and when he grabbed her wrist, she thought he'd broken it. But she managed to pull away, pushing him over a boulder. He hit the floor, and she took a second to check and then rub her wrist.

He aimed the gun.

Heidi launched herself on top of him, knees slamming his gun arm to the floor. He grunted in agony, arm pinned at the bicep, striking out with his other arm. Heidi raised an elbow to fend off the attack. She bore down, putting all her weight on his gun arm.

Bodie swung Gurka around. They pushed each other around the cave, gasping and struggling to gain control. Gurka's face was dripping with sweat, his scars turning more livid as his anger and frustration rose.

"We help you find this," Bodie hissed in his opponent's face. "One of history's greatest treasures. And you want to blow us up with it? What of Caruso's family? What of Lucie?"

Gurka fought back, matching Bodie's strength. "R24 *does not care about you or any of your family.*"

The scarred man heaved Bodie around so that his back was to a crate and then smashed him hard against it. Bodie felt the impact deep in his bones; it jarred every nerve in his body. But he held on desperately. Gurka's sweat was making his arm slippery. Gurka smashed him once more into the crate and wrenched his arm free.

Turned the gun on Bodie.

Who ducked and rolled an instant before the shot was fired. Without stopping, he jumped up, striking Gurka under the chin with the top of his skull. The bullet impacted the side of the crate. Gurka let out a muffled groan and fell back, staggering, collapsing to his knees. The blow seemed to have befuddled him. The fingers grasping the gun opened reflexively, and Bodie stooped down to grab it.

Cassidy used her strength and fury, lifting Nina off the floor and smashing her down onto a rocky ledge. The impact made the woman scream as her spine struck rock. When Cassidy let go, Nina slithered down to the cave floor among the fallen treasures.

But she held on to the gun.

Cassidy lifted a boot to smash her heel onto the woman's wrist. The gun's barrel inched toward her as Nina's own survival instinct fought intense pain. The weapon discharged, but it was too early. The bullet flew past Cassidy and struck a far wall. Cassidy kicked at the gun and sent it spinning off across the floor.

Heidi yelled as Vash bucked her off. His gun arm was free, the weapon tracking her. A moment of panic made her freeze. There was no way of stopping his shot, but then Yasmine saved her, diving

242

bravely in front of the gun and stomping on Vash's chest and arm. Heidi felt a flash of relief that Yasmine was right there with them. Pantera had actually tackled Heidi, pulling her out of the way of a shot that never came. Heidi rolled and then managed to sit up quickly, checking the cave.

Bodie and Gurka struggled by a crate. Cassidy looked to have gotten the better of Nina and was leaping for a discarded gun. That left Jemma and Gunn, who had climbed up on a ledge during the melee, grabbing weapons for the fighters to use, turning even now with several flashing blades in their hands. Caruso stood with his back to a crate, keeping deliberately clear of the action.

And finally there was Lucie, whom nobody had forgotten, but who had been placed with Dudyk essentially for this kind of situation. Dudyk was R24's fail-safe, their best, most vicious, and deadliest fighter. His remit was to kill Lucie and then help his team.

Heidi needed a gun.

Lucie saw Bodie start the fight and knew she was dead. Dudyk carried a handgun in his waistband with three spare clips of ammunition. He also carried a military knife, which he now pulled from its sheath. The metal made a rasping sound as it skimmed the leather. Together, they watched the fight for a while, and then Lucie took a step backward.

"No, please, Dudyk."

"Stay still. I have my orders."

"Please. I . . . I'm no fighter. I'm not even a relic hunter. I've never done a single brave thing in my life, but I helped someone like you."

Dudyk held the knife easily. "You told me your fears."

"That's not bravery. It's being human."

There was silence between them, a moment of shared introspection.

Gurka's strained command rent apart their connection.

"Do it, Dudyk! Kill her now!"

Bodie flung Gurka once more at the crate and smashed a fist into the man's arm. The gun lay on the floor between them, but Bodie ignored it, knowing he'd only catch half a dozen blows bending down.

"No," he shouted into Gurka's face. "Tell him not to do it. She's a bloody *historian*, not a thief or a relic hunter like us."

"She's an enemy." Gurka brought his forehead down sharply, smashing it onto the bridge of Bodie's nose. "And like you, she dies now."

They struggled, the gun between their feet. To their right, Heidi was reaching for Vash's discarded gun, fingers brushing the handle.

"You're just like us," Gurka hissed into his face. "Impassioned. Driven. Focused. And selfish. You care only for yourselves."

"We're nothing like you!" Bodie shouted back.

"Kill her!" Gurka screamed.

And Bodie stopped for just a second. He saw Dudyk clench his fist around a wicked eight-inch blade, grab Lucie by the back of the neck, and then plunge it forward at the same time. He saw Lucie's shock, heard her gasp, and saw her stop moving as Dudyk held her in position, his head close to hers.

Lucie slumped to the ground. Dudyk held the knife at his side and turned around. "It's done."

Bodie's brain shrieked as Gurka smashed an elbow across his face, making him see stars. Blood sprayed his shirt. He staggered. Lucie's meaningless death wrenched at his heart. A properly trained military man might be able to compartmentalize the debilitating grief, but Bodie couldn't. His legs were jelly. Gurka was stronger.

Dudyk took hold of Lucie's body, gripping her tightly under the arms, and dragged her behind a crate, off the field of battle. He then reappeared with his gun drawn.

Gurka smashed Bodie to the ground. At that moment the huge Belenko appeared at the entrance to the cavern, probably worried when Vash hadn't returned to his watch. With a bellow, he ran straight at Heidi and Yasmine, tackling them around their waists and bearing them untidily to the ground.

They all struck hard and rolled wildly. Heidi's head became a messy blur, full of pain and crazy images. When she looked up again, the scene had changed.

Belenko held a weapon over them. Dudyk pointed a gun from farther away, covering the whole cave. Bodie was on his knees, bleeding profusely from the face. Even Cassidy looked shell shocked, devastated at the loss of Lucie. Heidi watched as she turned and took stock of the situation, saw all the guns pointed at her friends, and then refrained from picking Nina's gun up off the floor.

Bodie looked up. Gurka staggered away, grabbed the gun, and then aimed it at Bodie's head. For a moment there was no sound in the chamber other than the panting of all the fighters. Gunn and Jemma stood frozen close to Pantera, to whom they had been bringing weapons.

"The explosives," Gurka breathed at Vash and Belenko. "Quickly, prepare them. I want to blow this place sky-high."

He then strode past Dudyk, staring the hard man in the eyes and saying nothing. He didn't stop walking until he'd reached the place where Dudyk had stashed Lucie's body.

Dudyk called after him. "It is done, brother. I did as you asked." He strode toward Gurka.

"I see," Gurka said. "I see what you did."

Then he turned and shot Dudyk through the stomach.

CHAPTER FORTY

Bodie was made to sit upright. His hands were secured behind him with zip ties. Soon, Cassidy and Heidi were forced to sit at his side, similarly secured, and then all the others. After that, their ankles were also fastened. Nina tied them as Gurka covered them with handguns. Dudyk was dragged, groaning, into their midst, where Gurka proceeded to slap and kick him, clearly so angry that he believed the pain of the gunshot was not enough.

"You let her escape? You let that blonde bitch go free? I thought you were with us. I thought of you as a *brother*." He spat the words at the groaning Dudyk and smashed the man's knees with the butt of his gun.

"Gurka," Nina said. "We must hurry."

"But this is not good enough." Gurka indicated the broken Dudyk. "Not good enough for one who betrays R24." The scarred man then went over to pick up one of the explosives and, deliberately, bent down to meet Dudyk's eyes as he strapped it to the man's back.

"There," he said. "You will feel my vengeance."

Bodie gave up trying to figure out why Dudyk had saved Lucie; he was only glad that he had. They had been positioned in front of the first crate, facing the entrance, with the entire Amber Room at their back.

"Find her," Gurka said to Nina when she'd finished with their bonds. "She can't have gone far."

To Bodie, he said, "I always knew we were better than you. This is more than you deserve."

Bodie said nothing as he watched Vash start placing charges inside the chamber that, assumedly, would run all the way to the cave's front entrance. R24's hope was to bring most of it down and escape as the CIA and whoever was left out there searched through what remained. The charges weren't especially complex—mere slabs of plastic explosive with detonators attached, joined by sets of wires—but would easily do the job.

As R24 worked and hunted for Lucie, Bodie held an arm up to his face, blotting some of the blood that still seeped from his wound, and started working on an escape plan. He was distracted by Cassidy kicking Dudyk.

"Hey, hey! What the hell did you do with Lucie?"

"She is alive," the man said, struggling to speak through pain. "Faked the stabbing. Told her to . . . to collapse. And hide. To . . . hide."

Bodie was thankful for that. He heard Cassidy ask why, but when Dudyk didn't answer, he turned his attention to Nina as she returned to Gurka at the front.

"Wherever she is, she's dug in deep," the woman said. "I can't see her."

"We have no time," Gurka said. "She will die down here anyway. We have to go." He started to walk away and then stopped, casting a glance over all the flashlights that still illuminated the cavern. "Die in darkness or in light?" he mused, staring mostly at Bodie. "It pleases me more to let you see each other die. That would be better."

He waited as Nina came back to them and looped a thick rope through their arms, joining them all together, before tying it off around one of the reinforcing bars at the top of a crate. *It was the final nail in their coffins,* Bodie thought. Tied as they were, they couldn't hope to climb the crates or untie their bonds. Gurka and Nina made a sudden departure, gloating no longer, staying focused and concentrating on the next part of their plan.

Dudyk groaned.

Bodie glanced at him. "If someone can place their boot on his stomach, it might help slow the bleeding."

"I am done for," Dudyk said. "Save . . . save her."

Caruso tried to hide the tears from Bodie as the thief swiveled his head, checking on everyone. "I am truly sorry, Dante," he said. "We failed your family."

They were never going to be spared. Caruso knows that. But sometimes, knowledge cripples hope. And hope is what truly gets us past every hurdle.

"It was an act, you know," Caruso said. "Sometimes. My forgetfulness."

"Duh." Cassidy spoke up, twisting her hands so hard against her zip ties that she ripped her skin. "I knew that."

"You did?" Bodie asked. "And never shared."

"Thought you knew, boss." She managed a smile.

Bodie shook his head. Even facing death, Cassidy was seeking to lighten their burden. But he knew Caruso's sickness was far from an act—it was clear only the proximity of his lifelong passion made him fully lucid.

"Before we die," he said to Caruso, "please explain how you first found those clues. Who left them? A German soldier from the train? An undercover agent from the Second World War? Or someone else?"

Caruso sighed. "It is nothing so dramatic. But I'm surprised you don't know? Even now."

"Don't be an ass." Heidi's wrists were bleeding too as she fought the bonds.

The group shifted and twisted as they talked, but the ties were holding. Bodie managed to clamp the rope attaching them to the crate under his armpit and pull, but the bonds didn't budge. A sense of fate and finality settled within him.

"I left the clues," Caruso said. "In reverse. I created that long, wide-ranging route on the way home to help safeguard me and the Amber Room. In case"—he shook his head—"anything bad happened."

"You left the clues?" Jemma had positioned herself so that she could tear at Gunn's ties. "Presumably, then, you could have led us right here?"

"Yes. But my route created conflict. Opportunity. You just weren't good enough to escape R24."

"Thanks," Cassidy said dryly, staring at the ground. "I blame myself for that, mostly."

"No," Bodie told her. "It's nothing to do with you. Gurka told me that they were similar to us. They'd just gone down a darker path. I understand that. They're our equals."

"I helped along the way." Caruso shrugged. "When you appeared to need me to."

"But something still doesn't add up," Bodie said and saw Pantera nod at the same time. "If not by following clues, how did you find the bloody Amber Room in the first place? Surely not by chance?"

Caruso's voice took on a sad note. "I truly wish I'd never found it. Now, I have lost everything. My poor family." He hung his head before continuing: "I spent days and days rummaging in the basement of Königsberg Castle, through every box in those cellars. In the end, I found more than the single pane of glass that I showed you. There were really three. The second showed this valley, and the third showed the location of the cave."

Bodie digested that. "And these panes were in situ at the castle between 1945 and 1968, when they blew the castle up?"

"Yes and no. The three panes were placed in separate walls of the castle. I know that because the boxes were marked. They were not together. I rummaged through countless boxes before connecting all three."

Bodie could have gone on, but precious minutes were ticking by. His wrists were scraped raw, dripping blood, as were everyone else's. They couldn't move, couldn't take cover.

"Wait," Dudyk moaned then, interrupting them. "Wait, I can help you."

But a shriek suddenly rang around the cave. Bodie whipped his head toward the noise and saw Lucie running from a far corner. His heart leapt. The blonde girl ran across the floor.

Her eyes were focused in the middle of the group. "No, oh no. What did you do, Dudyk?"

She stepped across Bodie and fell to her knees beside Dudyk. Gently, she reached down and cradled his head in her arms.

"Thank you," she said. "For saving my life."

Dudyk's reply was audible to all. "You told me to stop fighting for others and fight for myself. Well, I chose to fight for you instead."

She hugged him hard, making him groan. Tears fell down her face. "Shit, don't die. You can't die. Just hang on."

"Hey, Luce." Cassidy's voice interrupted in a way only she could. "Sorry to intrude, but if you don't start cutting us free, we're *all* dead."

Lucie whirled around, still not leaving Dudyk's side.

"Just think," Cassidy said with determination. "What would Cross do?"

Lucie started tugging at Cassidy's ties, making the redhead grimace in pain. Lucie wrenched even harder, lost in her distress, in desperation, in panic.

"Caruso," Dudyk muttered. "At least I can tell you where . . . where your family is." He dissolved into a racking cough as he gave them an address before going absolutely silent.

Lucie whirled around. "No! Oh, dammit—"

Dudyk's head lolled to the side. The hand he'd been using to close the gunshot wound fell away. Lucie put a hand gently to his cheek. "Poor guy," she said. "From birth, some people never stand a chance in life. He was one of them."

Bodie shuffled. "I'm really sorry, Luce, but just go grab one of those bloody knives. *Now!*"

Lucie cried out in despair and started to move. But then, as if to drive home the fact that they were about to die, a shout traveled down the cavern's passageways from the front of the cave.

Belenko's voice.

"Charges ready! Take cover. They're set for ninety seconds!"

Lucie rose instantly to her feet, body rigid. "I can't save you in ninety seconds! I can't cut you all free." And she ran from them, eyes streaming, face red, deserting Dudyk and Bodie and the entire team.

Bodie met the disbelieving eyes of all his friends.

Caruso voiced everyone's thoughts: "It's over now."

CHAPTER
FORTY-ONE

Even in the midst of hopelessness, faced with death, Bodie did not give up.

Due to the cave's acoustics, they could hear the raised voices of the members of R24. It seemed they had gathered close to the crashed plane, taking cover behind some rocks there, close to the entrance. They could see the lower valley floor outside but still couldn't raise their mercenaries on the radio. The mountains were clear; it was the valley that worried them. The choppers were idling away down there, surrounded by heavily armed men as several of their number used radios.

Still, R24 had no idea they were the CIA. Bodie hoped the Bratva had survived but had no way of knowing. His life was currently measured in seconds.

And to their credit, not a single person tied with him sat there and accepted it.

"The knives," Jemma said first. "When we grabbed the knives earlier, some fell to the floor."

It took a huge joint effort, but the bound group quickly rolled themselves around the first crate and nearer the cave wall. The rope that entwined them and secured them to the crate pulled taut. The person closest to the wall—Pantera—lay down and stretched as far out as he could, reaching for the hilt of a sharp blade.

No matter how hard he strained, how much skin he took off his own and others' wrists, his questing fingers stayed a good six inches short. The seconds ticked down. They rolled again, trying to reach a pile of treasure that contained at least one cutlass and a pitted bayonet. This time it was Gunn reaching, cursing, but still coming up short.

They were strung out all around the crates. Bodie, counting down in his head, knew that half a minute had already passed. Their next attempt was to reach the explosives—maybe they could defuse enough of the row to save the cavern they were inside.

But that goal was even further out of their reach. Cassidy was closest and grasped again and again until those behind her groaned in agony at the constricting bonds.

The seconds counted down.

Twenty-five, twenty-four . . .

Lucie left them all behind, her friends, her fears, her expectations, and her best future. It had been a quick, horrible calculation. Yes, she could have cut some of them free, and they could have cut others free. But ninety seconds was not long enough to liberate everyone *and* escape the cave. Of course there were options, but Lucie didn't have time to go through them.

So she ran, leaving her friends behind and Dudyk, who had saved her life. She ran across the cave to the first exit, reaching the tunnel in seconds. She didn't slow. She entered the next cavern, the large interior one where the airplane's skeleton lay. Now, she stopped just inside the entrance and reached down for something.

A piece of plastic explosive.

254

It wasn't rocket science, and she hadn't expected it to be. She pulled the tiny silver detonator out of the plastic, thus making it and all the deadly packages behind her—leading back to the Amber Room chamber—safe.

At least, unless the larger blast reached them.

She scooped up the plastic explosive and ran to the next one, repeated her actions, and moved again. She stayed low and quiet, collecting the explosives and counting the seconds down in her head.

Sixty-five . . . sixty-four . . .

The trail of plastic explosives ended as she approached the plane, but she noticed that the wires connecting them snaked all the way to the entrance. R24 must have rigged a smaller explosion either at the front or just inside the cave entrance to further confuse matters. Lucie assumed they had a route and a plan worked out for when the chaos began.

She carried four packets of explosives in her hands.

She could hear her enemies speaking, talking of the choppers in the valley and ridiculing the "useless" mercs who had died at their orders. She heard Nina laugh and Gurka curse Dudyk's name. Her fingers were clenched tightly around the explosives.

Shit, calm the fuck down.

Forty-four . . . forty-three . . .

The seconds slipped away with frightening rapidity. She had risky work to do. She approached the rear of the plane, using its sizable bulk to hide her approach. The cockpit reared above, its disturbing skeletal pilot staring down with those large round eye sockets. Nina was talking now, voicing aloud her wish she could see "Guy Bodie and his band of clowns" meet their ends. Lucie crept forward on tiptoe, stepping lightly. The plastic explosives felt warm against her side.

Not far now.

She hesitated for a second, wondering just who the hell was taking this risk. Lucie Boom? Starched historian? No, not her. This was a different Lucie, a *new* Lucie, who risked everything for her friends and had seen a wicked sworn enemy give his life for hers.

Mixed emotions rose. She fought them off. Halfway down the length of the plane, she spotted an explosive placed across to her right. She followed the wires with her eyes and saw it led outside, where other charges would be set.

To the far left or right of the entrance? To give R24 just enough time to escape?

Sounds reasonable.

But they wouldn't be expecting this.

Twenty-four . . . twenty-three . . .

Lucie clasped the explosives tighter and inched away from any cover afforded by the plane.

◆ ◆ ◆

In the final twenty seconds Bodie cast aside mounting regrets. If only he'd created more than one opportunity to escape. If only they'd made more of the one they'd had. If only . . .

He let it go.

And looked first at Cassidy and then at Jemma and Gunn. Disbelief was written on all their faces. Cassidy never stopped fighting, twisting her ties, using the slick blood that coated her wrists to gain better purchase for her cut and scored fingers. Next were Pantera and Yasmine, the first his oldest friend, the second his newest and someone he hadn't really had a chance to get to know yet. His plan had been to help her fight the infamous Lucien—but that was gone now.

He nodded to Caruso and felt a twist in his soul, seeing eyes that clearly showed the anguish the Italian felt for his family.

And finally, he turned to Heidi, who was seated next to him.

Fourteen . . . thirteen . . . twelve . . .

"Looks like we get to quit the CIA after all."

"That's right. Make our deaths about you and your family."

"It's about you too," Bodie said. "Family is a sense of belonging, and it feels like you belong."

"I wish . . ." Heidi placed her blood-soaked hands atop his own. "I wish we'd had a goddamn chance, Guy Bodie."

"Me too." He held her eyes until the very last moment. "If we had more time, I would say to hell with all the CIA shit and ask you out on a date, Heidi Moneymaker."

Her eyes brightened, but then a terrible rumbling began, and the explosion overcame them.

Lucie felt exposed as she crabbed sideways away from the plane into the middle of the cavern. The seconds ticked away in her head. This was going to be close. She felt a moment of surprise and selfless confidence when she realized she hadn't factored enough time into her plan to allow for her own escape.

Fourteen . . . thirteen . . . twelve . . .

She placed the plastic explosives on the floor and reconnected the detonators. One blast would now set them all off. She crouched and started pushing them toward the front of the plane, closer to the rocks where R24 was hiding.

Nina's voice rang out, tinged with malice. "Shall I order Caruso's family killed?"

"Yeah, but let's get out of here first."

Lucie clenched her fists and dragged the charges a little closer.

"Hey! It's the blonde. Stop her." Nina's voice again.

Six . . . five . . .

"Nina, stop!"

Nina halted beside a rock, Vash at her side. Lucie dropped the charges, showed empty hands, and then bolted for the only refuge she could see.

The crashed plane.

"Hey!"

She ran headlong. Numbers flashed behind her eyes. *Three . . . two . . .*

At full speed, she jumped and made it through the open rear door, rolling clear across the aisle to the other side of the plane.

The explosion, now five times the force it should have been and more localized, was enormous. Lucie's eardrums were pounded with a hammerblow as the deep blast shook the mountain. A wave of fire swept the chamber, escaping through the entrance as well as funneling along the inner passageways. Lucie was curled into a ball, head between her arms, but heard the skin of the plane disintegrating and felt the whole heavy structure shift. A wave of heat scorched her back, but she was out of reach of the flames. She screamed as her jacket, shirt, and then back were scorched. The material burst into flames. Lucie rolled onto her back to quench them, intense pain bringing her to the brink of passing out. The mountain was rumbling, loose rocks and rivers of shale tumbling from above. Her ears rang. The explosion passed her, sweeping the cavern floor, obliterating the rocks behind which R24 had made its hiding place, and shot outside, swelling as it left the cave, mushrooming upward into the daylight.

As the noise diminished, nothing moved in the cave.

CHAPTER
FORTY-TWO

Bodie flung himself low when the explosives detonated, stubborn to the end, desperately looking for a way to survive. The whole mountain shook. The floor vibrated with enough force to dislodge some flashlights and dozens of boxes from the ledges around the chamber. The crates storing the Amber Room rattled. Dust and rocks fell from above, mostly fragments, but a boulder the size of a chair crashed down only three feet to Cassidy's left. More rumbling and shaking, and one of the crates split apart, sending amber panels spilling out. Bodie had split seconds to prepare for the explosives Gurka had placed close by to detonate.

But then the noise faded away.

A moment later he looked up and was greeted by a scene from a madman's dream. The dislodged flashlights were now shining their beams in haphazard disarray; shafts of light speared through the cave in all directions. A cloud of dust billowed from wall to wall and up to the ceiling, hitting rock and rolling back on itself.

The plastic explosives just beyond Cassidy's reach were intact.

From the random light he could see many of the ledges had lost their treasures. Boxes and sheets and ripped parchments were heaped upon the cave floor. Two of the eighteen crates had split asunder. Bodie couldn't tell much more. Slowly, he moved, feeling fire in his wrists as sore, broken skin rubbed rope and sharp plastic.

He reached out. "Heidi, you okay?"

"I'm not dead, so that's a good start."

Small chunks of rubble spilled from his back as he sat up. At his request everyone, including Caruso, sounded off that they were alive and injury-free. There was a lot of coughing and choking and groans of pain, but they had survived.

"What happened?" Pantera wondered.

Galvanized by the thought that R24 could be upon them at any minute, he fought his bonds. "It might be wishful thinking, but check that rope."

"The one that was attached to the top of the crate?" Cassidy asked. "Yeah, I got it here." She held the loose end in her right hand.

"You're free?"

"We're all free, dumbass. Just gotta find something to cut these zip ties."

Bodie crawled with her, determined to help. Together, they found the sharpest old knife—a Nazi bayonet attachment. Bodie turned his back on her and held it firmly with the blade sticking out. Cassidy rubbed the ties along it, missing twice and cursing in pain. Eventually, though, her zip ties broke. She took the blade, sawed through the plastic that bound her legs, and then turned to Bodie.

One by one, as those released picked up knives, everyone in the cave freed each other. Bodie worked soundlessly at first, squinting against the dust and watching the walls carefully for further rock-falls, but Yasmine's next question made him take note.

"Why didn't these charges detonate? The wires are still attached."

"Something went wrong. Maybe they came loose farther along. Heidi and Cass, cover the tunnel. Get ready for Gurka and his pals coming back."

The two readied knives and ran into position. Yasmine and Pantera joined them, treading carefully. Bodie assumed they were experiencing the same loss of balance he was and took a moment to hold himself still.

Then he rose, taking a last look at the dead Dudyk and wondering what might have happened to Lucie. In a few moments, the whole group was waiting at the tunnel entrance.

"Ready?" Cassidy asked.

"Are you?" Bodie caught her eyes, questioning her insecurities of the last few weeks.

"More than ever," she said confidently. "This is how Cross would want me to go on."

She was first into the tunnel, Bodie a step behind. They traversed the passage carefully and emerged into the larger cavern on the other side. Bodie stopped short when he viewed the scene beyond.

It was a wrecked and ruined tableau, a nightmare of war memory. The old Junkers was ripped apart and spread all over the cavern. Its body, tail, and cockpit had been burned and singed, half-melted. Shattered boulders and sharp rocks lay everywhere.

And there were bodies too.

Smashed against the wall of the cave, as if propelled there by the hand of a violent giant, two were spread eagled against the rock wall, while two others lay crumpled at its base. Their clothes were blackened and flesh burned to ruin by the explosion. Bodie winced but had to be sure. The whole team walked toward the lifeless remains.

"Belenko and Vash," Cassidy said, halting. "I can tell by what's left of their clothing and their size. I see Gurka too."

"The woman?" Jemma asked with trepidation.

"Has to be Nina . . . oh, wait . . ."

Bodie flinched. The woman's body was badly burned, the hair gone and part of the skull. From the height and build it might be Nina, but it could also be Lucie.

"Wait here," he told them. "I'll check."

"Not alone, you won't." Cassidy walked with him, and he soon realized that Heidi was a step behind. Yasmine too. Together, slowing, they approached the body. Bodie's heart was hammering faster than when he'd been awaiting the explosion.

"I can't believe you're checking on the enemy first," said a prim, clipped voice, "instead of the girl who saved your asses."

Bodie spun and saw Lucie immediately, standing amid the wreckage of the plane. She was leaning heavily on a seat, face and body blackened, clothes tattered, but she was standing—and she was okay.

Pantera was past Bodie and at her side quickly, helping her out of the wreckage and assisting her to a boulder. With a flourish, he swept it clean.

"Your seat."

"What happened?" Gunn asked. "What did you do?"

Bodie listened to the tale as the dust settled, as the mountain ceased rumbling, and as the noises of approaching soldiers filtered through the cave's front entrance. As they came closer, he managed a wry smile at Heidi.

"You?" he asked. "Or me?" He was asking who would stave off the soldiers' initial assault and start running them through what had happened.

Heidi linked her arm with his and dragged him along. "Let's go together."

CHAPTER
FORTY-THREE

From an open, clear, and essentially boundless vantage point, Bodie felt freedom for the first time in a week. With Heidi at his side, they were still being questioned by the CIA suits, but the open air, the vast views, and the lack of guards felt like a slice of heaven.

Heidi handled most of the questions. The entire process was made easier by her knowing one of the questioners and, of course, by her superiors vouching for them back at Langley. Bodie took the time to relax, to test his wounds, to stretch out his muscles and bask in the warm, healing rays of the sun.

"This feels good," he said, sitting back. "Bloody good."

The rest of the team was sprawled out close by, across the foothills of the mountains. CIA agents wearing flak jackets and camo and carrying semiautomatic weapons walked between them. Others manned the perimeter, watching the open valley, the mountains to both sides, and the choppers. Reinforcements and archaeology experts had already been called in to assess the monumental find.

The first thing Lucie did on seeing the authorities was relay to them the address where Caruso's family was being held. The information was passed along, and even now, thirty minutes later, a rescue operation was underway. Caruso couldn't stop pacing and wringing his hands, and the team took turns standing with him.

As soon as it seemed appropriate, Bodie asked the main guy, a mop-haired thirtysomething who Heidi called Carl, if they knew anything about the battle on the other side of the valley.

"Friends of yours?" Carl asked with a raised eyebrow.

"Not exactly," Bodie said, and Heidi laughed. "But they did help us out, and I'd like to see them leave here alive. And free."

"Which ones?"

"Not the mercenaries," Bodie said.

"Ah, well, if the mercs were wearing military fatigues, carrying HKs, face masks, and all the best gear, then they're all dead. The other guys—a mishmash of shapes and sizes, some wearing jeans, others chinos, all of them sporting the tattoos of a particular Russian brotherhood—are doing pretty well."

"Still up there?" Heidi asked.

"Yeah, haven't moved. Feels like they're waiting for something."

Bodie nodded. The freedom of the day started to recede. It hadn't lasted long. "They are," he said softly. "Me."

He wanted to go alone, but the entire team insisted on accompanying him. Without haste, they walked across the valley floor, bypassing the silent choppers, forged the narrow river, and then started up the same easy pass that R24's mercenaries had used to launch their attack. It was a relatively short walk, and not without trepidation, but Bodie thought he knew how the Bratva worked by now and wasn't unduly worried.

First, they would be waiting to see which team of relic hunters had survived. The Bratva bosses would have different plans for R24 than they would for Bodie's crew.

Hopefully.

Second, they would want to finish their business with Bodie once and for all. Lay everything to rest.

They reached the cliff top as the sun began to dim in the west, and they headed inland, seeing the Bratva camp up ahead. It wasn't far and consisted of a small group of tents around one large campfire. Bodie wondered if they'd had any issues with wolves or panthers as he approached but decided not to broach the subject.

The first man he saw was the bearded giant he remembered speaking to him at the battle. Cassidy had already pointed out that they were being watched from cover, but it didn't matter.

"I am Alexei," the man said as he approached. "And you are Guy Bodie."

They met where several obstinate tufts of brush created a miniature forest amid a stretch of barren, brown land. Both men's boots kicked up dust as they came to an abrupt stop.

"You look the worse for wear, my friend," Alexei laughed.

Bodie nodded wryly. "As do you," he said, looking over the big man's bandaged arms and two gashes along his left temple. "Was it a good fight?"

"Ah, they were American pussies," Alexei guffawed. "Went down like weak Russian vodka."

"They weren't all American," Cassidy said. "I remember hearing a couple of British soldiers too."

"Even easier." Alexei grinned. "They were your cheap supermarket vodka, nothing more."

Cassidy smiled back, and Bodie turned to show he wasn't armed. "We're here to talk."

"Of course. You must come with me. First, we wrestle, and then we eat. Then we drink. And then, if we're still able, we will talk."

"First we . . . what?"

Alexei ushered them past the tent line and over toward the large campfire. A man was already lighting it, tending the flames. The sun was at their backs, glowing orange as it sank between the peaks. The evening was still and burnished and beautiful. The Bratva gathered around, some eyeing the newcomers suspiciously, others with distaste, and still others with a quiet acceptance. The first wrestling match was taken by the Bratva, two strong soldiers who whipped off their shirts and set about flinging each other left and right close to the flickering flames. When they were done, they shared vodka, spitting a mouthful each into the flames before swallowing three more.

Bodie and his team found themselves relaxing in the Bratva's company, an odd turn of fate but a welcome one. Soon, it was Bodie's turn to wrestle, and despite voicing his reluctance, he climbed to his feet to face a small man with strong, thick arms. The Russian pulled his shirt over his head. Bodie did the same.

Instantly, Cassidy let out a wolf whistle. "Hey, put it away, man. That should come with a health warning."

Heidi laughed out loud. "Yeah, cut down on your doughnut intake."

"You wanna borrow my body, pal?" Pantera catcalled.

Bodie ignored them all. "What are the rules—" he began.

But the short man was on him before he'd finished speaking, wrapping those arms around his chest in a grip of iron. Bodie felt all the air leave his body and fought with every screaming muscle he had left, but he couldn't break the hold. When he sank to his knees, the short man pulled away and cheered, reaching out for the vodka.

Bodie swallowed it too, relishing the smooth taste.

"That is Southern Cross," Alexei bellowed. "The best that Dmitry Kovalenko ever made, bless his cold, dead soul."

Bodie knew the name but didn't have the strength to remember why. Slowly, he staggered back to his people and slipped his T-shirt back on. Alexei held out spread hands to them.

"Anyone else?"

Their lack of movement made him guffaw and turn to his own men. "They are all pussies, yes?"

Laughter rang out. Some slapped the ground with open palms. It stopped abruptly when Cassidy stood up. "Feed me first," she said. "And then I'll take you out, Alexei. And I don't mean to dinner."

There was a shocked silence, but then Alexei roared his approval. Meat was found and roasted over the campfire. More vodka was passed around. Bodie began to feel comfortably numb as full night fell and the smell of roasting meats made his mouth water.

As they ate, Alexei sat down beside him.

"You eat and drink to end our feud," the Russian told him. "It is good between us now."

"And Jack?"

"The bald one is free also. And his family. But you must remember the matter of your onetime debt is yet to be settled. And the Bratva will not take no for an answer. And it might only be you, not your team."

Bodie remembered they had demanded he do them a single service at some time in the future. The knowledge that he might have to do it without his friends raised new implications and ambiguities. He didn't like it. "Will it be legal?"

Alexei slapped the ground hard and guffawed. "That depends on which country you are from and which authority you work for, my friend. One man's crime is another's act of necessity. Today, the CIA love you. Tomorrow . . . who knows?"

"Good point. And thank you . . . my friend."

They toasted and ate. The night wore on. Cassidy put up a great performance against Alexei and earned his respect before he dumped her unceremoniously on her ass. Grinning and calling for more, he pulled her to her feet, but she held up a hand.

"Another time," she said. "Another place. I've gained one too many bruises during the last few days to make this a fair match. Whaddya say, Alexei? I'll kick your ass later?"

The bearded Russian grinned and shook her hand. "I'll kick your ass later."

Around him, Bodie knew his team was content. They sat close to each other. Only Lucie sat with a downcast expression. Heidi shouted in joy when Carl called her to say his team in Germany had safely rescued Caruso's wife and child. They were fine. Alexei gave them a card, stating that if they ever needed a hand, he would be there.

It was then that he saw her—the black-haired woman from the earlier battle. She stalked toward him now, a dripping sponge in one hand, a wickedly curved blade in the other.

"I have never seen her without a weapon," Alexei said in matter-of-fact tones. "Even when she makes love."

Bodie shuffled, unable to take his eyes from her as she approached, finally zeroing in on him.

"I am Tamara," she said. "I saw you at the battle. I like you."

She slipped fluidly into a seated position at his side, blocking Heidi out, and gave him a winning smile.

Bodie started to answer but found the words catching in his throat. Pantera chuckled as he tried again.

"Oh, hi . . . I'm . . . well . . ."

"You don't know?" Tamara leaned close to his face and started dabbing at the cuts and bruises with the sponge. The cold water felt good, the attention even better. Bodie grinned and let her work.

When he heard Heidi's grunt of disapproval, the grin wavered, but only a little.

"Do we *all* get a turn?" the curly-haired agent asked.

Tamara turned and said sweetly, "Would you like a turn?" before rising slowly and making her way back to a tent. Close to the entrance, she turned and smiled at Bodie.

Yasmine also soaked cuts and bruises with a towel and water to Bodie's left. As he pretended not to notice Tamara, Yasmine caught his eye.

"Lucien next," Yasmine said relentlessly. "He will pay for what he did to me and what he did to Cross."

"I promised you that back at the safe house," he said, sitting back as Yasmine finished. "And I meant it then. Even more now, because during this nightmare, you've proved yourself beyond any doubt."

"Thank you." She nodded solemnly.

"Don't be humble," Cassidy said. "We don't accept people easily. You've earned it."

"I can help with Lucien," Heidi said, shuffling forward so that Bodie could see her. "But all this talk of leaving the CIA has to stop." She paused. "For now. It only breeds insecurity and undermines my position."

Bodie recalled their recent admissions. Was it because they had been about to die? Or was there much more to their relationship than a deathbed declaration?

"Happy to stick around," he said with purposeful double meaning, "and see what happens."

She understood and looked away, but not before he saw her smile. He took it as a sign to lean in and whisper, "What I said back in the cave . . ."

She suddenly looked uncertain, innocent even. "Which bit?"

He nudged her and grinned. "You know. I mean . . . a date. There's a lot to consider."

"Yeah, I guess there is. Your gang. My bosses. Everyone's future. And how you decide to deal with the CIA."

"Rain check?" he asked.

"Maybe," she said, "but I won't be around forever."

The conversation reminded him of the Forever Gang and Darcey, the first girl he'd ever kissed. There was no great story, no special hook. He'd simply leaned over and kissed her lightly when they'd been in the dark, in the back row at the movies, because that was what a boy was supposed to do. It was a sweet, brief, innocent expression, never repeated. Who knew what might have happened between them in years to come if his parents hadn't died a week later.

Uncharted love, never explored. The knowledge of what might—and should—have been had left an everlasting burden on his heart.

Always. Even now. He didn't want that to happen between Heidi and him.

"I'm going to find them," he said quietly.

Heidi cocked her head. "Who?"

"The Forever Gang. My childhood friends. I lost them, but they . . . they were my second family. And I was torn from them too. I want to know what happened to them. Where they are now. I want . . . to know."

Heidi placed her hand on his arm. "I will help you."

Bodie clinked glasses with her. "You're a star," he said and then turned serious. "Did you contact your daughter?"

"Ah, yeah, yeah. It's not good. Doesn't matter that I was friggin' abducted. Doesn't matter that I'm okay. What matters is that this job always comes between us."

Now Bodie leaned across. "I know it's not the same," he said. "But you will always have us. We understand. We take the risks and lay it on the line for each other. And we'll never let you down."

It didn't feel odd to Bodie that the relic hunter team was essentially his third family. The other two had been ripped apart. This one, he vowed, would endure forever.

No matter what confronted them.

AUTHOR'S NOTE

While *The Amber Secret* is the third part of the Relic Hunters series, it shares the same themes of escapist adventure, camaraderie, and cinema-style action as my Matt Drake series, starting with *The Bones of Odin*, which is also available for the Amazon Kindle.

Keep up to date with all my latest news and giveaways by following me on Facebook—davidleadbeaternovels—or at my website: www.davidleadbeater.com.

ABOUT THE AUTHOR

David Leadbeater has published twenty-three Kindle international bestsellers and has sold over three-quarters of a million e-books on Amazon. He is the author of the Matt Drake series, the Alicia Myles series, the Chosen trilogy, and the Disavowed series. *The Amber Secret* is the third in his Relic Hunters series of action-packed archaeological thrillers.

For a list of his books and more information, please visit his website, www.davidleadbeater.com. You can also join him on Facebook for news and paperback giveaways: www.facebook.com/davidleadbeaternovels.